Murder at Monticello

⌒

A HOMER KELLY MYSTERY

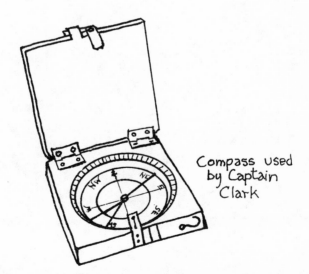

Compass used
by Captain
Clark

Murder

at

Monticello

A HOMER KELLY MYSTERY

Illustrations by the author

⌒

Jane Langton

V I K I N G

VIKING
Published by the Penguin Group
Penguin Putnam Inc., 375 Hudson Street,
New York, New York 10014, U.S.A.
Penguin Books Ltd, 27 Wrights Lane,
London W8 5TZ, England
Penguin Books Australia Ltd, Ringwood,
Victoria, Australia
Penguin Books Canada Ltd, 10 Alcorn Avenue,
Toronto, Ontario, Canada M4V 3B2
Penguin Books (N.Z.) Ltd, 182–190 Wairau Road,
Auckland 10, New Zealand

Penguin Books Ltd, Registered Offices:
Harmondsworth, Middlesex, England

First published in 2001 by Viking Penguin,
a member of Penguin Putnam Inc.

1 3 5 7 9 10 8 6 4 2

Grateful acknowledgment is made for permission to reprint excerpts from
The Field Notes of Captain William Clark, 1803–1805, edited by Ernest
Staples Osgood, Yale University Press, 1964.

PUBLISHER'S NOTE
This is a work of fiction. Names, characters, places, and incidents either
are the product of the author's imagination or are used fictitiously, and
any resemblance to actual persons, living or dead, business establish-
ments, events, or locales is entirely coincidental.

LIBRARY OF CONGRESS CATALOGING-IN-PUBLICATION DATA
Langton, Jane.
Murder at Monticello : a Homer Kelly mystery / Jane Langton.
p.   cm.
ISBN 0-670-89462-1
1. Kelly, Homer (Fictitious character)—Fiction. 2. Jefferson, Thomas,
1743–1826—Homes and haunts—Fiction. 3. Charlottesville (Va.)—Fiction.
4. Monticello (Va.)—Fiction. 5. College teachers—Fiction. I. Title.
PS3562.A515 T6 2001
813'.54—dc21   00-043369

This book is printed on acid-free paper. ∞

Printed in the United States of America
Set in Stempel Schneidler
Designed by Ann Gold

For Meg Ruley

To Captain Meriwether Lewis esq. Capt. of the 1st regimt. of Infantry of the U.S. of A.

. . . The object of your mission is to explore the Missouri river, & such principal stream of it, as, by it's course and communication with the waters of the Pacific ocean . . . may offer the most direct & practicable water communication across this continent for the purposes of commerce.

Beginning at the mouth of the Missouri, you will take observations of latitude & longitude, at all remarkeable points on the river. . . . The courses of the river between these points of observation may be supplied by the compass the log-line & by time. . . .

. . . Given under my hand at the city of Washington this 20th day of June 1803.

TH: JEFFERSON Pr. U.S. of A.

Author's Note

Most of the chapters in this book begin with passages from the journals of Captains Meriwether Lewis and William Clark, leaders of the expedition that was first imagined and then brought into being by President Thomas Jefferson. Other passages are taken from the journals of Sergeant John Ordway, Sergeant Patrick Gass, and Private Joseph Whitehouse.

Together they form a continuous sequence from the departure of the expedition on May 14, 1804, to its return to St. Louis on September 23, 1806.

Except in a metaphoric sense, they are not related to the ongoing narrative. They are a story in themselves.

Murder at Monticello

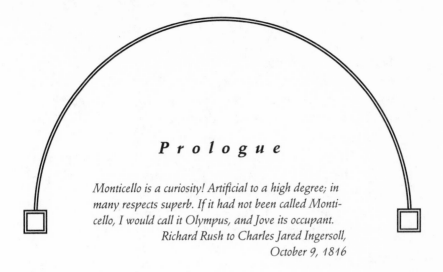

P r o l o g u e

*Monticello is a curiosity! Artificial to a high degree; in
many respects superb. If it had not been called Monticello, I would call it Olympus, and Jove its occupant.*
Richard Rush to Charles Jared Ingersoll,
October 9, 1816

The houses of the great men and women of the past are different from those of ordinary dead people, because so much
trouble has been taken to stop time in its tracks.

It often fails. Worn away by the tramp of visitors' feet, the living surface of the floor has been embalmed in polyurethane. The
chairs on which the deceased once sat have been reupholstered.
No stain from a fallen tear blots the starched handkerchief in the
glass case. Too many flower arrangers have stood gazing at a
vase, studying the effect of one more delphinium.

Sometimes a few fragments are snatched from the clearing
out of attics—the hairshirt of Savonarola, Darwin's rolling chair,
the teacup of Emily Dickinson. But often the place has been fal-
sified by centuries of tidying up.

In the life of the original owner the house might have been a
godawful mess, but now all the books are neatly shelved, not
scattered on the floor and stepped on. The papers are stored in
acid-free folders, not coffee-stained in drifts on the desk or lost
under the bed. The sticky glass on the mantelpiece and the half-
empty bottle have given way to the delphiniums.

The house of Thomas Jefferson is more evocative than most. The painted buffalo hide speaks of him, though only a copy of the one sent by Lewis and Clark from the Missouri River. Other memorials are the household gadgetry and the mastodon jawbone from Kentucky. The engraved copies of the Declaration of Independence are of course a powerful reminder, but keenest of all is the sharp gaze of the bust of Thomas Jefferson by Jean-Antoine Houdon. How those eyes flash and pierce!

Jefferson's mind and flesh are gone, but a breath of life still remains in the house he called Monticello.

Chapter 1

Rejoice! Columbia's Sons, rejoice!
To Tyrants never bend your knee,
but join with Heart and Soul and Voice
for Jefferson and Liberty.

Patriotic song, 1800

"Homer Kelly, is that you?"

"It is indeed. Who's this?"

"It's me, Ed Bailey. You know, your old friend Ed in Charlottesville, Virginia? Listen, Homer—"

"Oh, Ed! Well, hey there, it's good to hear from you. Just a sec." Homer shouted at his wife, "Hey, Mary, pick up the phone, it's Ed in Charlottesville."

"Ed! Hello, Ed!"

"Mary, bless your heart. How are you, dear?"

"Fine, I'm just fine. How are you, Ed?"

"How am I? I'm patriotic, that's how I am. I've got an American flag right here and I'm standing at attention and saluting. No, hold it, wait a minute, gotta shift the phone, person can't salute with their left hand."

Ed was shouting, so Homer shouted too. "Well, okay, Ed, good for you. What the hell are you talking about?"

"Fireworks," cried Ed. "You know fireworks, Homer? *WhizzzzzzBOOM?* Hey, Mary, you like skyrockets? *Sssssssss-BANG?*"

Mary made a face and held the phone away from her ear. Homer carried on. "Of course she likes skyrockets, Ed. We're *crazy* about skyrockets. What skyrockets do you mean exactly?"

"Fourth of July, naturally. You guys got anything against the Fourth of July?"

Homer laughed. "Oh, come on, Ed, what are you talking about?"

"Big celebration at Monticello, Fourth of July."

"Monticello?" said Mary. "You mean Thomas Jefferson's Monticello?"

"Of course I mean Thomas Jefferson's Monticello. You gotta come. Bicentennial celebration, election to presidency, big deal, fireworks, *zzzzzz*—"

"Okay, okay, you mean Jefferson was elected to the presidency in 1801 on the Fourth of July?"

"Nah, nah, not the Fourth of July! It was February, but who the hell wants to celebrate in February? Besides, the Fourth of July was when—you know, *KABLAM, KABLAM!*"

"Oh, for Christ's sake, Ed, we get it. You mean the fourth of July in 1776, when the founding fathers signed Jefferson's Declaration of Independence. Is that it?"

"You got it." Ed whispered a soft *kaboom*.

Mary gave up and went back to the news on television, but it was just as bad. By some ghastly coincidence it was reporting a murderer on the loose in Albemarle County, Virginia, and now it was zooming in on target practice in the firing range of the Charlottesville Police Department, *SPANG-ITY BLAMMITY BLAM.*

When Homer came in at last, grinning, she turned off the TV. "Homer, what on earth was Ed talking about?"

"He wants us to come. Big celebration at Monticello on the Fourth of July, two hundredth anniversary of Jefferson's election to the presidency. Sounds great."

"But he's drunk. He's positively smashed."

"Oh, sure. I'll call back in the morning. He'll be cold sober in the morning. How about it? You want to go?"

Mary thought it over. "Well, I think so, Homer. As a matter of fact, I'd love to."

"Good. I'll tell him we're coming."

"Isn't Charlottesville where Whatsername is? You know who I mean, Homer, one of our old students, Fern somebody. I wrote a recommendation when she applied for a grant at Monticello. I'll bet she got the job."

"Oh, sure, I remember Fern. Wasn't she that funny girl who whistled through her teeth?"

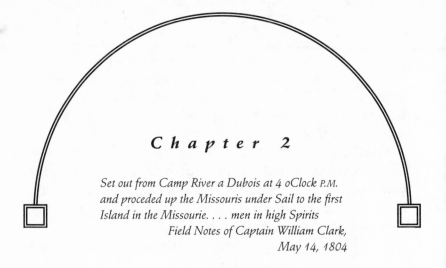

Chapter   2

*Set out from Camp River a Dubois at 4 oClock P.M.
and proceded up the Missouris under Sail to the first
Island in the Missourie. . . . men in high Spirits*
Field Notes of Captain William Clark,
May 14, 1804

It was May 14, the anniversary of the day the Lewis and Clark expedition had set out on the waters of the Missouri River, abandoning their first winter camp.

George Dryer was aware of the significance of the day as he shopped for supplies in the Bargain Mart on Hydraulic Road in Charlottesville. George, after all, knew more about Lewis and Clark than any of those high-toned professors.

With a couple of new shirts under his arm, he stopped to read a big handwritten sign on the bulletin board beside the checkout counter:

NEIGHBORHOOD MEETING
ON THE SAFETY OF OUR DAUGHTERS

It gave him a jolt. At once he decided to go to the meeting, hoping to hear himself talked about.

In the auditorium of St. Anne's Belfield Upper School on Ivy Road, George sat in the back, behind forty or fifty mothers and fathers. He was not disappointed. The worried parents talked fervently about the monster who was threatening the young women of Albemarle County. They were urgent with questions about the protection of their children.

It was so thrilling, George could hardly control himself. He wanted to stand up and talk a blue streak. With difficulty he kept his mouth shut.

The female sitting next to him was a good-looking olive-skinned woman, Latino or Native American. It occurred to George that she looked a lot like Jeanie. And probably the Mandan squaws had looked just like that.

He spoke to her as they left the hall, and she told him how worried she was about her little girl. "She's only fourteen, so vulnerable. Do you have a daughter?"

"Three of 'em," said George, the long-suffering father. "You live in Charlottesville? I'd be glad to accompany your little girl when she goes out. Where do you live?"

She told him gratefully that it was right around the corner.

"I'll walk you home," said George. "Can't be too careful."

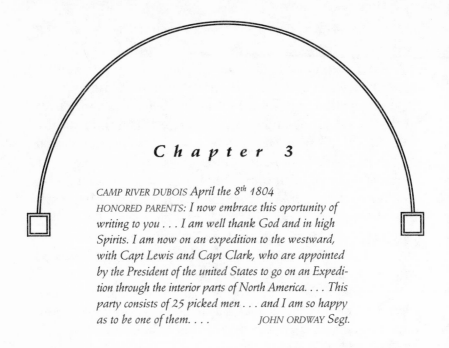

C h a p t e r   *3*

CAMP RIVER DUBOIS April the 8th 1804
HONORED PARENTS: I now embrace this oportunity of
writing to you . . . I am well thank God and in high
Spirits. I am now on an expedition to the westward,
with Capt Lewis and Capt Clark, who are appointed
by the President of the united States to go on an Expedi-
tion through the interior parts of North America. . . . This
party consists of 25 picked men . . . and I am so happy
as to be one of them. . . .   *JOHN ORDWAY Segt.*

O n the day after the meeting that had been called to pro-
tect the wives and daughters of Albemarle County, two
hikers exploring the woods in McIntire Park came upon the
strangled and disfigured body of a woman.

Ed Bailey saw it all on television, the ambulance pulling
away from the scene, the interview with the hikers. The boy
hiker was excited and talkative, the girl was deeply affected
and could hardly speak.

Wisely, Ed decided to say nothing about this sordid episode
to Homer Kelly.

Therefore Homer had no inkling of the ugly news from
Charlottesville as he lugged a stack of books down the great
staircase of Widener Library in Harvard Yard. All the books
were about Thomas Jefferson. Homer was reading up.

In the downtown mall in Charlottesville, the president of

the Society for Jefferson Studies was also unaware of the savage attack in McIntire Park. Augustus Upchurch was shopping, going from store to store. In a moment of abandon he bought several bow ties in jolly colors, seeking a dashing and youthful effect. He had a certain young lady in mind. His wife would have hated the new ties, but she had been dead for years.

And in the woods around Thomas Jefferson's house at Monticello, a trespasser walked his motorcycle up the hill from Route 53 and pushed it higher and higher through the undergrowth of hackberry and spicebush.

He was careful not to tread on the delicate blossoms of lady slippers, or crush under the wheels of his bike the green canopies of jack-in-the-pulpit. Moving up and up, away from the road, he found a level place at last and parked his bike, breathing hard. It had been a long, steep climb. Then he set to work unpacking his tent and lashing it to a pair of oaks and a hickory tree.

The trespasser too had not seen today's edition of the *Charlottesville Daily Progress*.

Nor had any copies of the *Richmond Times Dispatch* or the *Washington Post* found their way to the very top of the hill into Thomas Jefferson's house—neither downstairs, where batches of tourists were moving through the beautiful rooms, nor upstairs, in the office of Curator Henry Spender, nor still farther upstairs, to the very top of the house, where Fern Fisher was beginning her first afternoon on the job.

⌒

Fern was a middle-sized big-boned woman with clever eyes, a cheerful expression, big feet, a gap between her front teeth through which she could utter a piercing whistle, and a lot on her mind.

For the moment she was content to bask in her working

quarters. Nobody else in the world had as good a place as this.

As an office, the Dome Room of Thomas Jefferson's Monticello was an inconvenient place to get to, because you had to climb three long flights of breakneck stairs. But once you made it to the top, the great glowing room was a reward.

It was a huge round space with the sun's eye staring through an oculus at the top, throwing down a blob of light that moved silently across the floor with the turning of the earth.

The dome was actually a shallow octagon resting on octagonal walls, but the enclosed space felt hemispherical, like the sky above. With its six round windows it was a collection of circles, echoing and re-echoing the most perfect of shapes. Thomas Jefferson had designed the room himself, following the divine Palladio. *Palladio,* he had said, *is the Bible.* There were domes in Palladio's Bible, and Jefferson had built one.

Afterward he had not known what to do with it. It had become a playroom for his grandchildren, a storeroom, and leftover attic.

But Fern knew what to do with it. Her grant had come through, her wonderful grant. The stipend was small, but the working space was magnificent.

She was eager to get started, but there was a job to do first. "It's just routine," Mr. Spender had said. "Everybody has to fill out a questionnaire."

She looked at it. There were all the usual queries.

Name, etc. Fern wrote the answers neatly. *Address: 222 South Street, Lewis and Clark Square, Charlottesville.*

Most of the questions were easy, but there was a final question, *Honors, prizes, awards?* Fern balked and dropped her pen.

It was silly, because at twenty-three, Fern had achieved a

few things. She was a Ph.D., she had taught classes, her dissertation had been published. It had won a prize.

Folding the questionnaire, she wondered why it didn't ask for *Shameful episodes,* because she would have answered that one truthfully—*Rotten marriage, miserable divorce, three coy self-descriptions in three personals columns, three embarrassing blind dates. And after that—well, never mind.*

Now, how to begin? Fern picked up the letter from the grant committee and read it again. They had laid out in precise language exactly what they expected her to do.

> In awarding this grant to Fern Fisher, the Society for Jefferson Studies wishes her to write a book in celebration of the two hundredth anniversary of Thomas Jefferson's election to the presidency.
>
> We assume that Ms. Fisher is aware of the increasing chorus of criticism, in particular the attacks upon his personal life.
>
> The members of the Grant Committee hope that her book will restore to our third President the distinction he deserves in the eyes of his countrymen. She will not, of course, ignore the burden of the attacks against him, some of which may be justified, but she will remind the citizens of the United States, who have perhaps forgotten, how important to the formation of this nation were his life and thought.

Fern closed the folder. God, it wasn't much to ask. What if the book was impossible? What if she couldn't do it?

Well, of course they were right, she did revere Thomas Jefferson, there was no question about that. And of course it was true that the great man was getting a raw deal. But—Fern scraped back her chair and jumped up—the committee's high expectations made her feel like a rebellious child.

For most of the day she arranged her books and set up the computer that had been paid for by the Grant Committee.

"There's no electricity up here," the curator had explained as he led the way upstairs. He pointed to the cable taped along the baseboard. "So we've connected you to the second floor. It should work all right."

And it did. When Fern hooked up all the wires and plugged in all the plugs, her monitor glowed softly, the tiny lights on her printer shone green, the lamp turned on—not that she needed a lamp in the middle of May, there was so much light pouring down from the round opening above.

The snaking cables were an insult to the architecture. Fern did her best to shove them out of sight.

It took her the rest of the afternoon to organize everything. By the time she was done, the footsteps of the tourists downstairs were fading. The guides were bustling around down there, talking cheerfully. Fern leaned over the banister and listened to the gentle Southern voices.

"Those women weren't even *listening*. What do they come here for anyway?"

"Didn't somebody tell you? They're interior decorators. I suppose they were disappointed. Not enough curvy furniture and gold chairs."

"Ah, that explains why they kept complaining about the lack of flower arrangements. One of them offered to make gigantic bouquets for every room in the house."

"Heaven forbid."

Fern had her own key to the house, her own freedom to come and go. When everything was silent downstairs, she put her freedom to the test. She descended the two narrow flights of stairs and walked boldly into the entrance hall. One of the evening guards was there, but he knew who she was, and left her alone.

Fern went from room to room, touching everything with

her eyes—the Parisian clocks, the great French mirrors, the handy furnishings of Jefferson's study. She was trying to magic herself into a proper excitement, the necessary fervor to begin.

Unknown to Fern as she circled the house from room to room, someone else moved slowly around the hill below the house, treading softly like a hunter with a quiver of arrows.

⌓

Set out early, Killed a Deer last night, examined the mens arms, & Saw that all was prepared for action. . . .　　　*Field Notes of Captain William Clark,*
May 24, 1804

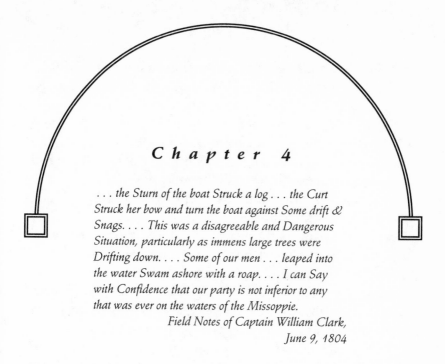

Chapter 4

*. . . the Sturn of the boat Struck a log . . . the Curt
Struck her bow and turn the boat against Some drift &
Snags. . . . This was a disagreeable and Dangerous
Situation, particularly as immens large trees were
Drifting down. . . . Some of our men . . . leaped into
the water Swam ashore with a roap. . . . I can Say
with Confidence that our party is not inferior to any
that was ever on the waters of the Missoppie.*

Field Notes of Captain William Clark,
June 9, 1804

ext day, after revving up her computer and staring for a
while at the empty monitor, Fern decided impulsively to
take a walk. She snatched up her jacket and hurtled down the
breakneck stairs.

A startled face looked out halfway down. "Be careful!"
warned Henry Spender from his office on the second floor.

"Of course," murmured Fern, plunging down the rest of
the way, landing with a thump, and bursting out of the corridor into the entrance hall.

A crowd of tourists looked at her, and Gail Boltwood's
pleasant voice paused for a second, then went on serenely, "If
you look up at the balcony you'll see a copy of the painted
buffalo robe that was sent to President Jefferson by Meriwether Lewis." All eyes obediently gazed upward.

What Fern needed, she decided, was to explore everything,

not only the house but the surrounding garden and hillside, because every square inch of Monticello had been fashioned according to Jefferson's own design.

There was no more personal house in the world. Every roof and chimney, every carved molding, every drapery at a window, every outbuilding, every vegetable in the garden had come into being as an act of his creative will.

Fern dodged past the tourists who were waiting outside and headed for the path called Mulberry Row.

Below the path lay the vegetable garden. It was a long strip of level ground, carved out of the mountainside and buttressed by a wall of rock. The grassy hillside was green and inviting. She sat down and stretched out her legs and admired the long straight rows of lettuces and cabbages and the pea vines twining around brushy twigs. Had the garden been as perfect as this in Jefferson's time? There was a memoir by one of his slaves, a man named Isaac, who remembered his master working in the garden *in right good earnest*.

Fern shut her eyes, imagining Thomas Jefferson planting Alpine strawberries, or the Arikara beans collected by Meriwether Lewis, or Lewis's sweet-scented currants. Did they prosper? Did the strawberries come to his table?

She didn't know, but it was easy to picture a tall man crouched on one knee, digging the beans into the ground, then standing to look down, erect in an old coat, his reddish-gray hair pulled back, his ruddy skin freckled. *Oh, a hat, he needed a hat against the sun*. At once Fern invented a broad-brimmed straw hat and clapped it on his head.

She was pleased at the ease with which she had evoked him. Walking farther along the path called Mulberry Row, she could almost see him moving ahead of her, mounted on his horse Caractacus, swaying a little as the horse moved gently beneath him.

She hardly needed to close her eyes to see that the horse was a long-legged bay and that the rider's boots were narrow and black, like the pair standing side by side near his bed. The rippling shadow of horse and rider mingled with the tree shadows cast by the morning sun. Singing, surely he'd be singing. Slave Isaac had said so—*hardly see him anywhar out doors but what he was a-singin.*

At once Fern reminded herself severely that Isaac's memoir was not politically correct, because his interviewer had set it all down in dialect. Still, it was pleasant to add melody to her vision of Thomas Jefferson riding along the path in front of her.

She smiled. Her task would not be so hard after all, if she could go on like this every day, calling up visions of Thomas Jefferson actually doing things, moving around his mountain-top, walking purposefully from room to room in the building he had designed entirely alone, the house he had pulled down and built up again over the course of half a century.

Yes, oh, yes, this was the right way to begin—envisioning the man himself in hallucinatory images, right here on his own ground. The visions would be like incantations, the calling up of a spirit.

Horse and rider were gone, but Fern moved on down the sloping brick path, not caring where it was going.

It led to the burial ground. This too had been planned by the master of the house. An iron fence enclosed a level acre of hillside. It was full of gravestones.

There in front of her rose his own monument, the obelisk with the famous inscription that made no mention of his presidency. And there—Fern caught her breath—who was that coming away from the cemetery, moving straight away from the obelisk as though he had melted through the fence?

It was the liveliest vision so far, a tall, lank figure resurrected from the grave. His long shabby coat was green this time, but his red hair was still pulled back with a ribbon or a piece of string.

As a vision, he was very nearly real. But then he faded like the others. Moving into the woods, he was soon lost among the expanding leaves of spring.

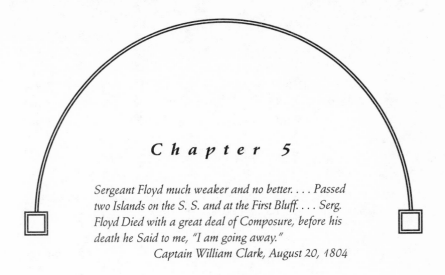

Chapter 5

Sergeant Floyd much weaker and no better. . . . Passed
two Islands on the S. S. and at the First Bluff. . . . Serg.
Floyd Died with a great deal of Composure, before his
death he Said to me, "I am going away."
Captain William Clark, August 20, 1804

In Concord, Massachusetts, in the Kellys' house on the Sudbury River, Homer had another call from Ed Bailey, his old friend in Charlottesville.

"Hey, Homer, guess what? I've got the tickets for the Fourth of July celebration at Monticello. Nothing to it. I said you guys were truly distinguished, you know, a coupla *Hawvawd* professors. But what really bowled them over, I said you were the District Attorney of Cambridge, Massachusetts. They were really impressed."

"Good God, Ed, you didn't say that? It's been years since I worked in the DA's office, and then, for Christ's sake, I was only an assistant, not—"

"Well, whatever. Anyway, you can't deny you've solved a lot of murder cases."

"Or not solved them," said Homer, speaking the simple truth. He changed the subject. "Listen, Ed, do you happen to know an old student of ours, Fern Fisher? She's got a grant. She's working at Monticello now."

"Don't know her. Heard of her, that's all. Old Upchurch's little pet."

"Upchurch?"

"Augustus Upchurch. There's this bunch of old fuddy-duddies, Jefferson groupies. Upchurch is head groupie. He gave her a grant. She's supposed to write this truly worshipful book."

"Well, good luck to her," said Homer doubtfully.

"Jesus, Homer, I forgot why I called. How'd you like to come down early? My landlord's taking off until August, so you guys could stay right here until then. Come early, stay a while, enjoy the wonders of Albemarle County, the state of Virginia, the whole goddamn sunny South. See, I just have the third-floor apartment, the rest is all yours. Big ugly house, three bedrooms, two baths, no rent. Landlord just wants somebody in the house. He's scared about crime—you know, serial killers on the loose. You just have to feed the dog."

"Feed the dog! How big is the dog?"

"How big? Oh, I'd say"—there was a pause—"maybe twelve inches. Toy poodle."

"Oh, for Christ's sake, Ed, I was just kidding about the dog. What do you mean, come early? My God, Ed, we've got our hands full. End of semester, final papers, final exams, general hysteria, helltime, kids flunk out, parents skin you alive."

"Tell me about it," groaned Ed, who taught a bunch of courses himself at the University of Virginia.

"But anyway, thank you, Ed, I'm really grateful, but I'll have to talk to Mary. She's looking forward to a general collapse, keeps talking like a prelapsarian female."

"Prelapsarian?"

"You know, before the Fall. Garden of Eden before the snake—in other words, before Harvard University. Keeps talking about cooking and sewing, picking flowers, she's never going to open another book. I'll talk to her, let you know, call you tonight. Oh, say, Ed, before you hang up, what's all this about killers on the loose?"

"Sorry I brought it up. By the time you get here it'll be all over. There's this creep prowling around, killed a buncha women, another body turned up today, you must've seen it on TV. Holistic practitioner."

"Holistic—?"

"Oh, I don't know, some woman. Anyway, it's okay, not to worry, cops've got all these clues. Police labs, you know. Bits of fiber, pieces of skin, blood under the fingernails, pubic hair, you know the kind of thing."

"Pubic hair? Did you say pubic hair? Jesus! He's a rapist?"

"God, I don't know. Carves 'em up and kills 'em. Or else kills 'em and carves 'em up. I forget which comes first. There's this self-proclaimed eyewitness, swears he's got red hair."

Homer put the Charlottesville killer out of his mind and went back to his stack of books about Thomas Jefferson. They were depressing. When Mary walked in and pulled off her jacket and kissed him, Homer looked at her unhappily. "This book really tears him apart."

"Who, Thomas Jefferson? Ah, yes, of course." Mary shook her head sadly. "It's the revisionist police. Those people can't stand a genius. It's all the rage right now, tearing down the sacred image of the noble founding father."

"Oh, right, I suppose so." Homer stared dreamily at the book and said, "Ed Bailey called again from Charlottesville. Wants us to come early for the celebration at Monticello, stay in his house free of charge. What do you think?"

"Oh, I don't know, Homer. Did you see the news last night? That serial killer in Virginia, he's murdered another woman."

Homer grinned. "Well, maybe I could lend the local investigation a hand." Then, seeing the look on his wife's face, he said quickly, "Joke."

"Well, it better be a joke, Homer. I thought you just wanted to bask in Jefferson history."

"Of course I do." Homer closed the book and looked at the picture on the jacket, a painting of a thin-faced man with a narrow nose, a strong chin, and sandy hair. "Christ, now I don't know what to think. The arguments against him are so convincing."

In some portraits the eyes stare directly into yours and follow you around the room. But the man on the cover of Homer's book did not look back at him. Instead he gazed serenely to one side, as though unaware of the revelations packing the pages bound so thickly together under his chest.

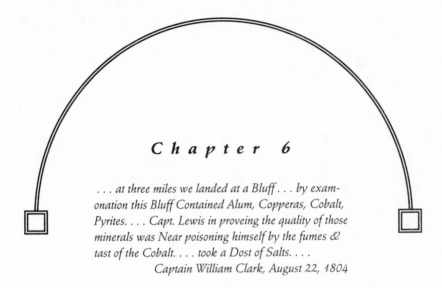

Chapter 6

... at three miles we landed at a Bluff ... by exam-
onation this Bluff Contained Alum, Copperas, Cobalt,
Pyrites. ... Capt. Lewis in proveing the quality of those
minerals was Near poisoning himself by the fumes &
tast of the Cobalt. ... took a Dost of Salts. ...
Captain William Clark, August 22, 1804

God, they were all over the place, crawling around the body like maggots! George pushed ahead, trying to see better, but a big woman in uniform kept saying, "Keep back, come on, move back." He pressed forward anyway, but then a barrier was set up and he had to retreat. Somebody stepped on his foot.

George suppressed an impulse to respond with a savage shove. Instead he leaned over the strip of yellow tape and stared at the body and drank his fill. They still hadn't covered it up, even though there were cameras all over the place. George chuckled with delight. One guy had even climbed a tree.

Most of the daily papers and all the news programs on TV contented themselves with images of the police ambulance, the crowded backs of the forensic team, and an interview with the Charlottesville Chief of Police, who was beside himself with frustration. There was a photograph from a high-school yearbook of the unhappy murdered girl, an acupuncturist in a chiropractic clinic on Massie Road.

But one of the papers regularly brought home by Augustus Upchurch, president of the Society for Jefferson Studies, was more shameless. The color picture on the front page had been taken from high in a tree.

Augustus was drawn to the story. The ghastly photograph both repelled and attracted him.

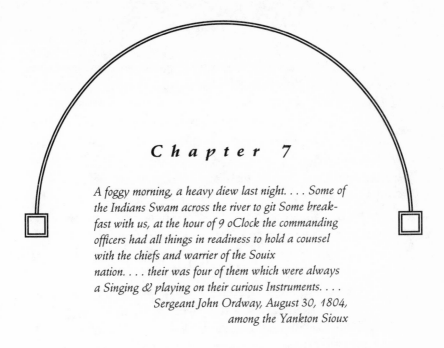

Chapter 7

A foggy morning, a heavy diew last night. . . . Some of
the Indians Swam across the river to git Some break-
fast with us, at the hour of 9 oClock the commanding
officers had all things in readiness to hold a counsel
with the chiefs and warrier of the Souix
nation. . . . their was four of them which were always
a Singing & playing on their curious Instruments. . . .
Sergeant John Ordway, August 30, 1804,
among the Yankton Sioux

When Fern went out next day, there was fog all around
the mountain. Monticello was a castle on an island—
blue sky above, soft billows below.

It was too early for visitors. They would soon be here in
droves, riding up in the shuttle bus from the gatehouse, but
for a little while Fern would have Mulberry Row to herself.

She walked along the path briskly. Leading her on was
the hope of calling up another vision like the firmly three-
dimensional spirit that had astonished her yesterday in the
burial ground.

Mulberry Row had been Monticello's factory street. Small
signs marked the sites of the Weaver's Cottage, the Stable,
the Joinery, and the Nailery.

Fern paused at the sign for the Nailery and stared at the
grass around it, straining her imagination, trying to shape a
building in the air, a cluttered dark space with anvils and fiery

kilns, where iron rods had been wrought into nails by young black boys, with Jefferson himself explaining the nail-cutting machine.

The picture refused to come. All she could see was the ground where the structure had stood and the vegetable garden below. This morning two volunteers were already at work in the garden plots, bowed low over their weeding. Today there was no ghostly master of the house inspecting the neat rows of spinach and the feathery heads of carrots.

The only image forming in Fern's mind was of the house servants of two hundred years ago, kneeling beside the long beds, harvesting fresh produce for Jefferson's table.

Then Fern corrected herself. *Servants* was a euphemism. Even the household servants had been slaves.

Slaves. The word rose up and smote her, because Jefferson's plantations had been worked entirely by slave labor. Some of the slaves had been highly skilled. In the Joinery, John Hemings had made furniture for his master's use. Slaves had manufactured the bricks and built much of the house themselves. They had fetched and carried, harvested the fields, cared for the stock, washed the linen, raised the vegetables, pruned the orchard, built the encircling roads, and waited on table. Even the French-trained chef, James Hemings, had been a slave.

A slave. Fern tramped on, heading once again for the graveyard, the word pounding in her head. It had been her sensible position on the question of slavery that had so pleased the Grant Committee.

Well, it hadn't been the whole committee. It was really just Mr. Upchurch. His was apparently the deciding vote; in fact, perhaps it didn't matter what the others thought, because only Mr. Upchurch had been present at the final interview.

They had sat in a small room in the headquarters of the Society for Jefferson Studies in Charlottesville, just the two of

them, Fern and Mr. Upchurch. He was a dignified white-haired old man with pink cheeks.

There had been very few questions. All the members of the Grant Committee had read Fern's application. They were pleased, Mr. Upchurch said, with her qualifications.

"Thank you," murmured Fern. Was the interview over?

No, there was a pause. Mr. Upchurch's face bunched itself together as if in gastric distress. Leaning forward, he uttered the word "Slavery."

"Slavery?" said Fern, not sure what was coming.

"It's what they can't forgive him for," went on Mr. Up-church, "the fact that he had so many slaves."

Oh, of course, thought Fern. Glibly she comforted Mr. Up-church. "But all those Virginia gentlemen had slaves. All those great men who were the backbone of the American

Revolution, every one of them was the owner of a plantation worked by slaves."

Mr. Upchurch leaned back, looking relieved. "That's what people so often forget. George Washington had slaves at Mount Vernon, so did James Madison at Montpelier and James Monroe at Oak Hill."

Bravely Fern grasped the thorn. "I think of it this way, Mr. Upchurch. You see, it's such a common fault among historians, judging the past by the present." She leaned forward eagerly. "Suppose that a hundred years from now everybody is vegetarian. I mean on moral grounds. The very idea of butchering animals for food would be repugnant—the thought of cattle prodded into freight cars, and slaughterhouses dismembering hogs, and supermarkets selling carcasses cut up and packaged as bottom round and sirloin steak."

Mr. Upchurch looked stunned.

Fern had invented this little allegory only recently. "What would they think of *us?* I mean, looking back? They'd never forgive us. All our heroes, all our famous writers and artists, all our great scientists and statesmen—their achievements would be rejected with disgust because they were carnivores with blood running down their chins."

Mr. Upchurch gasped. Then he laughed with delight. "Of course, of course!" He slapped his knee and sat back, beaming. But then his face scrunched up again. His voice dropped an octave and he whispered the name of Sally Hemings.

Fern was ready. She had been expecting it. At once she said calmly, "But it could just as well have been his brother Randolph who slept with Sally Hemings. He had the same DNA. Why do people pick on Thomas Jefferson? I mean, it's inconceivable that he could have fathered all those children."

Mr. Upchurch relaxed. He was charmed. "The award is yours, my dear," he said, and shook her hand. "I know your book will be everything we hoped for."

But now the book was on hold. Fern ran along Mulberry Row and down the sloping brick path to the graveyard. This time there was nothing within the iron fence but the obelisk and all the other monuments and stones memorializing various Jeffersons, Randolphs, Carrs, and Eppeses.

No tall figure moved among the graves, whether living or dead or in between.

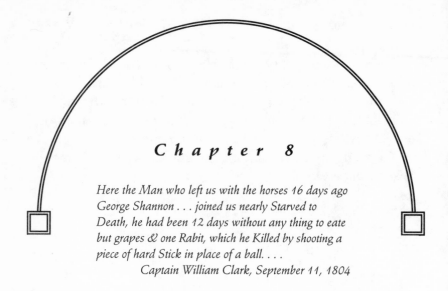

Chapter 8

Here the Man who left us with the horses 16 days ago
George Shannon . . . joined us nearly Starved to
Death, he had been 12 days without any thing to eate
but grapes & one Rabit, which he Killed by shooting a
piece of hard Stick in place of a ball. . . .
  Captain William Clark, September 11, 1804

"Welcome to Monticello," said Gail Boltwood, opening the tall glass door to admit another batch of tourists.

They gathered around her politely as she explained the Great Clock over the door, and the cannonball weights, and the days marked on the wall. "Do you see the holes in the floor? The weights have to go down into the cellar to reach the other days of the week."

Then Gail showed them the mastodon bones in the glass case. "The President hoped the live animal itself would be discovered in the West, because he didn't believe in the extinction of species. If the bones existed, then the creature itself must be out there somewhere."

"You mean he didn't agree with Charles Darwin?" asked an earnest tourist.

Gail smiled gently. "Darwin published his theory many years after Jefferson's death."

"I see," said the humbled tourist.

They were not all so humble. Today there was a crude visitor with only one thought in his head. "Is it true about Sally Hemings? Did he really have sex with a slave? I mean, they've got the DNA to prove it, right?"

Gail was used to the question, and she handled it with scholarly good taste. "Perhaps it's true. But perhaps the children of Sally Hemings were fathered by another member of the family. Some people have suggested Thomas Jefferson's nephews, the sons of his sister, but their DNA would have been quite different. But Thomas Jefferson's brother Randolph is plausible, or one of his sons. Theirs would have been exactly the same."

The scandal-monger would not be denied. "But it's true, right? Every one of her five kids was born nine months after he was right here at Monticello. You know, back from Washington or someplace else. Isn't that a fact?" He grinned right and left, looking for agreement, but the others were too polite to accuse their long-dead host of scandalous behavior.

With relief they followed Gail as she walked ahead of them into the parlor. Reverently they looked down at the maple-and-cherrywood geometry of the floor and up at the molding along the top of the wall—copied, Gail told them, from a Roman temple in a book.

She was a good guide, Gail knew that, but perhaps she was too pedantic. A Roman temple in a book! Why would anybody care about that? Well, they were lucky she didn't tell them *which* Roman temple and *which* book, because it was the personal things they cared about, like *which* slave he had slept with, how *rich* he had been exactly, and was it true he had *died poor?*

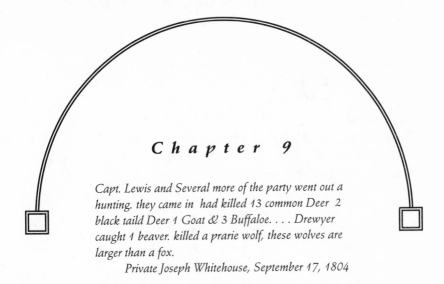

Chapter 9

Capt. Lewis and Several more of the party went out a hunting. they came in had killed 13 common Deer 2 black taild Deer 1 Goat & 3 Buffaloe. . . . Drewyer caught 1 beaver. killed a prarie wolf, these wolves are larger than a fox.
Private Joseph Whitehouse, September 17, 1804

Bright sunlight poured from the top of the dome. Fern could barely see the words on the monitor. She squinted at it and typed a word, then stopped and listened. There was a heavy thumping on the stairs.

Soon it turned into the sound of gasping, and there in the doorway stood Mr. Upchurch, blowing out his cheeks and wheezing. He was wearing a gentlemanly seersucker suit and a shocking-pink bow tie.

Fern leaped up. "Oh, Mr. Upchurch, hello."

"Good morning." He smiled, and asked how she was coming along. Did she have an outline the committee could see? Had she written a chapter or two?

"Oh, Mr. Upchurch, it's too soon. A writer can't—I mean, they have to have some—" She had been about to say *personal space,* but it was a phrase she detested, and she stopped.

But Mr. Upchurch understood at once. He too was a writer. He too knew the necessity for time to allow the creative process to work its mysterious will.

"Oh," said Fern, relieved, "you're a writer, Mr. Upchurch?"

"Just now and then," said Mr. Upchurch modestly. "Little occasional pieces like a genealogical study of my family, *The Upchurches of Rappahanock Valley,* which several newspapers have been good enough to praise. Don't you find"—Mr. Upchurch became confidential, one writer sharing his experience with another—"that good things come into your head when you least expect it? Happy strokes? I once found an entire chapter writing itself in my head while walking my dog."

Fern heartily agreed, and mentioned the inspiration to be found in the aisles of a supermarket. "The green broccoli, Mr. Upchurch, the scarlet tomatoes, the purple grapes."

"Golf!" exclaimed Mr. Upchurch, his eyes shining, and at once he began describing the flow of soul occasioned by the sunlit putting green, the ramble from one hole to another, the flight of the ball over the fairway.

At last he said goodbye and went away, descending the staircase heavily.

Fern listened until the sound of his footsteps faded. Then she went to one of the round windows and peered down at a cluster of visitors boarding the shuttle bus. No, Mr. Upchurch was not getting on the bus. He was walking downhill in the direction of the staff parking lot. Well, of course, as a big giver to the Thomas Jefferson Memorial Foundation, he didn't have to park at the bottom of the hill.

Mr. Upchurch was gone. It was safe to go out.

Once again Fern walked along Mulberry Row and descended to the vegetable garden. There were tourists here too, stooping to read the markers.

"Hey, honey, look at this, purple broccoli."

"Wow, look at the size of those cabbages."

Fern found the stairs to the orchard, where some of the peach trees were beginning to set fruit. Wandering along the grassy verge of the vineyard, she was surprised to see Thomas

Jefferson himself, once again, standing stockstill below her. He was staring up at Carter's Mountain, the round green hill that blocked the view of the distant range of the Blue Ridge. Even though he was the offspring of her own will, Fern was startled by the solidity of his shoulders. He was not transparent, like the man she had imagined in the garden, through whom she had clearly seen a shovel. This apparition was standing motionless in the posture that was Jefferson's own, arms crossed on chest, back perfectly straight. Fern remembered what slave Isaac had said—*Mr. Jefferson was a tall strait-bodied man as ever you see: nary man in this town walked so straight as my Old Master.*

Well, of course she knew exactly what he was thinking. He was looking a little sideways, staring westward, worrying about the men he had sent out on a dangerous mission, wishing he could see beyond Carter's Mountain and the Blue Ridge and the Alleghenies and straight across the eight hundred miles of intervening wilderness to the little band of men working their way up the Missouri River. He'd be worrying about the dangers they were facing, wondering if they would ever come back.

The clothes of this visionary Jefferson were a little odd— he was wearing a loose blue jacket and long blue trousers. She had never imagined him in anything but breeches buckled at the knee. Frowning at her creation, she commanded it to change its pants.

It didn't. It still stood there stubbornly with its arms crossed, looking out. Then, to her surprise, it lifted a hand to its face. There was a trickle of smoke.

Shocked, Fern started forward, but then she slipped on the sloping grass and gave a small cry.

At once the face turned toward her. Instantly the vision tossed away its cigarette and plunged downhill, vanishing in the trees.

◠

Tom waited until the woman went away. Then he climbed back to the orchard and poked in the undergrowth until he found the cold cigarette stub. He put it in his pocket and got the hell out of there.

The woman had seen him twice. The first time he had been taking a shortcut around the graveyard, and he had assumed she was just a tourist. This time it was clear she was a member of the staff.

What in the hell would happen now? Would they scour the woods? Make him clear out?

Goddamn her anyway.

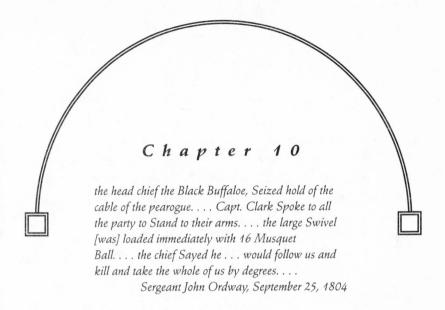

Chapter 10

*the head chief the Black Buffaloe, Seized hold of the
cable of the pearogue. . . . Capt. Clark Spoke to all
the party to Stand to their arms. . . . the large Swivel
[was] loaded immediately with 16 Musquet
Ball. . . . the chief Sayed he . . . would follow us and
kill and take the whole of us by degrees. . . .*
Sergeant John Ordway, September 25, 1804

George sat down with his book at a table in the Charlottesville Public Library and copied out a passage in his
meticulous small hand—*The Chin-nook womin are lude and carry
on sport publickly.* It was another find. There were plenty more,
he was sure of it. George vowed to pounce on them all—no
problem for a guy like him, a real brain, not like those party-
ing bastards on Fraternity Row who never cracked a book.

Then George moved to another table, where he could
watch the librarian. She was pulling on her coat. It was
lunchtime. A younger woman was taking her place. They
were chatting. The older woman was explaining something
in a whisper. She was leaving.

He studied the new one intently. He'd never seen this one
before. She had dark hair in pigtails. She was fat, just like Jeanie.

She was possible, quite possible.

To Fern's alarm, Mr. Upchurch began dropping in without warning.

Hearing his heavy step on the stair, she would sigh and prepare her face for a smiling welcome. And there he would be again, the dignified old gentleman, wearing another of his crazy neckties. Sometimes Fern wondered which was the real Augustus Upchurch, the dignity or the craziness? It was a silly question. Mr. Upchurch was a sweet, foolish, kindly old dear, and that was all.

He was always delighted by her growing stack of feeble pages. One day he asked if he might borrow them and bring them back next morning.

"Oh, no, I'm sorry, Mr. Upchurch. I can't let anyone see a first draft." Shrewdly Fern flattered him. "Of course, you of all people know what first drafts are like."

"Oh, of course." His scrunched-up face attested to the torments of the writer.

But why did he keep coming?

She should have guessed why. He was lonely. Augustus Upchurch lived all by himself in a gloomy ten-room house, he had no hobbies, he had nothing to do all day, and his old friends were either dead or in Miami.

Fortunately, his son Roger lived only a few miles away, on Jefferson Lake Drive, not far from Monticello, and Augustus was usually invited for Sunday dinner. Until the arrival of Fern Fisher, it had been the highlight of his week, because Roger and his wife were the parents of twin daughters who were their grandfather's joy.

Everything else had fallen away. Augustus Flaminius Upchurch had once been a highly respected elder statesman in Charlottesville, as well as a successful businessman with a chain of printing shops all over the state of Virginia—but in the fifteen years since his retirement the shops had been totally transformed.

The thump and rattle of the old machinery was gone, and so were the craftsmen in inky aprons who had worked so swiftly in the dark clutter of the old shop, nimbly scooping up letters with their dirty fingernails, reading the chases backward and upside down.

The new equipment merely clicked and hummed in pale rooms harshly lit with fluorescent lights. Teenagers with clean pink hands sat staring at a dozen screens.

The first time he had wandered into the new building for a visit and a cheery cup of coffee, hardly anyone had known who he was.

"Whodja say you want?" the child in the office had asked him, sipping her Diet Coke.

And then the young proprietor had hurried out of his office—busy, bored, and interrupted.

Augustus told himself gloomily that he should never have retired. He could have learned the new way himself. It couldn't be all that difficult. He would take a course at the university. But he didn't.

He had begun to feel his age in other ways. Augustus often reflected on the passage of time, wondering if there had been a particular moment when the slippage had started. An instant before that moment, he had been at the apex of success and esteem. An instant after, the descent had begun.

Around him teemed a younger race, fiercely ascending, edging him aside. They were jovial middle-aged men and women jiggling with energy, throwing themselves into the world's work. They failed to appoint him to committees. He was never invited to dinner.

Fortunately, the Society for Jefferson Studies remained. For twenty years he had been its president. The other elderly board members still looked up to him. They spoke his language. They were his friends. In fact, one was too friendly by far.

Flora Foley was a widow, and when Martha Upchurch had died at last, Flora had attacked on all fronts.

She might have made more headway if she had not been such an old hag, such a genuine fright. Her cheeks hung in swags, her black wig swore at her face, and her face swore back. Augustus was embarrassed that such an old crone should think him fair game. Why weren't younger, more attractive women making eyes at him?

They were not. It was only Flora Foley.

The other members of the board were kind and comfortable, but they met only once a month. The rest of the time Augustus didn't know what to do with himself.

In the past he had found fellowship in the Charlottesville Public Library, but now the old librarians had all retired. Their replacements were brisk and helpful, but there was no jocular exchange of gossip, just a dry *stamp, stamp* on the flyleaves of his books.

So the young woman at Monticello was an oasis, a social resource. Surely it was proper for him to show an interest, to ask how she was getting along?

Of course it was proper. Fern was immensely grateful to Mr. Upchurch, and she told herself that he had a perfect right to come.

At his fourth visit, he was interrupting nothing anyway. She had been falling asleep over the local paper, the *Charlottesville Daily Progress*. Even the gruesome news about another murdered woman hadn't kept her awake.

The tread on the stair woke her up. She jumped out of her chair. "Oh, Mr. Upchurch, I didn't hear you coming."

He always began by asking politely how the book was coming along, and she always politely lied that it was getting along just fine.

Once he had come so early, half an hour before the official

tours began, that Fern had given him her own personal tour of the house.

He was surprisingly ignorant. In Jefferson's Cabinet he was puzzled by the polygraph. "What's that thing on the table?"

"A Xerox machine," joked Fern. "No, no, of course it isn't, but it does the same thing. It makes copies. It's called a polygraph."

"Oh, yes, I see. The two pens are connected. You write with one and the other imitates every stroke. How ingenious." And then, to Fern's dismay, Mr. Upchurch invited her to lunch.

"Oh, thank you, but I'd better not." She racked her brain for an excuse, and simpered—if her eyelashes had been longer she would have batted them—"I've got to keep my nose to the grindstone."

"Well, that's admirable of you, I'm sure." It was clear he was disappointed.

When he was gone she hurried outdoors, abandoning the grindstone.

June in Virginia was a bower of flowers. The Canada lilies along the walk were chandeliers of orange bells. The sweet Williams and foxgloves were in bloom. But it was the trees that counted most. Fern wished that the man who had made a garden on his mountaintop could see these massive galaxies of leaves—the purple beeches, the tulip poplars, the sugar maples.

Elsewhere on earth people might be freezing, sweating, starving, scrabbling in garbage dumps for food, sleeping in gutters, dying. At this very moment a dangerous killer was threatening the town of Charlottesville. But here at Monticello such things were unimaginable. Here there was no starvation, no homelessness, no death.

Fern cast the tragic world aside. She had been invited into this paradise, and she might as well enjoy it.

In the back of her mind, or perhaps not in the back but smack in the front, was the man she had seen below the orchard, staring out at Carter's Mountain and smoking a cigarette.

He was not, after all, the resurrected ghost of a long-dead president of the United States. He was real.

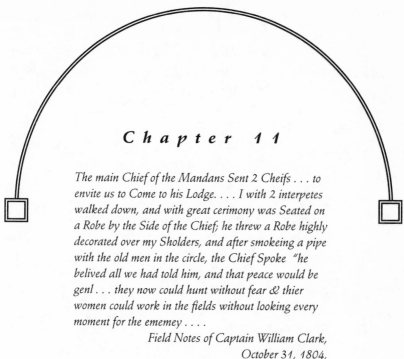

Chapter 11

The main Chief of the Mandans Sent 2 Cheifs . . . to envite us to Come to his Lodge. . . . I with 2 interpetes walked down, and with great cerimony was Seated on a Robe by the Side of the Chief; he threw a Robe highly decorated over my Sholders, and after smokeing a pipe with the old men in the circle, the Chief Spoke "he belived all we had told him, and that peace would be genl . . . they now could hunt without fear & thier women could work in the fields without looking every moment for the ememey . . . .

Field Notes of Captain William Clark,
October 31, 1804,
arrival among the Mandans

In Charlottesville, part of Market Street in front of the Jefferson-Madison Public Library was cordoned off with yellow tape. Half a dozen police cruisers and a police ambulance were double-parked on the street. On the side of each of the cruisers was the heraldic emblem of the city of Charlottesville, divided into quarters displaying the Rotunda of the University of Virginia, a Civil War cannon, a dogwood blossom, and a mysterious trio representing three Virginia presidents—Washington, Jefferson, and Madison. (Perhaps the city had something against James Monroe, the fourth president from Virginia.)

A stretcher emerged from the front door of the library, its contents covered with a plastic sheet. As it was carried down the steps, a woman leaped over the no-trespassing ribbon and catapulted forward. When an officer tried to stop her, she thumped him with her fists. It was Victoria Love, the director of the library. Her hair was in a frowze, her shoes were on the wrong feet.

Oliver Pratt, Charlottesville's Police Chief, was just in time to seize her arm as she tried to pull back the sheet.

"Now, ma'am," he said, "are you a relative?"

"A relative?" cried Victoria. "No, certainly not."

Someone whispered in Pratt's ear. The Chief nodded. "I see," he said to Victoria, easing her gently away from the stretcher. "You were her boss. Well, now, ma'am, just keep calm, and we'll soon straighten things out."

But Pratt himself was anything but calm. In fact, he was a jittering mass of confused rage. Still holding the director of the Jefferson-Madison Public Library by the elbow, he guided her to the corner of the street, where a woman officer from Forensics was holding something close to her eyes with a pair of tweezers. It was a bloodstained scrap of paper.

When Chief Pratt introduced Victoria, the woman from Forensics seemed pleased. "You knew the young lady? Well, then, maybe you can help us out. This was pinned to her clothing. What do you think it means?"

"Oh, my God," said Victoria. She stared at the paper and pawed at her breast, where she usually carried her glasses on a string. "Oh dear, I forgot my glasses. What does it say?"

The Forensics officer read it aloud. "It says *Sport publickly*."

"Oh, please," moaned Victoria Love, and she tottered away.

Chief Pratt looked at the strip of paper. "Spelled wrong, of course. Killers, lots of times they're illiterate, can't even read."

The officer from Forensics dropped her piece of evidence in a plastic sack. "Since when has carving up women been a public sport?"

A crowd had gathered across the street. One of them, a lanky guy with an orange ponytail, stood beside a small motorcycle. His overdue library books were weighing down his backpack. "What's going on?" he asked the guy standing next to him, a thickset man with a small head and an orange bristle cut.

"Dead female," said the man, his eyes shining with excitement. "Strangled, all carved up."

"Make way, you people," called out Chief Pratt, his voice shaking. "Car coming through."

It was the limousine of the Governor of Virginia, speeding to the scene of the latest attack on the young women of the commonwealth. He was eager to show his concern.

"High time he showed up," said the man with the bristle cut. "Must be feeling kind of helpless. This guy's too clever for 'em. They'll never catch him."

They stood back out of the way as the limousine pulled up to the curb. A couple of Secret Service men got out, and then the Governor—portly, red-faced, and grave.

The Secret Service men looked left and right. One of them, running his eyes along the barrier tape, saw the two redheaded men standing side by side.

He nudged one of the Charlottesville police officers, and wagged his head. "That eyewitness last month, she said he had red hair, remember?"

The police officer turned and saw only the redheaded guy with the motorcycle.

George Dryer had slipped away.

⌒

In his office at the University of Virginia, Ed Bailey unfolded the *Charlottesville Daily Progress,* glanced at the front page, saw the story about the latest victim, and decided once again not to pass along the news to Homer and Mary Kelly, who were driving down next week to join him in the house on University Circle.

Homer wouldn't be put off by the news, but Mary Kelly was skittish about the increasing number of murdered and mutilated women in the city of Charlottesville. *Females,* thought Ed, *God bless 'em, they're such timid creatures.*

He smiled with anticipation. Not only were the Kellys dear old friends, but, thank God, he would no longer be responsible for the care and feeding of Doodles, his landlord's little toy poodle.

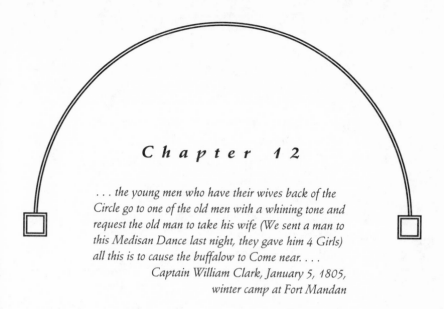

Chapter 12

*. . . the young men who have their wives back of the
Circle go to one of the old men with a whining tone and
request the old man to take his wife (We sent a man to
this Medisan Dance last night, they gave him 4 Girls)
all this is to cause the buffalow to Come near. . . .*
Captain William Clark, January 5, 1805,
winter camp at Fort Mandan

Fern was back at the family cemetery, a little off the path,
when she almost collided with him.

She said, "Oh," and backed up.

He backed up too. "Whoops, sorry."

The question burst out of Fern, "Who are you?"

"Tom," he said at once. "My name's Tom."

Fern gasped and whispered, "Oh, it is not."

"It isn't?" He looked at her in mock dismay. "Oh, sorry. I
guess I've had it wrong all my life. Maybe it's Ethelbert. Yes,
that's it, I remember now. Ethelbert Szybloski here, how do
you do?" He reached out a dirty hand and smiled pleasantly.
"Actually, my name's Tom Dean."

She laughed and shook it. "Fern Fisher." How could she
ever have been so carried away? This Thomas Not-Jefferson
had the right pigmentation, red hair and a fair skin blotched
by the sun. But he had a funny face with a big shapeless nose,
and he was wearing grubby jeans and a Laurel and Hardy

47

sweatshirt. His faded blue jacket was denim. His frayed sneakers were nothing like the tall narrow boots that stood so primly on the floor beside Jefferson's writing table. "But what are you doing here, Ethelbert—I mean, Tom? I keep seeing you. You're all over the place."

He coughed. "Forester. I look after the trees. You know, sycamore, oak, et cetera."

"Oh, is that it."

He turned away and pointed to the top of a pine rising above the other trees a long way off. "Canker sores, root rot. Gotta see to it. So long."

He loped away. Fern stared after him. Did trees get canker sores?

On her way back to the third floor, she put her head in the door of the curator's office. He was standing behind his desk looking at the mail.

"I didn't know Monticello had a forester," said Fern.

"A forester?" Henry Spender looked blank. "You mean Marcus Constable? He runs all kinds of things around here, not just the forest."

"Marcus Constable? But I met—well, never mind. My mistake."

The curator was staring at her, or, rather, through her. He seemed anxious. "Do you know anything about presidential protocol?" He heaved his shoulders nervously up and down. "It's this Fourth of July celebration. The President's coming and so are a lot of other important people in the administration, and I don't know who should be seated where."

Fern laughed. The opportunity to show off was too good. "What about President Jefferson's principle of pell-mell? Sit anywhere? Remember when he got in trouble because he didn't ask the wife of the British Minister to sit beside him at the table?"

"Oh, yes, the Merry affair," said Henry Spender absently.

"Big hullabaloo." Then he said, "Letter for you," and handed it across the desk.

A letter? Fern was pleased. It was her first at this address. Smiling, she reached for it, hoping it was from Jim Reeves, who had murmured in her ear, "Let's keep in touch."

But it was from one of the professors who had recommended her application for the Monticello grant:

> Dear Fern,
> Homer and I are so pleased to hear that you won that lovely grant. It sounds like a real plum. Will you be at Monticello this summer? We've been invited to the Fourth of July celebration, so we'll be coming to Charlottesville right after final exams. We hope to see you then.
>
> > Affectionately,
> > Mary Kelly
>
> P.S. Oh, Fern, we keep hearing about the Charlottesville killer. We trust you're being careful!

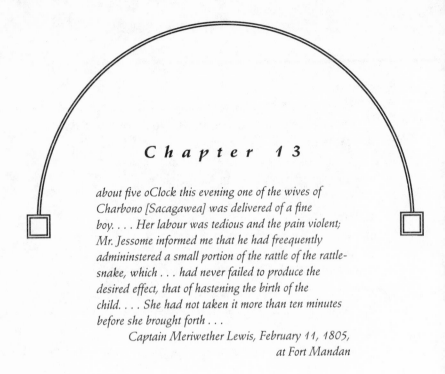

Chapter 13

about five oClock this evening one of the wives of
Charbono [Sacagawea] was delivered of a fine
boy. . . . Her labour was tedious and the pain violent;
Mr. Jessome informed me that he had freequently
admininstered a small portion of the rattle of the rattle-
snake, which . . . had never failed to produce the
desired effect, that of hastening the birth of the
child. . . . She had not taken it more than ten minutes
before she brought forth . . .
            Captain Meriwether Lewis, February 11, 1805,
                                    at Fort Mandan

There were too many books about Thomas Jefferson. Fern
was losing track. She had read only a few from front to
back, taking careful notes.

Of course, she didn't need to copy down the preamble to the
Declaration of Independence, because she knew it by heart:

> *We hold these truths to be self-evident, that all men are*
> *created equal, that they are endowed by their Creator*
> *with certain unalienable Rights, that among these are*
> *Life, Liberty and the pursuit of Happiness. . . .*

The memoir of the slave named Isaac was especially beguil-
ing, even though he referred to Thomas Jefferson as *Master:*

Old Master had abundance of books:
sometimes would have twenty of 'em down
on the floor at once: read fust one, then tother.

So were the recollections of Margaret Bayard Smith:

The children . . . now called on him to run with them, he did
not long resist and seemed delighted in delighting them. Oh
ye whose envenomed calumny has painted him as the slave of
the vilest passions, come here and contemplate this scene!

Fern copied this passage, underlining *vilest passions,* and
flipped open another book.

To Giovanni Fabbroni, 1778—If there is a gratification
which I envy any people in this world, it is to your country
its music. This is the favorite passion of my soul. . . .

"Oh, God, that's right," muttered Fern to herself, "he played
the violin." She underlined *favorite passion of my soul.*

But there were a lot of other books she was reading at the
same time, important books about Jefferson's championship
of the rebellion, his political opposition to John Adams, John
Jay, and Alexander Hamilton, his presidential accomplish-
ments and failures.

The trouble was that reading put her to sleep. Sometimes
her eyes closed. Then she would shake herself, jump up and
stretch, sit down, read another page, and begin to nod again.

So today, when Fern went outside for a brisk walk, it
wasn't to find the phony forester who looked so much like
Thomas Jefferson, it was to wake herself up.

But the imposter was looking for her. "Hi there," he said,
appearing suddenly from behind the South Pavilion.

Fern jumped and gave a small screech. Then, recovering her breath, she said innocently, "How are the canker sores?"

"Canker sores? Oh, those, they're fine. I just inject a little penicillin."

"Ah, I see. Well, what about the root rot?"

"No problem." The stranger whose name was Tom dismissed root rot with a wave of his hand. "Household bleach. You just pour a little around the base of the tree. Nothing to it."

"Oh, come on," said Fern, grinning at him, "that's silly. Tell me what you're really doing around here."

He looked at her accusingly. "Well, okay then, tell me what *you're* doing here. That's what I'd like to know."

"I asked you first."

He looked at her silently, and then said, "I'll show you." Gesturing with his elbow at Mulberry Row, he turned away and ambled down the slope.

Fern glanced back at the house and murmured, "I really ought to be getting back." But she knew it didn't matter. She was completely independent of everyone else. The tourists ebbed and flowed, the guides led them from room to room, the hired cleaners came and went, the windows were washed every day, the curator pursued his curatorial duties and worried about presidential protocol. Nobody noticed Fern's comings and goings.

Stepping sideways down the hill, she was acutely conscious of the stringy condition of her hair. She should have washed it last night, but she hadn't.

Tom wasn't looking at her anyway. He was walking ahead, not waiting for her to catch up.

It was a long way. They were descending into the woodland Jefferson had called the Grove, pushing deeper and deeper into the undergrowth, descending below the first Roundabout road and then the second.

"Hey," said Fern, when a branch lashed back in her face.

"Oh, sorry." He stopped and looked at her with concern. "Are you all right?"

She mopped at her eye. "You might tell me where we're going."

"We're almost there. This way."

And in a moment his camp appeared. It looked like something in a Boy Scout manual. His old-fashioned tent was slung between three trees, but there was no other miscellany of frontier life, no pot hanging from a teepee of sticks, no frying pan on a circle of stones. Only a small dusty motorcycle.

Tom lifted the tent flap. "Come in."

Fern ducked her head and went inside. At once the familiar fragrance of the sizing in the canvas walls charmed her, and the net-covered windows and the way the sunlight striped the translucent fabric. Memory rushed up—the delicious warmth of sleeping in a tent between her mother and father and waking up to the smell of frying bacon.

"Look," he said, showing her a card table covered with bottles, small bags, and sealed envelopes. "My pharmacopeia."

"Pharma—you're a doctor?"

"No, no. Well, not yet anyway. Actually it's not my pharmacopeia, it's Lewis and Clark's. I'm trying to collect samples of their medical supplies. Lewis made a list." He pointed at a small stoppered bottle. "Ipecacuanha." He picked up one thing after another. "Tartar emetic, mercury ointment, calomel." He opened a folder and turned the pages.

Fern stared at the dried leaves and flattened flowers. "I know, it's a—"

"Herbarium. Botanical specimens, samples of plants they mention in their journals."

The light dawned. "Oh," exclaimed Fern, "Lewis and Clark! That's why you're here, because the expedition was Thomas Jefferson's idea."

"Right. It was the one good thing he did."

"The *one* good thing!" Fern stared at him. "How can you *say* that?"

And then the argument began. It was soon obvious that Tom was the enemy.

It was too outrageous to need rebuttal, but Fern spluttered out the first things that came into her head, the Declaration of Independence, the Louisiana Purchase, the Virginia Statute for Religious Freedom—

He cut her short with one word: "Slavery."

"Slavery!" Fern remembered the word *passionately* that she had underlined so often in her notes. "But he was *passionately* against slavery! He was furious when the abolition of slavery was taken out of the Declaration, he hated the inhumanity of human bondage, and, good God, he persuaded Congress to end the slave trade. What more do you want?"

Tom led her outside and pointed up the hill. "How do you think he built this place? Oh, sure, he was the architect, but

who did the work? Who made the bricks, who did the plowing and harvesting so he could live like a king?"

Fern didn't want to hear it. Through her head shot the
facile excuse she had given Mr. Upchurch, that all the founding fathers from Virginia had kept slaves. Somehow it wasn't
enough. Looking around, she said angrily, "How do I get
back?"

Tom closed his mouth. Then he said curtly, "Follow me."

They said nothing all the way back. Fern trailed after him
blindly, gasping up the steep wooded hillside. She tripped
over tree roots, scratched her arms on briars, tore her shirt on
a thorn.

When the house showed through the trees, he stopped. A
little penitent, Fern smiled at him wanly and said, "Thank
you."

He nodded, his face solemn.

She walked away, a jiggling mass of self-doubt, feeling his
eyes on her back.

At least, she told herself ruefully, climbing the hill, this
man called Tom who was trespassing in Jefferson's sacred
grove had not brought up the name of Sally Hemings. Had
the master of Monticello slept with his slave or not? The evidence was against him.

Fern wasn't ready for that one.

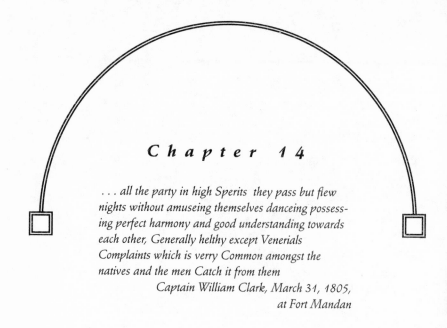

Chapter 14

. . . all the party in high Sperits they pass but fiew
nights without amuseing themselves danceing possess-
ing perfect harmony and good understanding towards
each other, Generally helthy except Venerials
Complaints which is verry Common amongst the
natives and the men Catch it from them
                    Captain William Clark, March 31, 1805,
                                  at Fort Mandan

There was something of which Augustus Flaminius Up-church was deeply ashamed, so ashamed that his mind refused to connect it with himself, because the real Augustus Upchurch had received the McIntire Award from the Charlottesville Chamber of Commerce and a citation from the Rotary Club of Richmond. And in 1978 the *Charlottesville Daily Progress* had called him Man of the Year. Augustus had a scrapbook full of flattering newspaper cuttings—although, looking at them recently, he had been surprised to see how old and yellow they were.

The shameful thing was his fascination with a pornographic tabloid he picked up at a convenience store on the other side of town, along with the *Richmond Times Dispatch* and the *Charlottesville Daily Progress*.

The porno sheet was always on the same place on the shelf, right next to a Christian magazine with headlines like HIDDEN BIBLE MESSAGES REVEALED.

At home he always dropped the respectable papers on the hall table, then carried the lurid sheet into his bedroom and turned the pages avidly, gazing at the sexy girls with their big breasts:

Strictly Hot Babes!
Wet & Ready 24 Hours a Day!
Gentlemen, Start Your Engines!
Live Sexy Coeds!
Horny Asian Sluts!

The sexy tabloid always ended up in a plastic trash bag. It had nothing to do with the rest of his life. It certainly had nothing to do with the charming young lady at Monticello.

But Augustus was aware that the world had two levels. When he got up in the morning the rising sun shone on the cars in which sober people were driving to work, his soft-boiled egg looked up at him with its cheerful yellow eye, his coffee steamed in the last of his wife's delicate cups, and the radio hummed softly with news about faraway wars. That was the normal everyday world.

But there was another one entirely, a swamp in which the supporting pillars of the good bright world were planted, their fragile foundations shifting sideways and threatening to collapse.

And of course, to his shame, he knew that he was part of it. The weird pages of the Adult Services section of the sexy tabloid appealed to his darkest inner nature. Maybe he was just a dirty old fart.

Well, no, of course he couldn't be that, because he wasn't really old. At least he didn't look nearly as old as he was. Whenever Augustus adjusted one of his jolly bow ties in front of the mirror he told himself that white hair didn't mean a thing. After all, plenty of young men were prematurely gray.

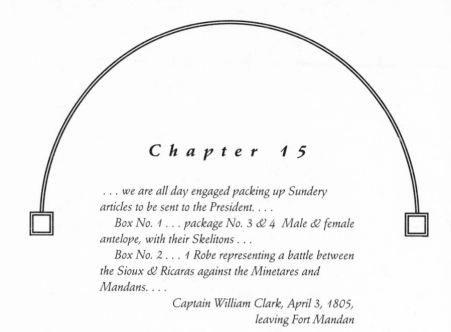

Chapter 15

. . . we are all day engaged packing up Sundery articles to be sent to the President. . . .

Box No. 1 . . . package No. 3 & 4 Male & female antelope, with their Skelitons . . .

Box No. 2 . . . 1 Robe representing a battle between the Sioux & Ricaras against the Minetares and Mandans. . . .

Captain William Clark, April 3, 1805,
leaving Fort Mandan

Tom rode back from a trip to Charlottesville with his backpack full of groceries. His camping cuisine was hobo-style—beans to be eaten from the can, bread and peanut butter, bananas, packaged cookies, Pepsi and bottled water. This time there were some oddities in the bag—a paper of pins and a roll of shelf paper.

His bike was small, only 250 cc's, but it was still a struggle to get it up the steep hillside. Halfway up, he stopped to catch his breath.

At once he was aware of something fluttering in the bushes. It was a cecropia moth, caught in a spider's web. The great wings were flailing. Tom leaned his bike against a tree, took out his pocketknife, and slashed at the web. At once the moth flapped up into his face and took off.

Do a good turn to fish or fox, and marry the king's daughter. Tom looked around dreamily for a beautiful maiden in floating garments and failed to see one. Instead he tripped over a tree root and fell flat.

It had been a bad morning. He had run into his mother in the supermarket. She had snatched at his arm and fixed him with her maternal gaze. "They do know you're coming back?"

"Who do you mean?" But Tom knew perfectly well what she was talking about.

"The medical school. I assume you're all set for next year?"

"Oh, I don't know," said Tom.

It had been like one of those fierce encounters on the Missouri River, when one of the men had come face to face with a grizzly bear. *Ursus horribilis horribilis,* that was his mother all over.

Now rolling his bike into the clearing around his tent, he found himself wondering if the big healthy girl he had met yesterday was a king's daughter in disguise.

It was too bad she was just another Jeffersonian sentimentalist, but at least she didn't seem stupid. Maybe she could be persuaded to the right way of thinking, if only she'd listen. Unfortunately, he had made her so mad she'd probably report him as a trespasser, and then his idyllic retreat in the woods would be over.

Now, forgetting about Fern, Tom unpacked the things he had bought in town. He put the groceries away in the cardboard box under the bed and pulled the wrapping off the roll of shelf paper.

His pharmacopeia took up all the room on the card table. Tom unrolled a short length of paper, cut it off with a pair of scissors, and laid it flat on his cot. The blankets were too soft for a desk, so he slid books under the shelf paper, picked up a pencil, and got down on his knees. Then, using a ruler, he drew a horizontal line.

The shelf paper was a time line. Eventually it would stretch all the way from May 14, 1804, when the expedition started up the Missouri River, to September 23 in the year 1806, the day of their triumphant return to St. Louis.

He made a spot with his pen. Above it he wrote carefully. "May 14, 1804, Capt. Clark sets off up the Missouri from the camp at River Dubois with the pirogues and the keelboat."

Then he sat back and looked at what he had done. To his astonishment his eyes were wet, he was filled with delight. He had made only a few scrawls on a piece of paper, and yet they propelled him through time and space, they carried him back and back. He was with the expedition on the river. The great journey had begun, and he was part of it.

⌒

Fern ate her paper-bag lunch on a bench at the far end of the west lawn. When she was finished she strolled along the North Terrace Walk and ducked into the tunnel that ran under the house from north to south. Blinded at first, she soon made her way to the foot of the stairs and climbed the three flights to the top.

Back in the Dome Room, she abandoned the latest timid chapter of her book and wrote a letter to her sister.

Dear Peg,

A person shouldn't forget another person's birthday, especially when that other person is one's own beloved sister. Happy birthday, darling Peg. I'm sending you an absolutely *unauthentic* bowl from the Monticello Gift Shop, accompanied by a guarantee that Thomas Jefferson *never* owned one like it in his whole *entire life.*

Of course you'll want to know how my new grant is working out. Well, naturally it's fabulous.

No, no, that's a rotten lie. The truth is, I can't do it. The moment I walked into my splendid office in Jefferson's house, every room of which is crammed with objects displaying the richness of his mind, the man himself disappeared. Thomas Jefferson I mean.

I should tell you that there's a strange person hanging around outside. At first I thought, aha, I've found him at last, because this guy is tall and skinny with red hair tied on the back of his neck the way the founding fathers tied theirs whenever they were signing a Declaration of Independence or making important remarks like *Life, Liberty and the pursuit of Happiness,* et cetera.

At first I thought he was a vision sent from on high to help me in my Quest. But alas he's only a human being, and pretty dumb at that. He thinks the only important thing TJ ever did was the Lewis and Clark expedition. How can he *say* that?

So I'm still all at sea. Please advise.

Love, Fern

P.S.—I forgot to answer your warning about the big bad serial killer. I know, I know, he's big news in Virginia. It's really boring, the way people talk about him all the time. But don't worry. I always drive straight home to my wonderful little apartment in Lewis and Clark Square, and then I go right in and lock the door. I'm not hitchhiking on a lonely road or walking around alone at night. So I'm fine. Don't worry, I'm being really careful.

P.P.S. Peg, remember when your Sunday-school teacher, Mr. Brisket, thought you were such a cute, cuddly little creature, he wanted to hug you to death and kiss you all over? Well, I'm beginning to have uncomfortable feelings about Mr. Upchurch, the old man who chose me for this award. He keeps dropping in and inviting me to lunch!

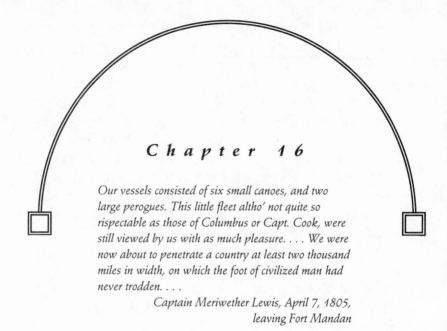

Chapter 16

Our vessels consisted of six small canoes, and two large perogues. This little fleet altho' not quite so rispectable as those of Columbus or Capt. Cook, were still viewed by us with as much pleasure. . . . We were now about to penetrate a country at least two thousand miles in width, on which the foot of civilized man had never trodden. . . .

Captain Meriwether Lewis, April 7, 1805,
leaving Fort Mandan

Mr. Upchurch's car was a large and imposing Mercedes Grand Prix, glittering with chromium trim. Fern hated it at sight, but when he opened the door for her, she climbed in.

He was a cautious driver. As he made his way slowly down the curving road encircling the hill, Fern caught a glimpse of Tom Dean kneeling among a clump of trees. He looked up and met her glance and gaped with surprise.

Fern wanted to roll her eyes and shrug her shoulders. *I'm just a kidnapped hostage.* But the car was creeping around another curve.

The hotel in Charlottesville where they had lunch was like the car, conspicuously luxurious. Mr. Upchurch pulled out Fern's chair, then sat down on the other side of the table and smiled at her tenderly. Fern could only gaze at his tie, mesmerized by its bold red-and-green stripes, which vibrated and jumped back and forth.

Wrenching her eyes away, she stared at the menu and ordered a salad. But it was impossible to say no to the glass of wine pressed on her by Mr. Upchurch, or to the hot rolls and turtle soup. Coffee came to the table in a steaming espresso machine. The little cups were piled with whipped cream. Fern sipped reluctantly, her stomach clenched with tension.

Afterward she asked to be taken back to work, partly to make a clean break with Mr. Upchurch and partly to make use of the rest of the day. But after the heavy meal in the hotel she found it impossible to concentrate. And anyway, on this first hot day of the season, the Dome Room was sweltering.

She went from window to window, unlatching the catches, pushing open the noble circles of wood and glass. They were hinged in the middle. The bottom half swung out, the top in.

Outside the house, on the west lawn, Henry Spender was working with a couple of groundskeepers and Howie Plover. Where should they put the caterer's tent? Would there be room for four-hundred folding chairs?

Howie nudged Henry Spender, and wagged his head at the open windows below the dome. "Looks kinda funny," he said, glancing at the curator.

Henry looked at Fern's windows, and his eyebrows went up. He said, "Mmmmm." But then he decided it didn't matter. As a curator he had the gift of distinguishing between trivialities and important matters. Briskly he turned back to the problem of the chairs.

Upstairs, behind the open windows, the magnificent chamber was still unbearably hot. Impulsively Fern decided to go right out and buy an electric fan.

She found one at the Bargain Mart on Hydraulic Road.

The Bargain Mart was often frequented by George Dryer.

He happened to be there at the moment, buying himself a bottle of hair color, because this morning on the news—George always watched the TV news—somebody who called herself a witness said the killer had red hair.

A witness? What goddamn witness? There'd never been any fucking witness! Still, the kooky female just happened to be right about his hair, so George was here to do something about it.

Slowly he walked up and down the aisle, examining the profusion of shampoos and hair conditioners and the forty feet of shelf space devoted to hair coloring. Studying the beautiful girls in Mocha Shimmer or Midnight Mink or Black Licorice, he decided on Cappuccino. Then once again he had to buy a bunch of shirts and long-sleeved sweats.

It was a joke, and it made George laugh, the way his back yard was like the places the cops dug up because they were full of bloodstained bodies, only his was a cemetery of bloodstained shirts. There wasn't much else you could do with a bloody shirt. No good washing it, no good burning it. You had to bury it.

In the checkout line, he was just behind a woman with long brown hair all down her back. She was lifting a big fan up on the counter. Interested, he watched her carry it outside. "Hurry it up," he said to the checkout girl, slapping down his shirts and his packaged hair color.

But the checkout girl was fiddling with the paper feed on the cash register. It was three fuming minutes before he could run out to the parking lot.

Naturally, the fascinating female was gone.

◠

The black pavement in front of the Bargain Mart was sending up such waves of heat, Fern dumped her new fan on the back

seat of her car, jumped in behind the wheel, and zoomed out of the lot. At home she went straight to her phone as usual, to see if there were any messages.

There was only one. Her sister had called from Indiana, responding to Fern's letter. Peg's recorded voice was loud and anxious.

"Honestly, Fern, did you read your letter before mailing it to me? Do you have any idea what you SAID? First you mention this nasty stranger in the woods, and then you insist you're in no danger from that scumbag, the creep who's still running around loose after murdering all those women. FERN, BE CAREFUL! CALL ME! And, hey, whatever happened to Jim Reeves?"

Fern flopped on a chair and pulled off her shoes. Funny, Peg hadn't mentioned the unwanted attentions of Mr. Upchurch. Because maybe Mr. Upchurch was a greater menace to her health and safety than Tom Dean. In fact, he had already made a dangerous sexual assault.

After depositing her on the walk in front of the East Portico, he had held her hand a little too long and asked her to call him Augustus.

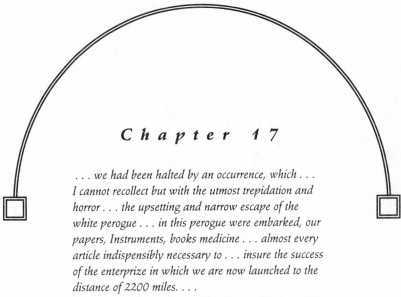

Chapter 17

*. . . we had been halted by an occurrence, which . . .
I cannot recollect but with the utmost trepidation and
horror . . . the upsetting and narrow escape of the
white perogue . . . in this perogue were embarked, our
papers, Instruments, books medicine . . . almost every
article indispensibly necessary to . . . insure the success
of the enterprize in which we are now launched to the
distance of 2200 miles. . . .*
Captain Meriwether Lewis, May 14, 1805

*. . . the Indian woman . . . caught and preserved most
of the light articles which were washed overboard.*
Captain Meriwether Lewis, May 16, 1805

The canvas walls of the tent were shivering a little. Tom Dean was at home.

Fern walked closer. She had found her way back to his hidden camp, after spending half an hour heading in the wrong direction.

The corners of the tent flap had been lifted and attached to poles, making a shady front porch. Fern stood at a polite distance and called, "Anybody home?"

There was a pause. The tent stopped shaking. Then Tom looked out and said, "Oh, hi."

She moved forward a few inches. "I just want to say I'm sorry I was so cross. I don't agree with what you said, but I shouldn't have been so rude."

"It's okay." Tom looked at her blankly, and then his face brightened. "Come in, I want to show you something."

His strip of shelf paper was pinned to the wall of the tent. It hung limply away from the sloping fabric.

He explained, "It's a time line for the travels of Lewis and Clark. Look, come close."

He talked excitedly, drawing his finger along the line from May 14, 1804, to the 21st. "This is where they set out on the Missouri River in earnest, Clark and Lewis and all the men together, in a heavy rain."

Fern stared and said nothing.

"Here they are at the mouth of the Osage River." Tom propelled her across the tent to a book lying open on his cot. "The Osage River, see? It's right here. It's Captain Clark's map for this part of the Missouri. Okay"—Tom pulled her back again to the time line—"so here we are again, June 2, 1804. Beautiful country, that's what they found. They killed a few deer." He looked at Fern fiercely. "That's the way they had to live every day. Every single day they had to kill deer, bear, antelope, whatever, or else go hungry."

"What if it rains?" said Fern.

"It did rain. It didn't matter. They went right on through rain and snow and starvation and every kind of obstacle."

"No, I mean, what if it rains on your tent? The paper will get wet."

"Oh, I know." Tom's cheerfulness faded. He touched the time line with a tender finger.

"Where do you live? Can't you do it there?"

Stubbornly he said, "No, I can't. I live here."

"But you can't stay here forever."

"I suppose not."

Then Fern spoke in a dream. "How would you like to see where I work?"

Surprised, Tom jerked his head up at the hill. "You mean up there? You work in the house?"

"Right. I'm trying to write a book about Jefferson. I have this really neat place on the third floor. I'll show you. Come on."

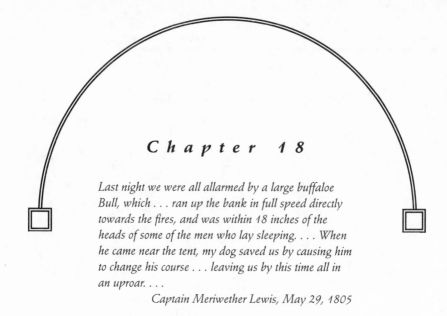

Chapter 18

Last night we were all allarmed by a large buffaloe
Bull, which . . . ran up the bank in full speed directly
towards the fires, and was within 18 inches of the
heads of some of the men who lay sleeping. . . . When
he came near the tent, my dog saved us by causing him
to change his course . . . leaving us by this time all in
an uproar. . . .

Captain Meriwether Lewis, May 29, 1805

Someone was knocking at the door of the curator's office. It was Gail Boltwood, Henry Spender's favorite tour
guide.

"Henry," said Gail, "there's a problem. A lot of people are
complaining about a bad smell."

"A smell?"

"I went to see for myself, and it's true. It comes from the
ice house. You know, that deep pit under the North Terrace
Walk."

Henry sucked his pencil. "Do you know what kind of
smell it is?"

"No, the iron railing makes it impossible to look down. I
think you'll have to get somebody with an acetylene torch to
remove the railing."

"Right." Henry made one of his usual sensible decisions.
"I'll call Howie Plover. He'll take care of it."

⌒

Tom followed Fern through the woods up the steep side of the mountain, and then through the field of daisies to the border of small trees at the end of the west lawn. Beside the Roundabout Walk, the foxgloves and Canterbury bells had given way to scarlet poppies and Texas bluebonnets. Tom stopped to admire the bluebonnets, because people said they were Lewis's pea.

He was falling behind. "Hold it a sec," he called to Fern. She looked back and waited for him to catch up, and then they moved quickly along the dependencies under the North Terrace Walk. Passing the ice house, Tom wrinkled his nose. There was something rotten down there. He wanted to look, but Fern was disappearing into a long stony corridor. He followed her in.

In the middle, the corridor opened out into exhibition spaces and offices. Fern stopped at the foot of a stairway, turned to smile at him, and then began running up the narrow steps.

Obediently Tom followed. As they climbed past the first floor, they could hear one of the guides lecturing to a flock of visitors—"The portrait over the mantel is Jefferson's daughter Martha at the age of fifty-one. She was the mother of eleven children."

Up and up. When Fern kept climbing past the landing on the second floor, Tom guessed where they were going. "You don't mean—it isn't the Dome Room?" She kept doggedly ascending, but at the last turn of the stairs, in a flood of sunlight, she looked back at him and grinned.

He stood in the doorway gazing around the lofty room. Then he said softly. "What a waste."

Fern was insulted. "A waste? What do you mean, a waste?"

"This room, these walls." He raised his arms in a gesture of wonder, and gave her a wild look. "Wait, I'll be back."

Astonished, Fern watched him stride to the door, then turn and begin plunging down the stairs. His footsteps were soft rapid thuds, going down and down. What did he mean, he'd be back? What made him think he could get in again by himself? She'd be damned if she'd wait for him downstairs.

Fern plumped herself down at her keyboard and brought up on the screen the chapter she had abandoned an hour ago, hoping it would look better than she remembered.

It was still pretty limp:

Thomas Jefferson was regarded as a kind master by the slave population at Monticello.

Tom was gone a long time. Fern could dimly hear the comfortable voices of the guides. Visitors from Boston, Minneapolis, and Los Angeles murmured their questions, the guides softly answered.

Probably he wasn't coming back at all. Well, good riddance.

At last there were footsteps on the stairs. Too many footsteps. When Tom appeared, he was accompanied by the curator, Henry Spender.

"This gentleman says he is a friend of yours," said Henry mildly.

"Oh, right," said Fern. Hastily she introduced Tom Dean, mentioning his interest in Lewis and Clark. Tom stood stiffly upright, looking sheepish.

Henry nodded and smiled politely at Fern. "Next time just let someone know you're expecting a guest."

"Yes, of course," said Fern, and Henry withdrew.

Tom had his time line under his arm. He strode across the floor and began to unroll it. "Look," he said eagerly, "there's room enough. There's room enough for the whole expedition." He swept his arm around the Dome Room.

Fern was speechless.

He unrolled the time line a little farther. Somewhere downstairs a door opened, sending a draft of air up the stairs to fling out the flimsy paper in Tom's hand. It rattled like a flag in the wind.

"Listen"—he was pleading with Fern—"it was Thomas Jefferson's expedition. Lewis and Clark, they were doing it for him. It's part of your story. It's the best part, the very best part." He brought the roll of paper to the table and spread out the first six feet. "It's the journey to the western ocean. It will fit on the wall. All of it, the whole thing, from beginning to end. Don't you see?"

Fern stared at it. "Well," she said doubtfully. "I don't know. I just don't know."

But Tom's sense of manifest destiny was very strong, and she gave in.

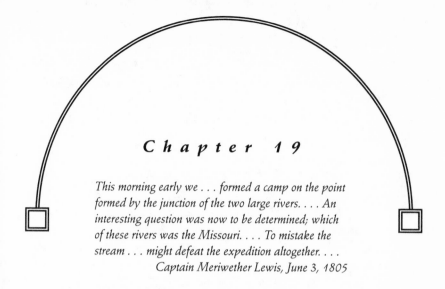

Chapter 19

This morning early we . . . formed a camp on the point formed by the junction of the two large rivers. . . . An interesting question was now to be determined; which of these rivers was the Missouri. . . . To mistake the stream . . . might defeat the expedition altogether. . . .
Captain Meriwether Lewis, June 3, 1805

There had been another killing. "The young woman was a hitchhiker," said the dapper reporter on Channel 10. "Several passing drivers saw her standing alone beside the road. Apparently, in spite of the warnings that have been broadcast throughout the entire commonwealth of Virginia, she accepted a ride from a stranger."

"Security measures are being instituted at the university," said the cute woman reporter, and she went on to talk solemnly about curfews and a buddy system. "Women students are urged not to walk alone after dark."

George was one of the first on the scene after his CB radio burst into noisy squawks, summoning a pack of cruisers to the place where he had dumped the girl.

A suspicious state cop asked him point-black what he was doing there.

"Heard the sirens," said George. "Just wanted to see what was up."

"Well, keep the hell out of the way. Get over there on the other side of the highway."

But it was too late. George had already seen the police photographer aim her camera at the new message pinned to this Jeanie's bra, and now she was focusing on one of George's artistic touches—the name tag he had taken from the Jeanie in the library.

He doubted they'd notice the mutilated ear or the careful pattern of the slashes. Too dumb, they were all too dumb. But it was what they always did first, the men with Lewis and Clark, they did the disemboweling so the meat wouldn't spoil. These ignoramuses, they didn't know stuff like that.

A lot of other drivers slowed down when they saw the cruisers with their flashing blue lights and the ring of uniformed men and women bending over something at the side of the road. A traffic cop from the Albemarle County Police Department stood in the middle of the highway making huge motions with his arm, urging the traffic forward.

The cop paid no attention to the inquisitive faces in the cars, but he couldn't help noticing a young guy on a motorcycle, because the kid pulled up near the taped barrier and pretended to fiddle with his engine.

When he took off his helmet, the officer thought he recognized him. Wasn't he a lot like the redhead who had been there at the public library when the body came out the door? Had the other kid been as funny-looking as this one?

The officer yelled at one of his colleagues, but nobody heard him. Frustrated, he watched the biker fasten his helmet and zoom out on the highway. He didn't even get the kid's license, because a couple of cars full of rubberneckers got in the way.

On the other side of the road, George Dryer was still watching, feeling more and more condescending. Oh, sure, those jerks had been to college, they thought they knew everything, only they didn't know shit. They didn't read great books like he did. They weren't worthy of somebody like him.

What George wanted was somebody with a high IQ, some genius out there somewhere, some great mind to catch on at last. *Somebody to give him credit.*

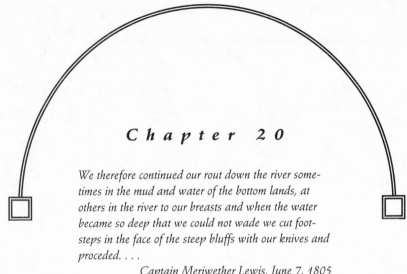

Chapter 20

*We therefore continued our rout down the river some-
times in the mud and water of the bottom lands, at
others in the river to our breasts and when the water
became so deep that we could not wade we cut footsteps in the face of the steep bluffs with our knives and
proceded. . . .*

Captain Meriwether Lewis, June 7, 1805

If Homer and Mary Kelly had great minds, their giant intel-
lects were absorbed at the moment in the task of driving
down to Charlottesville.

Mary was a steadier driver than Homer, who was apt to
fall asleep at the wheel. But by jolting himself awake with
strong coffee he was able to take his turn, while Mary read
aloud the letters that had passed between John Adams and
Thomas Jefferson.

Mile after highway mile streamed by, as the two old men,
long separated by political hostility, took up again their
youthful friendship by correspondence.

"Laboring always at the same oar—" read Mary, and then she
glanced up in alarm as Homer careened headlong into a traffic circle. "Watch it, Homer, watch it!"

Homer edged into the right lane, whirled the wheel, and
dodged in front of a truck. Somehow they came out alive,
and he said stuffily, "I am perfectly capable of driving this vehicle without supervision."

Mary took a deep breath, then went on calmly with Jefferson's letter—*"with some wave ever ahead threatening to overwhelm us and yet passing harmless under our bark, we knew not how, we rode through the storm with heart and hand, and made a happy port."*

When they pulled into a truck stop for lunch, they bought a copy of the *Washington Post.* "Good grief," said Homer, pouring ketchup on his French fries, "that weird homicidal maniac is still on the loose in Virginia."

Mary looked at him warily. "Now, Homer, it's none of your business."

"Of course not," said Homer stoutly. "But a person can take an objective interest in what's happening in the world, can't he? After all, it's one's duty as an informed citizen."

"Oh, Homer—"

He protested loudly. "After all, Thomas Jefferson himself wanted free public education. He said you couldn't have an enlightened citizenry unless they could read and write. You can't disagree with such a noble purpose, can you? All those little tots lisping their ABC's? Colleges full of scholars reading Shakespeare, et cetera?"

"Shakespeare has nothing to do with it," said Mary indignantly. "This killer is a crummy, disgusting, abominable human being, and the entire police force of Virginia is working on the case, and they're certainly going to nab him sooner or later, without your lifting a finger, Homer Kelly."

"No, no, of course not," exclaimed Homer, lifting his hands in innocent horror. "My interest is purely that of a spectator, nothing more."

"Glad to hear it," said Mary, looking at him darkly.

But as they paid for their meals, the man behind the counter said jovially, "That last poor girl, did you read how he carved her up?"

Mary hurried Homer back to the car and snatched up the

book. She had lost her place. As he turned the car back on the highway, she began reading another random letter from Jefferson to Adams in the middle of a page—*"It seems that the Cannibals of Europe are going to eat one another again. . . . This pugnacious humor of mankind seems to be the law of his nature."*

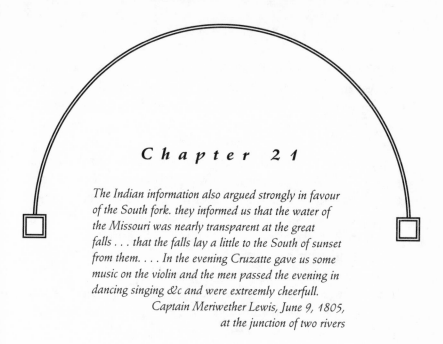

Chapter 21

The Indian information also argued strongly in favour
of the South fork. they informed us that the water of
the Missouri was nearly transparent at the great
falls . . . that the falls lay a little to the South of sunset
from them. . . . In the evening Cruzatte gave us some
music on the violin and the men passed the evening in
dancing singing &c and were extreemly cheerfull.
Captain Meriwether Lewis, June 9, 1805,
at the junction of two rivers

Tom got to work next day, unrolling his shelf paper all the way around the room, jamming his thumbtacks into the plaster wall and the wooden moldings, skipping only the two doors. Stretched over the round windows the paper was translucent, reducing the light only slightly.

Fern looked on with alarm. "Tom, hold it a minute. I don't know about all those thumbtacks. I mean, this place is a museum. It's all so perfect."

But it was too late. Tom carried on feverishly, thrusting the tacks into the wall with his thumb. In the powerful grip of the magnificent story, he was eager to record the emergencies that had come up every day and the beauty of the landscape and the roar of the Great Falls and the nearly impassable mountains and the urgent forward momentum of the two gallant captains in their drive to the western sea. "Hold this end a sec," he said. "Got any more thumbtacks?"

Fern shook her head. Oh, God, she should have put her foot down. How could she let this Tom person take over like this? Now he'd be here all the time, scribbling away on his sleazy piece of paper.

She tried to renege. "Listen, I don't know about all this. I mean, here I am with this big grant, and I'm supposed to be writing a book about Thomas Jefferson. Lewis and Clark were just a minor episode in his life. But here you are, taking up all this space."

"A minor episode!" Tom looked at her in horror.

Fern thrust out her lower lip. After all, it was *her* project, *her* office. She had a perfect right to tell him to piss off.

But to her surprise his face changed. He smiled and began talking like a rational human being. "Look, why don't you join me?" Leaving his roll of paper dangling from the last thumbtack, he walked back to the beginning, where he had pinned up the six-foot stretch recording the start of the journey. "See this horizontal line? My stuff about Lewis and Clark is just the top part. You can have all the rest."

Fern stared. She didn't understand. "What do you mean?"

He read his first entry. "May 14, 1804, Capt. Clark sets off up the Missouri from the camp at River Dubois—'*I Set out at 4 oClock P.M, in the presence of many of the neighbouring inhabitants, and proceeded on under a jentle brease up the Missouri. . . . A heavy rain this after-noon.*'"

"Well, all right," said Fern, "bully for Captain Clark."

"But what was Thomas Jefferson doing on May 14, in 1804?" Tom had the kind of complexion that flushed upward from the neck. Now it was patchy with excitement. "I mean, he was president of the United States, wasn't he? He must have been doing something important."

"That's right," muttered Fern. "He was in his first term as president in 1804."

Tom slapped the paper. "I'll write up here on top whatever

the Corps of Discovery was doing on any particular day, and you can match it with whatever Jefferson was up to at the same time." Again he swept his arm around the room. "See? There's miles and miles, and half of it's yours. How about it?"

Fern stared at the long stretch reserved for Thomas Jefferson. It was not just miles and miles, it was a continent of blank white paper.

"Can't you find out what he was doing from day to day?" urged Tom. "My God, you've got all those books. Is one of them a journal? I mean, after all, he told Meriwether Lewis to keep a journal. What about Jefferson himself?"

"Letters," mumbled Fern. "He wrote a lot of letters."

"Well, letters, then. Is there a letter dated May 14, 1804?"

It was a delicious question. Fern turned slowly and looked at her heaps of library books. For the first time she was captured by a strange kind of hunger, a passionate desire to fling open their pages, run her finger down their lovely indexes, ransack their beautiful chapters, looking for the answer to the question. *What was Thomas Jefferson doing on the day Lewis and Clark set off up the Missouri River?*

She had always thought of scholarship as meditative and serene. Could this really be scholarship, this greed to wrench the books open and tear out the pages, to gobble them alive, the dismembered facts red and dripping? She laughed, remembering that she was after all, a carnivore.

⌒

Outside, under the corner of the North Terrace Walk, Howie Plover set up a flimsy barrier of stakes and string around the ice house. Passing tourists walked around it, holding their noses. Then Howie put on his welder's mask and got to work with a torch. Blue flame attacked the iron gate at both ends, where it had been thrust deep into the stone.

When he could pull the gate free, he took a flashlight out of his toolbelt and pointed it into the pit.

Howie had suspected drowned rats, and his suspicion was right. Five bloated bodies floated in the shallow water at the bottom. The stench was overpowering.

Breathing through his mouth, Howie lowered a bucket on a rope and scooped them up. Nothing to it. Then he carried the bucket to his truck, hurtled down the mountain road, charged along Route 52 to 20, whirled onto Interstate 64 at Exit 121, found the Shadwell exit to Route 250, and at last turned off on a woods road and hurled the contents of the bucket into the Rivanna River.

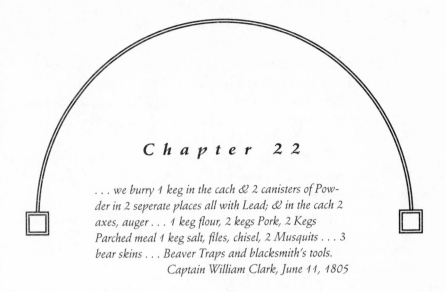

Chapter 22

. . . we burry 1 keg in the cach & 2 canisters of Pow-
der in 2 seperate places all with Lead; & in the cach 2
axes, auger . . . 1 keg flour, 2 kegs Pork, 2 Kegs
Parched meal 1 keg salt, files, chisel, 2 Musquits . . . 3
bear skins . . . Beaver Traps and blacksmith's tools.
Captain William Clark, June 11, 1805

"Jefferson was traveling too," said Fern, glancing up from the book. "May 14, the very same day. He was just back in Washington from Monticello. The carriage got stuck in the mud, it was raining, it was a mess, he was disgusted." She was flooded with excitement. She looked at the limp stretch of shelf paper. "I can't write on that."

"Of course not," said Tom. He detached his original six-foot stretch and slapped it on the table. "Here you are. Just fill in the bottom half."

Fern looked at Tom's sentences, rising straight up from the horizontal line. She pulled up a chair, picked up her pen, and whispered, "I'll be really careful."

He watched as she stared at the first piece of the time line, then turned it sideways and bowed over it, writing small, the words running neatly up from the bottom of the paper to the spot on the line that was the beginning of the voyage of discovery—*After a hard journey from Monticello, where he was present at the death of his daughter Maria, President Jefferson was back in Washington.*

She put down her pen and stood up, and then they both gazed at the six-foot piece of paper. Half a continent lay between Fern's entry and Tom's, but there was no separation in time. Godlike, they looked down at the small active figures poling their keelboat up the Missouri River while the founder of the expedition—far to the east, in another world—walked into the President's House in the city of Washington. The pure rain of heaven had fallen on all their heads alike.

When Augustus Upchurch appeared in the doorway, Tom and Fern were standing side by side, pinning the first piece of the time line back up on the wall.

They turned as one, and saw him.

Augustus had been about to invite Fern to a concert in Cabell Hall. After all, what could be more harmless? How could she refuse? They would sit together absorbed in the music. Afterward they would talk about it in high cultural tones, and then he would ask her where she lived and drive her home and kiss her lightly on the cheek.

But now his smile faded.

Rattled, Fern moved away from the time line and waved a feeble hand at Tom. "Mr. Upchurch, I'd like you to meet Tom Dean. He's helping with my research."

Augustus was still gasping from the steep ascent up the high risers of the stairs. His face was purplish red. His tie was Day-glo green. He frowned at Tom, breathing hard. "You're a volunteer?"

Tom nodded vigorously. Fern said, "Oh, yes, that's right, he's just a volunteer."

The interloper was young, no older than Fern herself. Suddenly Augustus felt superannuated and ready for the grave. He tried not to show his crushed feelings. "What's all this?" he said, walking to the time line, tilting his head to read the long slanting inscriptions.

They both spoke at once, explaining.

Augustus listened. Glancing around the room, he saw the prodigious length of the cooperative project, and his heart sank. He wanted to ask how this sort of thing would help with the writing of Fern's all-important book, but he didn't.

He also wanted to know whether or not they had permission to jam all those thumbtacks into the wall, but again he refrained.

Fern saw him glance at the crumbs of plaster along the baseboard. She hesitated on the brink of apologizing, then held her tongue.

Augustus could think of nothing else to say. He did not invite Fern to the concert. He did not even say goodbye. In a paroxysm of hurt feelings, he marched out of the room.

Almost at once there was a strangled shout and a heavy thumping, followed by a crash.

He had fallen downstairs. They clattered down the steps to the landing and helped him to his feet.

"Oh, Mr. Upchurch," cried Fern, "are you all right?"

He was not all right. By some miracle none of his bones had been broken, but a lump was rising on the back of his head, his dignity was shattered, and he was utterly miserable.

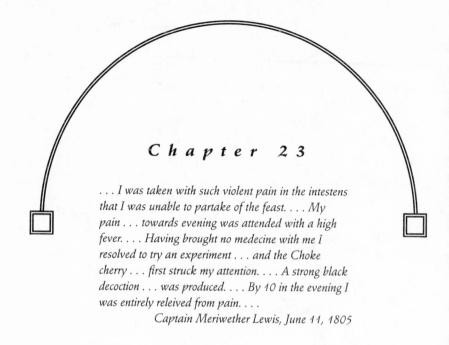

*. . . I was taken with such violent pain in the intestens
that I was unable to partake of the feast. . . . My
pain . . . towards evening was attended with a high
fever. . . . Having brought no medecine with me I
resolved to try an experiment . . . and the Choke
cherry . . . first struck my attention. . . . A strong black
decoction . . . was produced. . . . By 10 in the evening I
was entirely releived from pain. . . .*

Captain Meriwether Lewis, June 11, 1805

L ying flat on his back, Tom stared up at the top of the tent.
It was invisible, a blotch of darkness. He could be anywhere. Maybe in a vast cave with a thousand bats hanging
upside down over his head. Or in a wilderness camp on the
South Fork, and Captain Lewis and the other men of the exploring party were right there beside him, sleeping on the
ground.

But even in the pitch-darkness Tom could feel the close-
ness of the walls of the tent. And the freshness of the woodland air was tainted with the scent of asafetida from one of
the jars on the card table beside his cot.

The jar was part of his precious Meriwether Lewis pharmacopeia. For weeks Tom had been collecting samples of all
the medicines that had been packed in canisters and chests
and carried on the keelboat, portaged past the Great Falls of

the Missouri, and humped over the Rockies, all of those tinctures and powders and pills that had kept the men healthy, or at least had not killed them—mercury for the venereal diseases caught from the native women, salves for the eye problems that afflicted so many of the people in the tribal villages, and powerful purges for the cure of almost everything else.

But lately he had been neglecting his bottles and jars. He had forgotten the name of the next item on the list. What was the healing plant he had been looking for? He couldn't remember.

It was too bad. One of the reasons he had set up his tent in the woods around Monticello was to look for some of the wild herbs on Lewis's list—after all, this part of Virginia had been home to Meriwether Lewis as well as to Thomas Jefferson.

But there were other reasons. The second was that Jefferson's mountain was philosophically appropriate. The whole thing had been Jefferson's idea. The President had chosen and trained Meriwether Lewis as its captain, he had set him great goals. He had imagined the possibilities, the necessities and dangers, and then he had persuaded Congress to provide the money.

But there was a third reason why Tom was camping in the Monticello woods. It was an escape from his family. The big perfect house in Keswick Estates was only a few miles away, but here in the woods it felt like a thousand. He had fled from an overpowering mother, a demanding father, a domineering grandmother, and a younger sister in the most repulsive stage of sullen puberty.

The fact was, Tom had been a battered child. The punches and blows had been to the psyche, not the body. They had beaten him through the various stages of lower and higher education and thwacked him in the direction of medical school.

An ever-present scar was the cost of his education, never allowed to heal, always open and bleeding. *Do you know how much it's costing us to send you to medical school?*

They expected him to work the hardest, get the best grades, and be assigned to the best hospital. In other words, to become as successful as their friend Ronald Spark, whose medical practice was worth—*"What would you say, Janine? Seven figures?" "Oh, of course, seven figures."*

Dr. Spark was an eminent urologist, a specialist in diseases of the ~~intestinal tract~~. *urinary tract.*

Tom wanted nothing to do with the ~~intestinal~~ *urinary* tract. The only successful physician he cared about was Benjamin Rush of Philadelphia, who had provided Captain Lewis with his list of medicines, including his own famous thunderbolts for the complete evacuation of the bowels.

Tom had been working his way down the list. He had collected calomel and epsom salts and nitre and ipecacuanha, he was trying to figure out how to powder rhubarb and jalap. He wanted to know what clyster pipes and penis syringes looked like.

Laudanum had been more difficult to come by, because it was opium, and opium meant heroin. As a medical student with an earnest project, he had persuaded one of his professors to give him a prescription. But there were still a few things he had hoped to find growing naturally, plants he might find in the woods at Monticello. Exploring, he had come up with rhubarb and basilicum. He had collected bark from fallen branches.

But then the time line had occurred to him, and swept him away. The bottles and jars still sat on the card table in his tent, sweating on hot days, solidifying on cold nights, the labels darkening in the humidity, but now they were neglected.

The tent was nothing more than a place to sleep. Everything important had been carried up the hill.

Tom smiled in the dark, pleased with the way he had half conned, half persuaded the woman named Fern to let him use her wall. *She* didn't need it. She could write her dumb book in a closet. Let her scribble her sentimental garbage about Thomas Jefferson all over the lower half of the time line—the rest belonged to him.

It was too bad he couldn't accompany the words of the journals with a long continuous map of the terrain, but the river wouldn't cooperate. It would soon wander right off the paper, heading northwest.

The sloping walls of the tent were still invisible. But now the dark spaces around him were becoming the Dome Room, and over his head Tom could almost touch the wide concavity of the dome itself.

He reared up from the pillow, gripped by an idea. The dome! Why shouldn't he copy the maps made by William Clark—those wonderful maps drawn from measurements taken so faithfully every day with sextant, compass, quadrant, horizon glass, pole chain, and log line—why shouldn't he paint the windings of the river and the entire course of the journey right up there on the dome?

First, of course, he would need a ladder. . . .

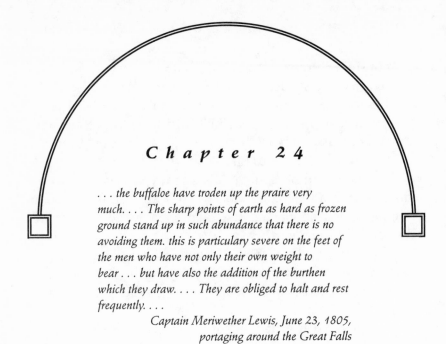

Chapter 24

. . . the buffaloe have troden up the praire very
much. . . . The sharp points of earth as hard as frozen
ground stand up in such abundance that there is no
avoiding them. this is particulary severe on the feet of
the men who have not only their own weight to
bear . . . but have also the addition of the burthen
which they draw. . . . They are obliged to halt and rest
frequently. . . .

Captain Meriwether Lewis, June 23, 1805,
portaging around the Great Falls

Augustus Upchurch could not see himself clearly. He was not aware of the intensity of his feeling for the young woman at Monticello. He knew only that the presence of the interloper in the Dome Room made him feel like an old fool. His hurt feelings simmered and boiled. Nursing his wounded pride, he decided to complain to Henry Spender. Surely the curator would be shocked by the strange things that were happening right over his head.

When the telephone rang in the curator's office, Henry was deeply engaged in planning the Fourth of July bicentennial extravaganza.

He had abandoned his keyboard. He was grasping a pencil tightly, checking and querying the items on a list.

1. President's helicopter, east lawn (Make sign visible from above?)
2. Phone-bank (Check AT&T)
3. Parking (Hire more shuttle buses?)
4. Security (What if duties overlap? Possible disaster? State Police, Secret Service, Ch'ville Police Department? Speak to Richard)
5. Food (Gail says caterers at loggerheads, possible catastrophe)
6. Chair rental, tents (Marcus Constable, no prob)
7. Fireworks (Richard going hog-wild)
8. Porta Potties (*Out of sight!* Howie swears, stack of Bibles.)
9. Music (String quartet, A-okay)
10. Setting up chairs (Howie again)
11. Name tags on chairs (Fern Fisher)
12. Invited guests (Jefferson descendants at each other's throats! God almighty!)

Scribble, scribble, scribble. In Henry's frenzied grip, the point of his pencil snapped. He jumped up, loped across the room, ground the point sharp as a needle, plunged back to his desk, and scribbled on without a pause. *Publicity, television, radio—*

He was just adding *Donors,* when the phone rang.

"Oh, Augustus," said Henry, "I'm so glad you called." (Surely the Society for Jefferson Studies would contribute a large sum.)

He didn't have a chance to say why he was glad, because Upchurch was in a tizzy. He was spluttering and shouting. Something must be terribly wrong. "What, the Dome

Room?" said Henry. "Did you say something's wrong with the Dome Room?"

"It's my Jefferson scholar, Miss Fisher. She's supposed to be working up there, writing a book."

"Yes, of course. I see her every day." The curator had the insane impression that young Fern was doing something unspeakable. "Is something the matter?"

Augustus choked. "Go and see," he said in a strangled whisper, and hung up.

Henry put down the phone and stared at his list. Then he slid back his chair and walked upstairs.

He found Fern sitting quietly in front of her keyboard eating a sandwich. No orgies were going on.

But there *was* something different about the Dome Room. A long strip of paper had been stretched all the way around it.

Fern waved her sandwich at the paper and explained. "It's a time line, Mr. Spender. For the Lewis and Clark expedition and the events of Jefferson's presidency at the same time. You know, from 1804 to 1806."

"I see. What a good idea." The curator smiled at Fern. "Please call me Henry," he said, and went back to his ever-lengthening list.

He was so absorbed that he paid no attention to the noises from the staircase, a succession of small rattles and bangs.

Tom Dean's aluminum ladder was an awkward thing to carry up the narrow stairs. He did his best to avoid knocking it against anything, but it was ten feet long. It kept bumping the wall on one side and crashing against the railing on the other.

Acquiring it had been a hell of a job. Since he couldn't carry a ladder on his motorbike, he had ridden the bike home, hoping to borrow his mother's second car, a flashy new sport-utility vehicle, if only she hadn't driven it away somewhere.

Fortunately, the car was sitting right there in the driveway. Unfortunately, his little sister Myrna was right there too, with her asinine girlfriend Nadine. They were lying flat on their backs on lawn chairs with their faces raised to the sun.

Nadine sat up and giggled at Tom. Myrna sat up and glowered. "Oh," she said, "you're back."

Tom yanked off his helmet, rolled his bike into the garage, came out again, and tried the door of the van. It was locked. He turned to his sister. "I just want to borrow it, bring it right back. Where's the key?"

Myrna said grumpily, "Mummy won't like it." Nadine giggled again.

"But it's only for an hour or two," protested Tom.

Myrna flopped back on the lawn chair and closed her eyes. Grudgingly she said, "Hall table." Nadine flopped back too.

The Bargain Mart on Hydraulic Road supplied everything required for living on the planet, except of course the finer things of life—poetry, music, and philosophical inquiry. But who wanted stuff like that when everything else was right here inside these cavernous walls? Certainly there were plenty of ladders.

Tom forked over two twenty-dollar bills, carried his purchase outside, and manhandled it into the van. One end of the ladder stuck out the back window. He tied his bandanna on the last rung. It was the first time the big SUV had transported anything but his mother and Myrna and the twits who were Myrna's little friends.

On the way to Monticello, he wondered where in the hell he could possibly park. Of course there was the visitors' parking lot, but he couldn't very well carry a ladder past all the tourists and the ticket office and the arriving and departing shuttle buses.

In the end Tom had no choice but to leave the big shiny car on the shoulder beside Route 53. It was illegal, of course, but he'd only be gone twenty minutes, just long enough to get the ladder up the hill to his tent and run back down.

Even so, he was away too long. When he got back he was disgusted to see a parking ticket under his windshield wiper. He thrust it in his pocket and drove the van back home.

Naturally, he'd pay the fine himself, but, God, he'd have to leave his mother a note, because the car was in her name and the Sheriff's office might call and complain. Tom's creepy sister had said, *Mummy won't like it.* Well, goddamnit, Mummy certainly would not like it.

The ladder was not easy to maneuver among the trees, but at least there was no one in the woods to ask what he was doing. When he carried it out into the open he was more conspicuous. Tom whistled carelessly as he marched across the lawn and around the South Terrace Walk and into the long passage under the house. There were staff members down there, and tourists looking at exhibits in glass cases, but nobody paid much attention to a working stiff with a ladder.

It was tricky, banging and bumping it up the three flights of stairs, but Fern was expecting him. She leaned over the railing, grasped the top, and backed into the Dome Room. The ladder came neatly through the door. Tom set it up and unfolded it.

"Oh, my God," said Fern. "It's so big."

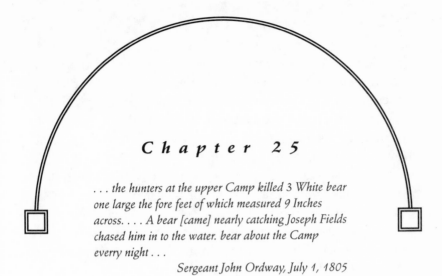

Chapter 25

*. . . the hunters at the upper Camp killed 3 White bear
one large the fore feet of which measured 9 Inches
across. . . . A bear [came] nearly catching Joseph Fields
chased him in to the water. bear about the Camp
everry night . . .*

Sergeant John Ordway, July 1, 1805

Ed Bailey had been right about the house on University Circle. It was not a handsome Jeffersonian edifice with white columns and classical detail, it was a homely pile of clapboards with a wraparound front porch. For Ed it was conveniently near the University of Virginia.

Homer and Mary settled in quickly. They had two floors to themselves. The guest bedroom was a shapeless space with ugly dressers and a deceased fern of immense size in a wicker stand. They hung their clothes in a cavernlike closet. Over their heads they could hear the soft thuds of Ed's footsteps in the attic apartment.

At first the telephone didn't work, but before long Mary noticed that it wasn't plugged in. At once she called Fern Fisher and made an appointment to visit her at Monticello.

There was a problem with the bathroom sink. "Ouch!" shouted Homer, the first time he tried to brush his teeth, because the faucet marked "H" was cold and the one marked "C" boiling hot. Downstairs, the kitchen worked pretty well after they mastered its eccentricities—the exploding coffeepot and the hiding places for pots and pans. In the parlor, the piano was useless, because half its keys were dead, but it sometimes struck a tringling note in the middle of the night.

The best part of the house was the front porch with its rockers and porch swing, as long as they didn't try to sit down in the collapsing lawn chair.

The house was under control, but for Homer the rest of the city was an enigma. Whenever he set out in the car, he lost his way.

"I kept going around in circles," he complained to his wife, coming back defeated yet one more time. "I just wanted to find the supermarket on Hydraulic Road, but you can't get there from here."

Mary took the crumpled map from his trembling hand. "Look, Homer, you just keep straight ahead on Preston Avenue. See? It turns into Hydraulic. Nothing to it."

"Preston Avenue! No, no, you forgot Grady! You gotta take Grady first, which turns into Preston, which turns into East Market, which turns into something else, and after a while you're on your way to Richmond."

"Homer, look. You take Grady to Preston and then turn sharp *left*. You see, right here you go *left*."

"Left? Left?" Homer was too excited to distinguish the blobs of color on the map, which was ripped and crumpled from being batted open in moments of crisis. "Where, where? Oh, God, I don't see it. Show me!"

Mary folded the map along its torn creases and said soothingly, "It's all right, Homer dear, we'll soon learn our way around." She whistled for the dog. It came bouncing to her on its tiny legs.

It was the teacup poodle. Its name was Doodles. "Your turn, Homer," said Mary, holding out the leash.

"Oh, God, not again." Homer looked down at the quiver-

ing little creature, which was looking up at him worshipfully
with black button eyes. "I always feel like such a fool."

The tiny dog threw its whole being into a paroxysm of
yipping. Mary thrust the leash into Homer's hand and controlled her laughter until they were out the door. Then she
watched from the window, rejoicing in the sight of her six-
foot-six-inch husband demurely following a fluffy little pow-
derpuff of a dog.

Then she stopped laughing, as the memory of their melodramatic sojourn in Venice welled up in her mind, as it did
so often without warning. Last year in Venice she had been
infatuated with someone else, a married man, a charming
stranger. She had abandoned all her New England inherited

principles, she had told herself they were prim and puritani-
cal and didn't matter any more. Now she winced, remembering, because she hadn't consulted her inherited principles at
all, she had simply been swept away. *Big mistake.*

Afterward she had tried to make it up to Homer. She had
kissed him and caressed him and lavished tenderness upon
him. Of course it was still necessary from time to time to
control his dangerous tendency to giddy euphoria and flights
of fancy.

Now she watched until Homer and Doodles turned a corner and were lost to view. Therefore, she was unaware that
another wild flight was about to happen. She did not see
Homer take a copy of the *Charlottesville Daily Progress* out of
the pocket of his jacket while Doodles squatted sweetly on
the grass next to the sidewalk.

On the front page was a photograph of the Governor of
Virginia, his mouth open, his fist raised high. He was hot under the collar about something or other. Oh, of course, it was
the serial killer. *Why doesn't the Charlottesville Police Department
DO something,* the Governor wanted to know. *Don't they have
a budget of six million dollars a year, paid by the hardworking tax-
payers of the city of Charlottesville? If they can find illegal stills in
the countryside and retrieve stolen cars, why don't they turn their attention to the monster who is threatening the innocent young women
of Albemarle County?*

Homer stuffed the *Daily Progress* back inside his jacket and
looked around vaguely. Where was he? Doodles had led him
astray. What was this crazy bridge? Why was that lumpy
wall painted pink and blue? Why did it say DAN ♥ MIGGY?

Homer shook his head, bewildered. The city of Charlottesville was a labyrinth of vanishing streets and mysterious apparitions. He walked home with Doodles and turned
her over to his wife.

At once Mary picked up the little dog and cooed, "Cunning

little sweetie," and kissed her nose, which was the color of violets.

"I think I'll try again," said Homer craftily. "I refuse to give up. This time I'll find that supermarket if it takes all day. Where's the stupid map?"

"Oh, good for you, Homer," said Mary. "This time be sure to turn sharp left on Preston Avenue."

But Homer was in the grip of transport. His heart beat high, his eyes glittered with crazy lights, he consulted the map and drove in the opposite direction.

He would just drop in on the Chief of the Charlottesville Police. Just make him a friendly little visit, because the poor guy was in terrible trouble.

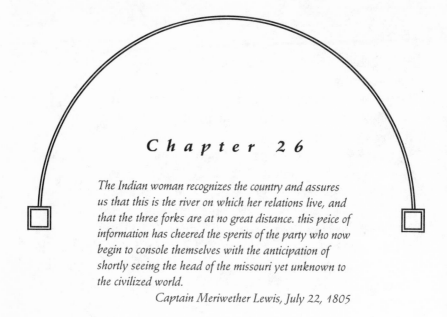

Chapter 26

*The Indian woman recognizes the country and assures
us that this is the river on which her relations live, and
that the three forks are at no great distance. this peice of
information has cheered the sperits of the party who now
begin to console themselves with the anticipation of
shortly seeing the head of the missouri yet unknown to
the civilized world.*

Captain Meriwether Lewis, July 22, 1805

Fern was soon accustomed to the slight scraping of Tom's
ladder on the floor as he followed the Missouri a few degrees of longitude farther west. Slowly the winding river advanced over the surface of the dome, climbing miraculously
over the shallow ribs and continuing on its way.

The time line too was growing longer and longer.

Fern's latest entry was Jefferson's speech to the tribal chief-
tains, sent to him by Lewis and Clark:

*My children, White-hairs, Chiefs & Warriors of the Osage
nation . . . It is so long since our forefathers came from beyond
the great water, that we have lost the memory of it, and seem
to have grown out of this land, as you have done. . . . I sent a
beloved man, Capt. Lewis . . . to learn something of the
people with whom we are now united, to let you know we
were your friends. . . .*

Tom looked over her shoulder. "Oh, right," he said. "The Osage chiefs. They all came to Washington."

Fern looked up. "Have you read it? Jefferson's speech?"

"No, I haven't. Are you finished? My turn."

She stepped back and he began writing quickly, recording a journal entry by William Clark:

Sent out Sjt. Pryor and Some men to get ash timber for ores, and Set some men to make a Toe Rope out of the Cords of a Cable. . . . Drewyer our hunter and one man came in with 2 Deer & a Bear, also a young Horse.

Fern looked at his entry and smiled. "The spelling is certainly amusing."

Tom took offense. "Oh, I suppose you think Jane Austen was a better writer?"

"Well, my God, of course I do."

"Well, how do you think Odysseus talked? Listen, think of those guys out there on an unknown frontier, living off the land, discovering places no white man had ever seen before, living with danger every day. They weren't writing pretty for the teacher. Whereas Jane Austen—"

"Oh, I guess she would have written better if she'd camped out in the wilderness?"

"*Whereas,* while they were writing their journals beside the river, Jane Austen was sitting on a velvet sofa writing novels about lovesick young ladies."

"Oh, she was not. You don't understand her at all."

Tom laughed. "Here, give me a hand. This piece is ready."

"Wait a sec," said Fern. "Did you bring the pins?"

Tom produced the paper of pins from his shirt pocket. Fern plucked out a few, remembering the way her mother had knelt on the floor to pin up a hem, with little Fern standing on a chair.

Together they picked up the new piece of the time line and fastened it securely to the long blank strip of shelf paper that ran all the way around the wall. Then they stood back to admire the twelve running feet of recorded time, from May to September in the year 1804, with its notes from the letters of Thomas Jefferson and the journals of Lewis and Clark.

"It looks great," said Fern.

Tom laughed. "What the hell are we doing this for?"

Somehow they had forgiven themselves for the absurdities of the eighty feet of shelf paper, the 160 thumbtacks, the tall, ridiculous ladder, and the assault on the dome. And they had forgotten Mr. Upchurch.

But Augustus had not forgotten them. One week after he had found the invader in Fern's lofty tower, they heard again the thump of his feet on the stairs.

At once the racing engines of their obsessions ground to a halt. Tom backed away, Fern turned to face the imposing figure of Mr. Upchurch as he walked in the door. Surrounding him rose shafts of normalcy, dull and bleak, gray and accusing.

Augustus was appalled. The boy was still here. Henry Spender had done nothing. Looking up, Augustus saw the vandalism to the dome, and gasped.

"It's the river, you see," gabbled Fern. "From Captain Clark's maps, the ones he made for Thomas Jefferson. We think he would have been pleased. The President, I mean President Jefferson would have been so *pleased.*"

Augustus didn't know what to say, or how to begin. "Well, my dear," he faltered, but then he couldn't go on. Once again he withdrew without saying goodbye. Stepping carefully down the staircase, gripping the steeply sloping banister, terrified of falling down, Augustus told himself that the poor child had been kidnapped. The threatening young stranger had led her astray.

What the helpless young woman needed was the advice and counsel of an older and wiser man, a truly loving friend. In fact—by the time he descended to the bottom of the staircase Augustus had worked out a plan.

He would send in a spy.

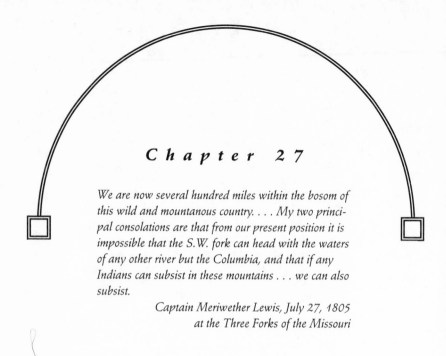

*We are now several hundred miles within the bosom of
this wild and mountanous country. . . . My two principal consolations are that from our present position it is
impossible that the S.W. fork can head with the waters
of any other river but the Columbia, and that if any
Indians can subsist in these mountains . . . we can also
subsist.*

> *Captain Meriwether Lewis, July 27, 1805
> at the Three Forks of the Missouri*

On his way to pay his kindly call on the beleaguered
Chief of the Charlottesville Police Department, Homer
again lost his way. After finding himself heading out of town,
he stopped to inquire the way at a gas station. The attendant
pointed to the left and said, "Nothing to it. You can't miss it."

Fifteen minutes later, at a convenience store, he bought a
bag of peanuts and inquired again. The woman behind the
counter pointed to the right and said he couldn't possibly
miss it.

But Homer had an infinite capacity for error. Before long
he was crossing the Rivanna River.

At last, by some miracle, he blundered in the right direction and found the Charlottesville City Hall on East Market
Street. By a stroke of luck, there was a parking place right out
in front. Homer swooped into the space, hopped out of his
car, and walked into the police station.

It was milling with uniformed officers. Their faces were grim. Was one of them Chief Pratt?

A reception officer sat behind a glass window. Homer edged in her direction and looked at her questioningly. "May I help you?" she said kindly, in the gentle accent he was already so fond of.

"My name's Kelly, Homer Kelly. I used to work for the District Attorney of Middlesex County in Massachusetts." Homer was telling the truth as far as it went. He did not confess that his job with the District Attorney was a quarter of a century back. "I wonder if I might see Chief Pratt."

The woman must have been out of her mind, because after a pause she said, "Certainly," and pointed down the hall.

Homer was flabbergasted. "Don't you need to ask him first?"

"Oh, I'm sure he'll be glad to see you." The officer did not explain that her chief was so frustrated, so apoplectic, he would grasp at any straw.

In fact, Chief Pratt hardly waited for Homer to introduce himself before he began to pour out his troubles. On his desk lay a newspaper with a couple of lurid headlines—

ANOTHER FOUL KILLING
MURDERED WOMAN WEARS
EARRING TORN FROM LAST VICTIM

Below was a color photograph of a body covered with a bloodstained sheet. The picture was overprinted with the words:

DO SOMETHING!

Homer listened humbly and watched in awe as the Chief ranted and raved and balled up the newspaper in his powerful fists. Hurling it across the room, he glowered at Homer and snarled, "He's here, God's whiskers, he's right here in

Charlottesville, I swear he is. Maybe we can't find him because he's in plain sight, like the purloined letter."

"The purloined letter?" Homer was charmed. "You mean
like the one in Poe's story? The police ransack the house for
a stolen letter but they never look at the one on the mantelpiece because it's in plain sight, so it can't possibly be the
right one, but of course it really is—you mean *that* purloined
letter?"

Pratt wasn't listening. He leaned forward and let off steam
like an overheated boiler. "You see, we think he has normal
middle-class habits. His victims aren't whores. The first two
were Sunday-school teachers, and then there was the librarian and the chiropractor, women like that. Well, of course
that hitchhiker was some kind of a New Age hippie, but that
kid was just asking for it, right? This one was a respectable
beautician."

Homer opened his mouth, but Pratt didn't wait to hear his
opinion, he just barreled right on. "Well, okay, we've got
people in all the branch libraries and we're trying to cover the
churches, but, Judas priest, Mr. Kelly, do you have any idea
how many there are in Charlottesville? Eighty-four—Lutheran,
Episcopal, Methodist, Pentecostal, Presbyterian, Jehovah's
Witnesses, Seventh-Day Adventists, Mennonites, Quakers, I
mean we got all kindsa churches except maybe Holy Rollers,
you name it, including twenty-three Baptist."

"A God-fearing town," murmured Homer encouragingly.

"So, okay, where does the bastard live? He's gotta sleep
somewhere, gotta room somewhere. Does he camp out in
the woods? Eat in restaurants?" Pratt rolled his eyes at the
ceiling, and swore by the bowels of Christ. "I mean, how
does he get his food? In a supermarket? Well, sure, we can
post people in all the big supermarkets and, like I said, in the
churches and so on, but what the devil are they supposed to

be looking for? Oh, there was some woman claimed she saw him, thinks he has red hair. And one of the county guys saw a redheaded kid on a motorbike"—Pratt scrabbled among the turmoil of papers on his desk and found a note—"little Honda, he said, only, goddamn him, he didn't get the license number, but he swears he's seen this guy coupla times, coupla different crime sites. But, jumping Jesus, maybe the description is phony anyway." Pratt tore at his thick white hair. "The goddamn killer's got some kind of vehicle, we know that because he picked up that poor hitchhiker. But, God's *teeth,* what kind of car?"

Homer didn't know, and he shook his head humbly. He was delighted to observe that Chief Pratt's exclamations were not anatomical but old-fashioned and theological, an exaggerated version of his own, because probably Pratt too had been brought up an earnest Christian, and what good were swear words if they didn't shock you a little?

Again the chief ran his fingers through his hair, front to back and side to side. "Oh, naturally, every single man, woman, and child in Albemarle County has called 911 because they saw a suspicious-looking car and scribbled the license number on their cuff, so we say thank you very much, and then of course we look it up, only it turns out the vehicle belongs to the rector of the Church of Our Saviour or an elderly orthopedic surgeon or a lady dentist. Christ Almighty." Pratt's face was a dark and passionate red.

Homer cleared his throat and asked a modest question: "Is this the first serial killer you've come across around here?"

Pratt looked at him scornfully. "Oh, God, no." He turned to a map on the wall beside his desk and tapped it with his finger. "Spotsylvania, Culpeper. We got 'em all the time."

No flies on us, thought Homer. "What about stolen cars? People steal cars around here the way they do in Boston?"

"Stolen cars? Mother of God, we got sixteen reports of stolen cars this week, tracked down eleven, mostly kids in the neighborhood, five outstanding, can't find 'em, owners mad as hell." With a savage motion of his arm, Pratt swept all his papers on the floor. "The guy's a smoker, we know that. Drops ashes on the bodies. Stands around admiring his handiwork, having a comfy cigarette."

Pratt surged out of his chair and stamped up and down. "The Governor, bloody Christ, we've got him on our neck, running for re-election, other guy's ahead in the polls, all the poor incumbent's got to run on is public safety, righteous wrath about this dangerous maniac on the loose, laxity in the police department, he's gonna reorganize public safety, turn it inside out, and guess who's at the top of his firing list, yours truly, that's who, God's britches."

Homer opened his mouth to say something sympathetic, but Pratt whirled around and jabbed his finger in the air. "Okay, I know what you're going to say, what about Forensics, right? Forensics, they always find something. Well, naturally they found something, this repeat pattern, he's got an MO."

"MO, right," said Homer. "Method of operation."

"It's the same every time, so we know it's just one guy, not different guys, because the pattern's always the same. Throttles 'em, probably with a piece of chain, we get bruises like from a chain, rips off their clothes, mutilates 'em with a sharp knife, could be an ordinary carving knife, hunting knife, we don't know what the hell, takes a memento, leaves it on the next victim. Like a rosary or the librarian's name tag or this earring. You know, whatever. Cigarette ashes, he's a smoker. And a note. Creep always leaves a note."

"A note!"

"Right. Pins it on the body someplace, or on the clothing, common pins like in sewing"—Pratt made little darting motions with his hand, stitching a piece of air—"pinned-on notes, can't miss 'em, stare you in the face."

"But doesn't that give you something to go on? What do they say?"

Pratt sat down again with a thump and closed his eyes. "Nutty, just nutty. We don't know what the hell they mean, they don't make any sense. Wait a minute." The Chief opened his eyes, reached down, snatched a paper from the floor, and handed it to Homer. It was a typed list of the messages left by the serial killer on the bodies of his victims.

Old bawd
Article of traffic
Presents neked
Pocks & venereal
All in scabs
Venerious & pustelus
Sport publickly

"Insane," said Pratt. "Uneducated guy, wouldn't you think? Can't spell worth a damn."

Homer stared at the list. "The spelling's odd, I grant you, but the words aren't exactly uneducated. This word *Publickly,* for instance." He glanced up at Pratt's tormented face. "There's this classy bar in Boston, calls itself Publick House, Publick with a 'K.' You know what I mean—ostentatiously old-fashioned."

Pratt took the list back from Homer and studied it. "That's right. I see what you mean."

"They probably have something to do with sex, wouldn't you say? *Venerious and pustelus,* meaning some kind of venereal disease? *All in scabs?* Symptoms of the same thing? This word *sport,* maybe it doesn't mean basketball or baseball, that kind of sport. Maybe—"

"Hey," said Pratt, "hold it. I gotcha. Wait a sec." He whirled around in his chair. "I just happen to have the complete *OED* right here."

Homer's jaw dropped. There they were, all twenty thick volumes of the *Oxford English Dictionary,* lined up on a shelf in the office of the Charlottesville Chief of Police, squeezed between catalogues of firearms and reference books on toxicology.

Pratt heaved the SOOT–STYX volume off the shelf, plopped it down on a reading stand, and flipped the pages to the word *sport.*

Homer stared enviously at the reading stand. It was a beautiful piece of furniture with a slanted top. In a flicker of resolution, he decided to make one for himself out of pine boards, because it didn't look all that difficult, you'd just need to cut the side pieces on the slant and screw a square piece on top and there you'd be with the reading stand of your dreams, and you could leave the dictionary open on the top and store the entire twenty volumes of the *OED* on a couple of shelves underneath, so handy, right there in the kitchen, next to the refrigerator, Mary wouldn't mind, she'd be delighted, and then they could look up words in the middle of a meal.

"Sport," said Pratt. Turning around triumphantly. "First meaning, *pleasant pastime, recreation, diversion.* Second meaning, *amorous dalliance.* So in this case, Professor Kelly, it must mean—"

"Please, Chief, not Professor. Call me Homer."

Pratt beamed at him. "Okay, Homer, and my name's Oliver. Anyway, what the hell, as I was saying, this weirdo is using the word *sport* to mean *amorous dalliance.* Using it in its archaic sense. But why? Where does it come from? Is it a quotation of some sort? A quotation from what?"

Homer laughed. "Chief Pratt, you're a man after my own heart. Those books must have cost a pretty penny."

"Money no object." Pratt smiled. His haggard face was transformed. "You see, I've got this project. I'm looking up old words in the language of Thomas Jefferson. Hobby of mine. You know, instead of building birdhouses or collecting stamps."

"The language of Thomas Jefferson? Why Jefferson?"

The learned police chief looked at him keenly. "Do the words *created equal* mean anything to you? *Self-evident? Pursuit of happiness?*"

"Oh, oh, I see what you mean."

"*Revolution? Republican? Traitor?*" Once again Pratt turned in his chair and reached for the *OED*. Then he changed his mind. "Hey, Homer, I've got a job for you." He plucked another book off the shelf and handed it across the desk.

Homer looked at the title in surprise—*The Mind of the Monster: A History of Serial Killers*. It was a steep descent from the sublime heights of Jeffersonian lexicography.

"You won't like it," said Pratt. "It's a disgusting book written by an idiot, but it may come in handy."

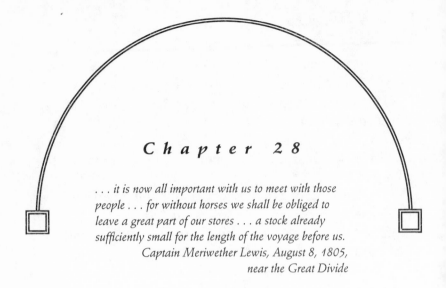

Chapter 28

*. . . it is now all important with us to meet with those
people . . . for without horses we shall be obliged to
leave a great part of our stores . . . a stock already
sufficiently small for the length of the voyage before us.*
Captain Meriwether Lewis, August 8, 1805,
near the Great Divide

When two people of different sexes and more or less the
same age find themselves in the same room for weeks
at a time, they size each other up. Well, the truth is, they size
each other up in the first fraction of a second, but as time goes
by, the first instantaneous judgment may change—growing
warmer or colder, or perhaps just more confused.

Both Tom and Fern were wary. In the past both had fallen
in love with, gone to bed with, fallen out of love with, or
been dumped by several different partners, and each of them
regarded people of the opposite sex with suspicion, however
plausible they might seem in the beginning.

Fern was leery of toothy smiles, artificially induced states
of rapture, and knives in the back. Well, it hadn't been a knife
exactly. Jim Reeves had broken up with her carelessly, like a
boy tossing a pebble into the sea. Oh, God, why didn't he
write?

Tom was cagey about beauty—in the past he had been led
astray by extraordinary gorgeousness, learning to his cost

that sometimes it was only skin-deep. He had figured out that you had to treat a woman the way the men of the Lewis and Clark expedition handled a deer they had shot for supper—you had to insert a sharp knife and pull back the hide and find out if the heart inside was the size of a pea.

But in Fern Fisher's case there was no question of excessive glamour. She was a big healthy woman with a lot of brown hair falling down her back.

And Fern could see that Tom's homely face with its big nose was a long way from the artificial charm of ex-husband Buddy. Nor did he seem in the grip of any mind-altering drug. As for a knife in her back, it was too soon to tell. It could happen in a flash—the skewer between the shoulderblades.

And there was always the probability that he was gay. The men she was attracted to often were. Fern watched for any sign, a particularly subtle understanding, an outrageous comic sense, a total blankness of response to the fact that she was female.

Tom was equally uncertain about Fern. She didn't seem to be giving off any pheromones, or whatever you called the invisible globules of sexiness pouring out of the female animal. Some women moved in a steamy cloud, but not Fern. The air around her was clear.

But of course it didn't matter anyway, because there was a gulf between them about the thing that mattered most, their opinion of Thomas Jefferson, the man who had built this house, who had arched over their heads this spacious dome.

The nature of their disagreement infuriated Fern. It was like a game of cards with someone holding nothing but trumps. Tom's trumps were from a suit called Slavery.

Fern would toss down on the table the Declaration of Independence, and—BANG!—down would come Tom's card to win the trick, because the man who wrote the Declaration had owned slaves. "Life, liberty, and the pursuit of happiness? What kind of liberty did his slaves have? What kind of happiness could they pursue?"

"But—"

"And anyway the Declaration was just a bunch of ideas that were floating around all over the place."

Fern was exasperated. "But Jefferson said so himself." She closed her eyes and the words appeared. *"Not merely to say things which had never been said before; but to place before mankind the common sense of the subject.* You see? That's all he was trying to do."

Tom looked at her slyly. "But I notice he bragged about it on his tombstone."

"Oh, God." Fern abandoned the Declaration of Independence and slapped down another winning card. "Okay, then, what about the Louisiana Purchase? He doubled the size of the country with a stroke of the pen."

"Was slavery forbidden in the entire new territory? It was not." WHAM.

Infuriated, Fern tried again. This card was a winner for sure. "What about Lewis and Clark? I mean, the expedition was Jefferson's idea from the start."

Tom looked at her pityingly, and pulled another trump out of his sleeve. "Don't tell me you didn't know about Clark's black slave, York? Poor York! He was with them all the way, but he never got paid, he never got a piece of land like the other men, and he wasn't freed either. You mean you didn't know that?"

All Fern's arguments collapsed. Struggling to hold her own, she threw down her last ace. "Well, for heaven's sake, what about the University of Virginia? He did it all. I mean, he persuaded the legislature, he designed the architecture, the whole idea was new, it was a model for all the schools that came after, it was—"

Tom said mildly, "Were black students admitted to the University of Virginia?"

So it was no use. All Thomas Jefferson's noble cards were swept off the table, leaving only Thomas Jefferson, Slaveholder.

⌒

George had to find another fast-food place. Twitchy-looking men in uniform kept showing up in the pizza parlors and Burger Kings in his neighborhood. He cruised around in his van, exploring the north side of town.

George was proud of the van, it was so invisible. It had once belonged to an electrician, and the back was windowless and empty. George had spray-painted the whole thing a dull gray. You could hardly see the vehicle, it was so blah.

Late one night he found a new Chuck Wagon way out beyond Shopper's World. There were no customers inside and nobody behind the counter but one woman flipping burgers. George sat on a stool and watched her pick up his order from the steam table and slide it on a plate.

She was not pretty. She'd probably be flattered if he asked her to come outside for a smoke. She had coal-black hair and a broad dark-complected face with high cheekbones. Indian blood for sure.

Sometimes George felt himself raised to a great height, looking down on the earth from above. This was one of those times.

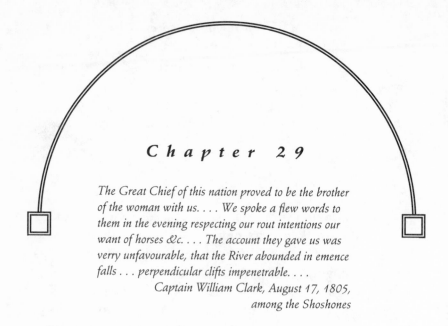

*The Great Chief of this nation proved to be the brother
of the woman with us. . . . We spoke a fiew words to
them in the evening respecting our rout intentions our
want of horses &c. . . . The account they gave us was
verry unfavourable, that the River abounded in emence
falls . . . perpendicular clifts impenetrable. . . .*
                    Captain William Clark, August 17, 1805,
                                        among the Shoshones

A new and ghastly suspicion had occurred to Augustus Upchurch. There had been another horrible killing, and this
time a high-school boy had come forward claiming to have
seen something out of the corner of his eye, the poor victim
walking out of a new fast-food place with a man.

There were now two vague descriptions. Both had been
turned over to a police artist. Bewildered, he produced a
sketch of the murderer's face that was a compromise between two wild extremes.

The resulting figment of his imagination was featured on
the front page of the *Charlottesville Daily Progress.*

To Augustus Upchurch it looked exactly like young Tom
Dean. He was profoundly alarmed. Poor darling Fern! She
might at this moment be in mortal danger!

At once he put into operation his plan to install a spy.

There was no question about who it should be. Flora Foley, his fellow board member in the Society for Jefferson

Studies, was perfect for the job. She was a fellow writer, turning out a new thriller every year. Her novels were never published, but they were packed with torrid and violent action. Her characters talked out of the sides of their mouths, using obscenities a quarter of a century out of date.

She knew everything about police procedure and the scene of the crime. She was informed about the proper care of bloodstained garments. She knew the importance of evidence tags. She sprinkled her manuscripts with the gruesome details of mortuary science, the consecutive degrees of putrefaction, the grisly succession of insects on a cadaver. She knew the muzzle velocities of firearms, the pockets of her characters bristled with snub-nosed derringers and .22-caliber Magnums. They carried duct tape, hand grenades and hunting knives. She had the lingo down pat—*aggravated assault, unnatural intercourse, unauthorized personnel.* Her characters never got out of a car, they *exited the vehicle.*

"Flora?"

"Oh, my God, is that you, Gus?"

It pained Augustus to be called Gus. "Flora, I wonder if I could drop in on you this morning? There's something I want to talk to you about, something very important."

"Oh, God, no, not this morning. I'm writing this big scene in the morgue. They've got the perp on the slab."

"The perp?"

"The perpetrator. They're sewing his mouth shut, only he suddenly wakes up. God, I can't stop now."

At once Augustus was aware of his half-digested breakfast. He swallowed, and went on bravely, "Well, what if I came over this afternoon?"

"Well, okay, sure. Come for a drink."

Flora Foley's apartment was something of a mess. As a talented and creative person, she had no time for stupid things like cleaning house. When Augustus appeared at the door, she pulled him inside, heaved a pile of papers off a chair, dumped a cat, and commanded him to sit down.

Flora had picked up her mannerisms from fifty-year-old movies, her tough talk with the cigarette wobbling in the corner of her mouth, her eyes narrowed against the smoke, her foul-mouthed vocabulary—although Flora's goddamns were pretty puny.

She sat opposite Augustus with her feet planted mannishly far apart and the paraphernalia of the hardnosed private investigator in her hands, the pack of cigarettes and the glass of bourbon. "Okay, I get it," said Flora. "You want me to hang out up there, keep an eye on the guy, ask him point-blank what he was doing last Tuesday at midnight, et cetera? Right?"

"Well, yes, I think so. But—"

Flora rasped her thumb on the wheel of her silver cigarette lighter, lit her cigarette, leaned forward, and tapped her visitor's knee. "Tell me this, Gus, do you think there's anything of a sexual nature going on? Killers, lots of times they're highly attractive to helpless young females. God, some women are gluttons for punishment. Does he kick her around? Is she black and blue? And listen to this, Gus, I'm telling you this, eyeball to eyeball. If he fucks her, *oohboy,* is she in trouble." Flora blew smoke from her nostrils, which produced a fit of coughing. Recovered, she gasped, "So, okay, how do I explain what the hell I'm doing there?"

Augustus waved away a cloud of smoke. "Tell Fern you're her new research assistant. You know the sort of thing. You'll get books out of the library and"—Augustus had no idea what a research assistant was supposed to do—"take dictation? You used to do shorthand, didn't you, Flora?"

"*Did* I? Christ, Gus, for twenty-five years I was executive secretary to the president of the Albemarle County Tobacco

Growers Association. My boss used to say to me, *Flora, you're a goddamned wonder,* and if I say so myself he was right." Flora dropped her smoldering cigarette into her glass, where it hissed and went out (an authentic gesture from an old Edward G. Robinson movie).

⌒

The Missouri River flowed still farther across the ceiling. Under Tom's meticulous brush it was now approaching the Great Falls, where the long and strenuous portage would begin.

The time line too was progressing. Fern had inscribed many good entries for the summer of the year 1804 in Jefferson's life. But this morning she had to take time out. Turning around suddenly, she bashed her forehead against a sharp corner of Tom's ladder and fell back moaning.

She had to sit down while he ran downstairs for a wet paper towel. While he was gone, feeling lightheaded and dizzy, she had a new notion about Thomas Jefferson.

She would tell it to Tom, she would make him see that it wasn't just the things Jefferson did or wrote or said, it was something in his very character that was significant. The nature of the country itself was still formless in some ways, capable of being shaped in any number of fatal directions. When Jefferson became president, he washed away the regal dignity of George Washington and the formality of John Adams with a pitcher of clear water.

Fern smiled, remembering the carpet slippers, the open door, the pell-mell seating at the dinner table. She closed her eyes and rehearsed a splendid conclusion—*If it's true that we Americans today—all of us, right here, right now—feel free of the baggage of royal protocol and kingly majesty, we owe it to the determined simplicity of Thomas Jefferson's presidency.*

Pressing the towel to her forehead, she tried to explain it to Tom. But her head was still throbbing. "Never mind," she said. "I'll tell you later." And soon she was back at work, bending over a new strip of paper on the table, recording the Burr-Hamilton duel and Jefferson's triumphant re-election.

Tom's part of the time line was farther along. Lewis and Clark had made their way halfway around the room. At the moment he was copying Captain Lewis's astronomical observations at the Yellowstone River. Softly he read the entry aloud as he wrote it below the line:

. . . observed Equal altitudes of the ☉ with Sextant and artificial horizon.

A.M. *9.h 41.m 13.s.*   P.M. *6.h 49.m 3.s*

It was at that moment that Flora Foley walked in and said a loud "Good morning!"

Their two heads swerved. Who was this strange lady?

She marched into the room, flat-footed, and stuck out her hand. "Flora Foley here. You're Fern Fisher?"

"Yes," said Fern. Doubtfully she shook Flora's hand.

"And who's this?" said Flora, staring at Tom.

Fern introduced him once again with exaggerated heartiness.

"Morning," muttered Tom.

Glowering, Flora turned back to Fern. "Listen here, Fern Fisher, I'm a gift to you from Gus Upchurch. How do you like that?"

Fern was appalled. "A gift from Mr. Upchurch?"

"Who else?" Flora spread her arms wide. "Here I am, my girl, your own personal girl Friday. See? I've brought my steno pad and pencil. Tell me, dear, what can I do to help?" Then Flora leaned forward and peered at Fern more closely.

MAY 4 1804

ARTICLES IN READINESS FOR +HE VOYAGE VIZ: 7 BARRELS OF SALT 50 KEGS OF PORK... ORDERLY BOOK CAPT. CLARK

After a hard journey through rain and mud from Monticello, where he was present at the death of his daughter Maria, President Jefferson was back in Washington.

MAY 14 1804

RAINED THE FORE PART OF THE DAY... I SET OUT AT 4 OCLOCK P.M., IN THE PRESENCE OF THE NEIGHBORING INHABITENTS, AND PROCEEDED ON UNDER A JENTLE BREASE UP THE MISSOURI... CAPT. CLARK

Jefferson's Minister to France, Robert Livingston, retires after successful negotiation with Talleyrand for Louisiana Purchase.

MAY 26 1804

THE POSTS AND DUTIES OF THE SERGT.S SHALL BE... WHEN THE BATTEAUX IS UNDER WAY, ONE SERGT. SHALL BE STATIONED AT THE HELM, ONE IN THE CENTER ON THE REAR OF THE STARBOARD LOCKER, AND ONE AT THE BOW... ORDERLY BOOK, CAPT. LEWIS

JUNE 4 1804

JUNE 2 1804

CAP LEWIS TOOK THE TIME & DISTANCE OF ☉'S & MOONS NEAREST LIMBS... GEORGE DREWYER & JOHN SHIELDS... JOINED US THIS EVENING MUCH WORSTED, THEY BEING ABSENT SEVEN DAYS DEPENDING ON THEIR GUN... CAPT. CLARK

Charles Willson Peale and Baron Humboldt dine with President Jefferson.

Her eyes narrowed to private-investigator slits. "My God, girl, what happened to you? You're black and blue."

"Oh, it's nothing. I ran into the ladder."

"You—ran—into—the—ladder. A likely story."

So the good times were gone. Well, of course, all the times up to now had been too edgy and argumentative to be called really good. But compared with the way things were now, they had been a golden age.

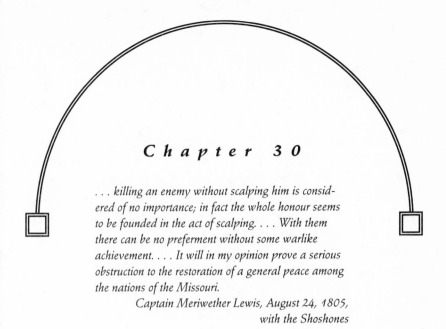

Chapter 30

... killing an enemy without scalping him is considered of no importance; in fact the whole honour seems to be founded in the act of scalping.... With them there can be no preferment without some warlike achievement.... It will in my opinion prove a serious obstruction to the restoration of a general peace among the nations of the Missouri.

Captain Meriwether Lewis, August 24, 1805,
with the Shoshones

George Dryer's childhood of neglect and abuse was no different from that of other bestial killers. Like many infant hoodlums, he had been thrown out of one school after another. Finally, expelled from the sixth grade, he had dropped out for good, heavily scarred by the contempt of women teachers, the ridicule of lady principals, and the taunting disdain of a hundred little girls. *And then there was Jeanie.*

George had long been finished with school by the time he moved to Charlottesville with his mother. The property she bought was a modest ranch house built in the 1950s. It became George's property when his mother vanished from sight.

Nobody in the neighborhood missed her, since no one had met her. They hardly knew George either, because he kept very much to himself. Luckily, there was no need for him to work, because his mother's savings were right there in the bureau drawer. In her checkered career, first as an exotic dancer and then as a chambermaid, she had been thrifty and tightfisted. The drawer held ninety-five thousand dollars.

The neighbors knew only that George kept the place tidy. It was all they cared about. He mowed the lawn regularly and clipped the hedge and whitewashed the rocks along the driveway and polished the gazing globe in the front yard— George was especially fond of the gazing globe. He liked to bend over it and watch his small face fill the whole round world.

He really cared about neatness. He liked to line things up— his shoes, his underwear, his razor and toothbrush, his set of knives. When not in use, his chain hung on a hook in the garage beside the garden rake and the shovel. The hose for washing out the back of the van was coiled in perfect order.

Of course, his back yard wasn't exactly neat, because it was the graveyard of all those bloody shirts. George had filled in the holes with dirt and seeded them with grass, but they were still visible. It was okay, next time he'd know where not to dig. There was plenty of room for more.

So far, George Dryer was not an exceptional psychopath. But in two ways he was different from other quiet and inoffensive mass murderers.

One was an episode with a girlfriend named Jeanie back in North Dakota. Jeanie had been an easygoing playmate until at last she grew tired of George's weird attentions. She had told him to get lost.

But he couldn't stand it. He couldn't let her alone. He had stalked her, grabbed her, kept her, showed her who was master, used her whenever he felt like it. *And then Jeanie—*

No, no, forget it, don't think about it. And somehow, by some sort of mental sleight of hand, George did not think about it.

The evidence was with him all the time, but he chose not to look at it.

The thing that Jeanie had done to him was absent from his conscious mind. It was missing, forgotten, and yet it surrounded him like a bleeding boil, a bloated translucent membrane pulsing with coarse blue veins. It was not neat and tidy, it was grotesque and horrible. George lived inside it, he saw the world through it, he was used to it, he wasn't aware of it at all.

The second thing that was different about George was even more unusual. He was a reader. The only public place he visited was the Jefferson-Madison Public Library.

All his life he had loved stories of high adventure—true tales of the Barbary pirates, true stories about man-eating sharks and tiger hunts, true histories of the slaughter of Allied forces on the beaches of Normandy, true accounts of the bloody battles of the Civil War.

And therefore, when he stumbled on Lewis and Clark, it had changed his life. George read their journals, skipping around, flipping the pages. He was thrilled by the sense of adventure, fascinated by the stories of the hunting and killing and butchering that kept them all alive. They were men, real men, heroes in the wilderness, fighting savages and rattlesnakes and grizzly bears and coming back alive.

And there was another thing. George pounced on something in the journals that no one else had paid any attention to—the way those randy white men slept with Indian squaws, all the way from the Mandan villages on the Missouri to the Chinooks on the Columbia River.

And one day he had been struck by an idea like a thunderbolt.

What if he himself was connected with the great expedition? Hadn't he been born in Bismarck, North Dakota? Wasn't

Bismarck very near the place where the expedition had spent a winter among the Mandans? What if a lot of little half-white, half-Indian bastards had been born to the squaws after the expedition took off up the river?

What if he himself was the descendant of a Mandan squaw and one of the men? One of the best men in the whole expeditionary force, one man in particular?

⌒

The day after Flora Foley began her job as a chaperone-spy in the Dome Room at Monticello, George was back in the Bargain Mart on Hydraulic Road, buying shirts. To his surprise and delight, he ran into the woman with long brown hair, the one he had seen here before. This time she looked even more like Jeanie, because she was wearing her hair in a pigtail.

Last time she had been paying for an electric fan at the checkout counter. This time she stood in front of a shelf in the housewares department studying the automatic coffeemakers.

At once George decided he needed a coffeemaker too. He moved up beside her and pointed to one and said, "Is that kind any good?"

Fern glanced at him. "I don't know. What do you think?"

George made a pretense of helping her choose. In two minutes he learned that she wanted a coffeemaker for her workplace at Monticello.

"Monticello?" said George. "Oh, sure. I never been there. Thomas Jefferson's place, right?"

Fern glanced at him again and decided she didn't want a coffeemaker after all. She walked away along the aisle of stoves and refrigerators, hurried past the racks of women's bathing suits, and ran out of the Bargain Mart.

Glancing back as she unlocked her car, she saw the too-friendly stranger racing toward her. Fern jumped in behind the wheel, slammed the door, started the engine, charged past him, and drove away.

Standing alone in the parking lot, staring after the disappearing car, George remembered what she had told him, the bitch who looked so much like Jeanie. She said she worked at Monticello.

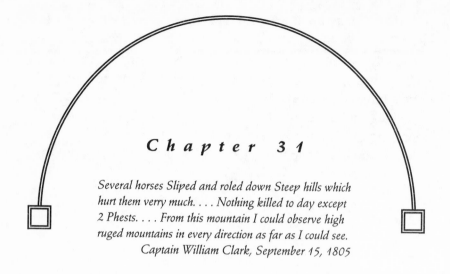

Chapter 31

Several horses Sliped and roled down Steep hills which hurt them verry much. . . . Nothing killed to day except 2 Phests. . . . From this mountain I could observe high ruged mountains in every direction as far as I could see.
Captain William Clark, September 15, 1805

The guide that morning, Gail Boltwood, was Henry Spender's pride. She knew everything there was to know about the building and rebuilding of Monticello, every detail of Jefferson's experimental farming, and a great deal about the lives of his slaves. She knew the background of every piece of furniture, every painting and Indian artifact, every useful Jeffersonian gadget.

If asked, she could talk about his political problems, his disastrous embargo, the rebellion of Aaron Burr in Louisiana, the embarrassing XYZ Affair, and the disappointment of the Missouri Compromise.

But this afternoon, as always, she was careful not to overwhelm her listeners. They were a typically miscellaneous lot. Most were the usual uninformed tourists, politely attentive. They were ignorant, they really wanted to know. "Did he live in this big house all alone?" "Did he die in this bed?" "Did he really design the house all by himself?"

As usual, a few were show-offs, eager to parade their little knowledge. "Where's the lapdesk?" asked a broad-shouldered man, eager to separate himself from the hoi polloi. "He wrote the Declaration of Independence on it, so where is it?"

"In the Smithsonian, I'm afraid," said Gail gently.

After that he kept erupting with identifications before she got to them, making a disjointed mess of the rest of the tour. He was bad enough, but one of the women was worse—another Sally Hemings enthusiast. She stared at Jefferson's bed and asked eagerly, "Is this where they made love?"

But there were a couple of other people in Gail's first morning batch of tourists who intrigued her, a tall woman and a tall bewhiskered man. Their faces were alive with interest, they smiled at the right moment. At first they said nothing, until Gail gathered her charges in front of the engraving of the draft committee delivering the Declaration of Independence to John Hancock. There they were, the founding fathers—John Adams, Thomas Jefferson, Benjamin Franklin, Roger Sherman, and Robert Livingston—all in a row.

"People forget," said Gail, "that they were putting their lives on the line. If the British had won the war, every one of the signers would have been hanged. Signing the Declaration took courage."

The whiskery male burst out, "My God, it could have happened. We could have lost the war."

Gail smiled at him. "It was a close call. And yet, according to Mr. Jefferson, not a hand trembled."

Homer Kelly was carried away. "Just picture it, all those founding fathers up on the scaffold! George Washington, John Adams, Thomas Jefferson, Ben Franklin with his little specs smashed, all of them choking and strangling and hanging by the neck."

"Homer, for heaven's sake." The tall woman was laughing and pulling on his arm.

But Gail was pleased. "Fortunately," she said, "we didn't lose the war, we won."

Not until the tour was over, and the rest of the group had been dispatched outdoors, did Homer and Mary Kelly introduce themselves to Gail Boltwood and inquire the way to the Dome Room, where they had an appointment with Fern Fisher.

"Oh, of course, you're the Professors Kelly I've heard so much about. She's expecting you." Gail led them to the foot of the stairs. "It's up two flights. They're awfully steep, I'm afraid. Look, there she is at the top. Fern!" called Gail. "Your visitors are here."

Naturally, they were stunned by the glory of the Dome Room. "Wow," gasped Homer.

There was too much to take in all at once—their old student Fern Fisher beaming at them, the redheaded guy on the ladder painting the ceiling, the long strip of paper running around the wall, and the homely old woman who was striding toward Homer, grasping his hand, shaking it vigorously.

"Flora Foley here," said the woman. "District Attorney Kelly? Well, well, I've heard of your exploits."

Homer protested that he was not and never had been a district attorney. "My wife Mary," he mumbled, pulling her forward.

Mary smiled politely, but Flora wasn't interested in Homer's wife. "I am the author of police procedurals," she said importantly. From somewhere in the air she produced a manuscript and urged it on him. "With my compliments, my latest, 'The Hacksaw Caper.'"

Homer wasn't prepared for its thickness and weight, and he almost dropped it.

He was rescued by Fern, who was eager to show them the time line. She touched the latest entry on the long strip of paper and explained: "You see, my part is Jefferson, it's what he was doing while Lewis and Clark were going up the Missouri. Look, here's July 11, 1804, when Aaron Burr killed Jefferson's political enemy in a duel—"

"Alexander Hamilton," murmured Mary.

Then Tom, perceiving that Fern's visitors were not complete fools, descended the ladder and explained his own part of the story, the daily adventures of Lewis and Clark.

"You see here," he said, pointing to his latest entry, "it's August 13, 1805. They think they've reached the headwaters of the Missouri, and now they're desperate to meet a local tribe with horses. I mean, they've got to have horses to get through the Rockies. They never expected the mountains to be such an enormous obstacle."

Mary listened politely. What an amusing face the boy had, what an eruption of orange hair. Earnestly she leaned forward and read Captain Lewis's account of the meeting of the Indian woman with her brother, Chief Cameahwait.

"It made all the difference, you see, that Sacagawea happened to be along," said Tom. "It meant the Shoshones would sell them the horses."

Homer repeated it in a whisper—"Sell them the horses, great God Almighty."

Mary saw at once by the look on his face what was happening. It was another love affair. From years of experience as his wife, she knew how easily Homer could fall in love at first sight with some vast new field of knowledge. He was a gulper, a swallower of information, a greedy grasper at more and more.

Once it had been Thoreau and Emerson, then Melville and Emily Dickinson, and still later on, with wild leaps across the Atlantic, the poetry of Dante, Darwin's *Origin of Species,* and last year—what madness!—Homer had spent the entire autumn in the Library of St. Mark's in Venice, gazing at manuscripts and early printed books. Since then, whenever his professorial duties permitted, he had been wallowing in the life of Thomas Jefferson.

And now it was as though he had taken one drink too many. Homer clutched the skinny arm of young Tom Dean and whimpered, "More, tell me more."

Mary turned to Fern and rolled her eyes, meaning, *My husband, you'll have to forgive him,* and Fern laughed.

But then Flora bore down on them and said to Mary, "This homicidal maniac, I must talk to your husband." Her eyes narrowed, and she whispered, "I have highly significant information about the identity of the perp. You know, the serial killer."

At once her eyes slid sideways to Tom Dean, who was talking and gesturing and snatching up maps and pointing at the ceiling and flipping the pages of a book, instructing his enraptured pupil, Homer Kelly.

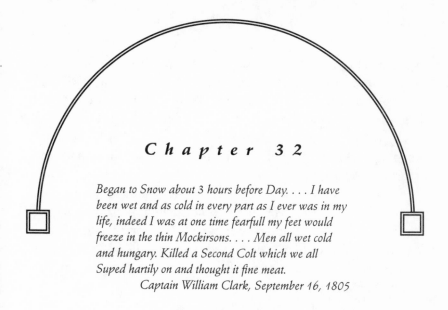

Chapter 32

*Began to Snow about 3 hours before Day. . . . I have
been wet and as cold in every part as I ever was in my
life, indeed I was at one time fearfull my feet would
freeze in the thin Mockirsons. . . . Men all wet cold
and hungary. Killed a Second Colt which we all
Suped hartily on and thought it fine meat.*
Captain William Clark, September 16, 1805

Flora left the Dome Room first. It was a clever move. Lurking on the South Terrace Walk, she watched the departure of Homer Kelly and Whatsername, his wife, and she saw the last group of tourists head for the shuttle bus. Where was that sly fox, Tom Dean? Was he still up there alone with poor gullible young Fern?

Flora was patient, but she almost missed him, because Tom didn't emerge from the East Portico along with everybody else. Luckily, she happened to glance down Mulberry Row in time to see him striding away down the hill into the woods.

Galvanized, Flora loped after him, her big pocketbook slapping against her side. As she bounded clumsily along the path she wondered how she was ever going to get home again, because it was a long walk in the other direction to the visitors' parking lot. Flora told herself pluckily that it didn't matter. Her investigation was more important. She would pursue it to the end.

She had to gallop along the path to keep him in sight. Then she almost missed the place where Tom left the path and dodged to one side. Slipping and sliding, Flora floundered after him. Oh, God, he was going so fast, she had to push her way recklessly through bush and briar, lashed at by whippy saplings. Where the hell was he going? Wasn't he ever going to stop?

She was soon exhausted. Her breath came in gasps, she wasn't used to exercise. She should have done more jogging in front of the TV. But her work was so important, who cared about touching their toes ten times or vacuuming the dust kitties under the bed or washing the sticky dishes from last night? Not Flora!

Oh, God, her heart was pounding. Oh, Christ, she was falling down! Flora screamed and landed on her back.

Tom stopped and turned around and helped her struggle to her feet. "It's okay," he said gently. "We're almost there."

"I was just—" she began lamely.

"Never mind," said Tom. "Here we are." He lifted the flap of his tent and said, "Come in. Be my guest."

Flora stared. She couldn't speak. It was the murderer's den. For a moment she panicked. Then her courage revived, and stoutly, valiantly, Flora Foley, the heroic private investigator in pursuit of Public Enemy Number One, the murdering monster of Albemarle County, the *Perp,* followed him inside.

"Mind if I smoke?" she said, staring around the tent with bulging eyes, pulling out her cigarettes, fumbling in her bag for her lighter, extracting it, and then dropping it from nervous fingers.

Tom picked it up. "Let me do it," he said, and with a gallant gesture he held the flame under Flora's trembling cigarette.

She inhaled and coughed. Her mind raced, trying to think of a crafty question, the kind that would nail a suspect and force him to admit his crime.

But Tom had had enough. "Excuse me," he said. "I'll be on my way. I've got an appointment with a hickory tree."

"What?"

He was nodding and smiling, standing by the open flap of the tent, sweeping his hands sideways in a polite gesture, *After you, dear lady.*

She had no choice. Flora ducked out of the tent ahead of Tom, who nodded again, smiled again, and set off down the hill.

Bewildered, Flora stared after him, then dropped her cigarette, crushed it underfoot, and began stumbling in the opposite direction.

It was hard work. Going downhill had been hard enough. Climbing against gravity was almost beyond her power. A small dead branch plucked at Flora's wig and snatched it off. She screeched, stopped, jerked at the fuzzy mop, and jammed it back on her head, not troubling to get it straight, not bothering to tuck in the straggling wisps of gray hair. Gasping, she leaned against a tree.

Think, Flora, think.

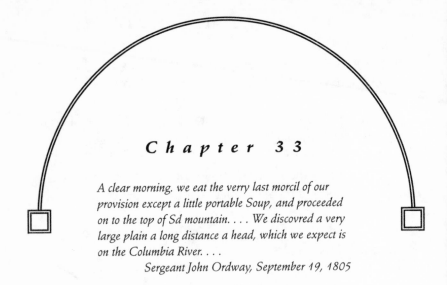

Chapter 33

A clear morning. we eat the verry last morcil of our provision except a little portable Soup, and proceeded on to the top of Sd mountain. . . . We discovered a very large plain a long distance a head, which we expect is on the Columbia River. . . .
Sergeant John Ordway, September 19, 1805

George wasn't equipped for business. He just wanted to check out the place. Therefore, he didn't stow any of his usual apparatus in the back of the van. He put on one of his new shirts and rolled up the sleeves because it was a hot day, but he wore his driving gloves because the steering wheel of the van was nicked and cracked.

He drove past the gate of Monticello, turned the van around, drove past the gate again, and headed back along the road for a quarter of a mile, then pulled over on the shoulder. It was the same place where Tom Dean had parked his mother's car and picked up a parking ticket.

George didn't know that, but he didn't want to leave the van where it could be seen, so he charged it up the slope, bashed through a barrier of low bushes, and crushed a thicket of maple saplings. Getting out to study the situation, he was satisfied that nothing could be seen from the road. He locked the van and began pushing his way up the mountain on foot.

It was heavy going. George heaved himself up and up, trampling the low canopy of maidenhair fern and sassafras on the forest floor. When he caught sight of a tent among the trees, he stopped and stared.

All was quiet. Through the undergrowth he could see a sparkle of reflected sunlight on something shiny. What was that?

Abandoning caution, he walked into the clearing. The shiny thing was a small motorcycle, propped against a tree. He saw at once that it was not chained to anything. What kind of careless shit would go off and leave a bike unlocked?

Cautiously George lifted the flap of the tent. Nobody home. Place a mess. Pair of pants on the floor, couple sneakers. Bed unmade, rumpled blanket, grubby pillow. Card table, lot of bottles, piece of chain—God, it was the lock for the motorbike. Jeez, what a jerk.

There was also a paper bag with apples and overripe bananas. George helped himself to an apple and took a bite. Then he reached under the bed, dragged out a backpack, and poked inside.

Heavy sweater, wrinkled pants, gray underwear, dirty socks, sealed envelope.

George picked up the envelope and looked at the address: *Registrar, School of Medicine, University of Virginia.*

At once he was filled with rage. Shit wanted to go to med school, be a fucking big important doctor.

In actual fact, the letter in Tom's backpack was not an application for admission, it was his notice to the med school that he was not coming back in the fall.

George didn't know that. His anger engorged his brain. He kicked the table. It collapsed. All the bottles fell off.

Then he paused, listening. Someone was coming. He picked up the fallen chain.

A face peered under the tent flap. To his surprise it was an old woman, a fucking fright in a black wig. She was opening her mouth, croaking. "What the hell are you doing here?"

George didn't have to think. Swiftly he lunged at her with the uplifted chain.

In the ultimate moment of her life, Flora understood her mistake. She had been wrong about Tom Dean. Struggling for air, her fingers clutching at her throat, she whispered one last word, *Perp*.

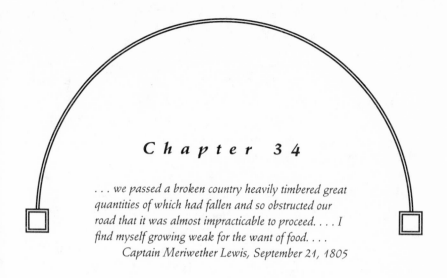

Chapter 34

. . . we passed a broken country heavily timbered great quantities of which had fallen and so obstructed our road that it was almost impracticable to proceed. . . . I find myself growing weak for the want of food. . . .
Captain Meriwether Lewis, September 21, 1805

Now more than ever, in this bicentennial year of his election to the presidency, the citizens of Charlottesville felt connected to Thomas Jefferson. He was a neighbor, after all—a dead one, but still a neighbor. Many of the things he had said and done were fresh in the mind.

They kept popping up in conversation—his role in the writing of the Declaration of Independence, his scientific studies, his interest in horticulture, his founding of the university, his passionate hatred of any kind of tyranny over the mind of man—from the dictates of the British throne to the local established church of Virginia—and of course his notorious DNA. In the local garden centers there was a run on the supply of *Jeffersonia diphylla,* the modest plant named for him by his botanist friend Benjamin Smith Barton.

Among the admirers of Thomas Jefferson were the son and daughter-in-law of Augustus Upchurch. Roger and Debbie Upchurch lived not far from Monticello, and they took a proprietary interest in its distinguished former occupant.

Not so, their ten-year-old twin daughters. The two girls took Monticello for granted. They cared little for the Declaration of Independence or the Louisiana Purchase or the Virginia Statute for Religious Freedom or any other celebrated achievement of the third President of the United States. Like Tom Dean with his paper time line in the Dome Room at Monticello, they cared for nothing about Thomas Jefferson but the Lewis and Clark expedition.

Ten years earlier the twins had been christened Bonni and Sherri, names they despised. Recently they had baptized each other in the water of the Rivanna River as Captain Meriwether Lewis and Captain William Clark.

This morning, sitting on the front steps of their comfortable house on Jefferson Lake Drive, they were engaging in target practice.

"Captain Clark," whispered Captain Lewis, observing a bison trotting along the sidewalk, "I reckon I'll git us some vittles fer supper." She cocked her finger and fired. "BANG."

The buffalo stopped and wagged its tail. "Reckon you missed," said Captain Clark.

Luckily, just then a grizzly bear streaked across the tulip bed. Captain Clark raised her rifle and shouted, "BANG," and the grizzly padded up to purr and have its ears scratched.

What they needed, they decided, was real wilderness experience. They had been forbidden to leave the house, but at this moment their parents were away at a neighborhood meeting in the school gym about the terrifying threat to the young women of Albemarle County.

"Let's go," said Captain Clark.

"Just for a little while," said Captain Lewis. At once they set off on their trusty horses for the woods.

Leaving their mounts in a tangle of wheels and handlebars in the bushes, they walked up a secret path. Almost immediately, only a few hundred yards from the road, they stumbled on the body of an old woman. She was sitting in the hollow stump of a tree like a queen on a throne, her balding head drooping sideways, her eyes staring. At once their jolly play-acting was abandoned, and they rushed away whimpering.

Their parents were still at the meeting, but their grandfather was just getting out of his car in the driveway. The two girls dumped their bicycles and ran to him and wrapped their arms around him and sobbed.

His first impulse was to call 911. His second was *not* to call 911. Grimly he said, "Where is she?"

Frantic with excitement, the two girls pointed their skinny arms and jabbered. "There's a path. It's by a big rock. We go there all the time."

"Now, children," said their grandfather, "you go right inside and lock the door. I'll go home and call the police."

But he didn't. Not yet. Instead, Augustus drove to the place where the big rock marked the path, parked his car off the road, walked up the hill, and found the body.

At first he didn't recognize Flora, because her black wig was gone. There was only a skim of gray hair on her scalp. Only slowly did he begin to recognize his old friend, the spying chaperone he had hired to keep an eye on Fern Fisher and Tom Dean.

A triangular scrap of paper was pinned to Flora's shirt, neatly inscribed. Augustus bent to look, but the words meant nothing to him. Shocked and confused, he turned away from Flora's body and moved clumsily down the hill. He was soon lost.

When he stumbled on Tom's camp, he was interested at once. Like Flora Foley before him, he poked his head inside the tent and walked in.

It was unoccupied. Augustus was not confronted with a killer, a murderer, a perpetrator. Grubbing around in the tent he found Tom Dean's name on the flyleaf of a book. At once he understood that the tent belonged to the dangerous young man in the Dome Room. Dean was camping illegally in Thomas Jefferson's sacred grove.

And there must have been some kind of violent scuffle. The table was tipped over, the place was a mess.

And Flora's body was only a few hundred feet away.

Augustus was filled with triumph. He had been right all along. Tom Dean was the murderer, the real serial killer, the threat to all the young women of Albemarle County, and most especially to dear, dear young Fern. Tom Dean had murdered poor Flora, right here in this tent, and then he had carried her body up the hill to that hollow stump and arranged her arms and legs as though she were sitting upright. What a cruel joke!

$$\frown$$

When the emergency line rang, the sergeant on duty at the desk picked it up and murmured, "Charlottesville Police, this message is being recorded, what is your emergency?"

There was a jabberer on the line. "Hey, listen, there's been a murder, a woman, in the woods at Monticello, right off Highway 53, you can't miss it. Path beside a big rock. Horrible, it's number nine, right? I mean, what's the matter with law enforcement? Why don't you apprehend this guy?"

"Sir, would you give me your name?"

"Bullshit, what is this crap?"

The caller hung up. Using another phone, the sergeant called the patrol officer assigned to Route 20. The patrol car's intercom burst into noisy life. "Big rock?" said the driver. "Yeah, right, I know the big rock." He swerved the car around and raced away in the other direction, his siren screaming.

At the desk in the Charlottesville Police station in City Hall on East Market Street, the sergeant rewound the 911 tape and listened to the message a second time.

In the weeks to come it would be replayed again and again.

∩

A hundred feet below Tom Dean's tent a cautious hand struck a match and lowered it carefully into the dry leaves. At once a little flame shot up and spread merrily in a ring, igniting the ferny undergrowth and rising into the lower branches of the trees.

∩

Back in his house on Park Street, Augustus Upchurch was at last ready to call 911 and tell his horrifying news. He was surprised and a little disappointed when the officer answering his call said, "Right, we know. They're on their way. Who's this?"

"You mean the girls called you?"

"Girls? What girls? May I ask who this is?"

"My name is Augustus Upchurch. Perhaps you've heard of me?"

"Can't say I have."

Of course he hadn't, thought Augustus indignantly. He was too young. The whole world was run by ignorant children. "But it must have been one of the little girls?"

There was a pause, and then the sergeant said, "Sorry, sir, I can't give information over the phone. Now, Mr. Upchurch, please give me your address and phone number, and tell me all about it."

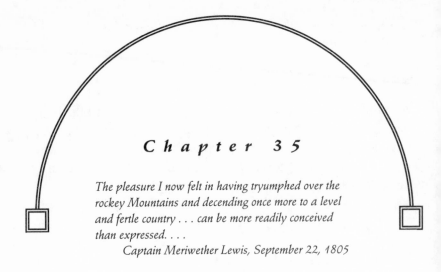

Chapter 35

The pleasure I now felt in having tryumphed over the rockey Mountains and decending once more to a level and fertle country . . . can be more readily conceived than expressed. . . .
   Captain Meriwether Lewis, September 22, 1805

When the patrol car braked to a stop beside the big rock, the fire in the woods was already sending flames high over the treetops. "Christ," said the sector officer at the wheel, and at once he called for help.

So the firefighters went in first. The fire turned out to be only a small local conflagration, easily controlled. By the time the smoke and flames died away, sirens were whining on the road. Soon the rest of the team was roaring up, jamming on brakes, and piling out. The five of them raced up the hill—the sector officer, the sergeant supervisor, a couple of detectives, and Marjorie Nightingale, the sergeant in charge of forensics.

They found the firefighters walking over the blackened ground under the dripping trees, checking for smoldering embers. "Where's the body?" said the sector officer.

One of the firefighters mopped his face and pointed up the hill. Then he gestured the other way. "Tent's down there."

Soon they were gathered around Flora, moving around her carefully, stepping back to make room for the police photographer with his battery-powered floodlights. When Howie

Plover came plunging down the hill gasping, the supervisor held up his hand and warned him to move back.

Howie had seen the smoke and flame from the house. Behind him stumbled Curator Henry Spender. Henry was flabbergasted. He had expected nothing more than a smoldering fire in the woods and a few firefighters. Now he was appalled to come upon a murder victim and a team of investigating police. His knees buckled, and he nearly fainted.

Howie caught him and led him to higher ground, where Henry soon recovered. "Who was it?" he whined to Howie. "I mean who was the dead person? What in the hell is going on?"

Howie shrugged his shoulders, and said damned if he knew, and Henry thought darkly that, whatever it was, it was just another example of the growing absurdity and incoherence of life on the planet. Where would it all end?

Oliver Pratt was the last official to flounder up the hill to the place where Flora Foley sat in pitiful majesty in her sylvan throne. Gasping, Oliver leaned against a tree, trying to recover his breath.

He was accompanied by an unofficial observer, the meddling outsider from Massachusetts. By a piece of blind luck, Homer Kelly had been talking to Oliver on the phone when someone barged into the Chief's office with the news about Flora Foley. Shamelessly eavesdropping, Homer heard the whole story. Without waiting for an invitation, he abandoned his astonished wife, leaped into the car, and raced unerringly, without a single wrong turn, to the very place on Route 53 where the fire truck and the police cruisers and the Chief's car were all gathered, their blue lights flashing.

Now Forensics Sergeant Nightingale moved around the body and explained. "Method of operation not quite the same. Oh, sure, she's been strangled, but she hasn't been disrobed or carved up."

Oliver stared wretchedly at Flora and said, "Mother of God, it's number nine."

Sadly Homer recognized the silly woman he had met that afternoon in the Dome Room in the company of Mary, Fern Fisher, and Tom Dean, the Lewis and Clark enthusiast who had swept him off his feet.

Silly or not, the poor creature did not deserve this ignominious end. "Look, Chief," he said quietly, "another note."

"Oh, of course, naturally," said Oliver bitterly, "another goddamned note."

One of the detective sergeants murmured, "Over here, Chief," and crooked his finger. "We found the killer's tent."

"His tent?" said Pratt. "What do you mean, the killer's tent?"

"Forgive me, Chief," said the sergeant. "I shouldn't have said the killer's tent. I should have said the suspect's tent. But one of the 911 callers said this kid was a dangerous maniac."

Fiercely Homer said, "What kid? Who called 911?"

But the detective sergeant was moving ahead of them, dropping slowly down the hill, making a wide detour around a faint beaten track among the trees.

Henry Spender joined the parade. "Come on, Howie," he said. "After all, we've got a perfect right. It's Jefferson's own grove, it's the private personal property of the Thomas Jefferson Memorial Foundation."

When the detective sergeant stopped, the others stopped too, and stood in a row—Pratt, Homer, Henry Spender, and Howie Plover—and stared at the big tent that had been roped to three trees and pegged securely into the forest floor. There were voices in the tent, a flash of light. The photographer was again at work.

Pratt repeated Homer's question. "Come on, Sergeant, who was it called 911?"

The sergeant explained. "The 911 call was from the man

who found the body, guy name of Upchurch. Well, no, Up-church wasn't the first. Somebody else called first, some kook, told us where to go. Crazy guy, pretty significant in the circumstances, we'll try to track him down. Then Upchurch called, said he knew the victim and he also knew this kid Tom Dean, and he said Dean was really dangerous." The sergeant nodded at the tent. "And he told us about the tent. Said it was Dean's tent, illegal trespass, shouldn't be here. And he was right. There's stuff inside with his name on it, Tom Dean."

Once again Henry Spender's knees were wobbling. With horror he recalled the warning call from Augustus Upchurch and his own failure to expel the interloper.

With trembling fingers he plucked at Chief Pratt's sleeve. "He's up there in the house right now," he said. "Tom Dean, I mean. I heard him go out. I can always hear them going and coming, because the stairs are right outside my office. And then just now"—Henry's face was deathly pale—"just now I heard him come back in. He works up there every day with a graduate student, her name's Fern Fisher, right up there in the Dome Room."

"Holy bleeding *Christ,*" said Pratt. He shouted at the others, and soon they were all galloping up the hill in the direction of the house. It was an improvised SWAT team, a police assault on the house at the top of the hill, an attack on the architectural masterpiece that was Henry Spender's precious charge. In the company of Howie Plover, Henry trailed wretchedly after Oliver Pratt, two detective sergeants, a supervisor, a sector officer, a couple of firefighters, Sergeant Nightingale, and a thoroughly wretched unaccredited inquisitive observer.

Homer had taken a liking to young Tom Dean.

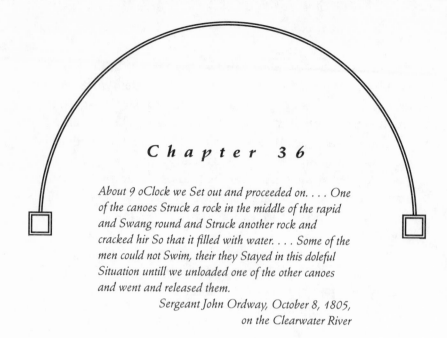

Chapter 36

About 9 oClock we Set out and proceeded on. . . . One of the canoes Struck a rock in the middle of the rapid and Swang round and Struck another rock and cracked hir So that it filled with water. . . . Some of the men could not Swim, their they Stayed in this doleful Situation untill we unloaded one of the other canoes and went and released them.

Sergeant John Ordway, October 8, 1805,
on the Clearwater River

"Clear the house," cried Chief Pratt, throwing open the glass doors of the West Portico.

Gail Boltwood and her group of tourists were in the parlor, where she had been naming the portraits on the wall. At once she shepherded her charges into the greenhouse and out to the South Terrace Walk, leaving no one in the parlor but John Locke and Benjamin Franklin, Christopher Columbus and Amerigo Vespucci.

Another group of visitors, in the entrance hall, was whisked out of the house the other way, leaving only the white busts musing on their pedestals—Voltaire and Turgot dreamily aloof, Alexander Hamilton frowning across the room at his old enemy Thomas Jefferson.

By some miracle, Homer was right behind Chief Pratt. "This way," he said breathlessly, gasping in the direction of the stairs, hoping to give Tom and Fern a little warning. But the stairs were too steep and Homer was too fat. He had to stand aside on the landing, puffing and blowing, while everyone thundered past him.

Henry Spender was gasping too. He limped up the stairs, nodded at Homer, and took refuge in his office on the second floor, just as Fern leaned over the railing and cried, "Hey, what is this?"

By the time Homer reached the top, Tom was already in custody.

He looked dazed, but Fern spoke up angrily. "What's he accused of?"

The arresting sergeant said smoothly, "Suspicion of arson and murder. Will that do for now?" He looked at Tom, whose skinny sunburned arm was handcuffed to the wrist of one of the detective sergeants. "Where were you, say, half an hour ago?"

Homer grasped the sergeant's shoulder and muttered, "Miranda warning?"

"Right," said the sergeant, and he began to recite it mechanically.

But Tom broke in. "I was in the woods. I left here about four o'clock. I've got a tent down there."

"A tent in the woods?" said Chief Pratt softly. "That's your tent? Did you meet anyone while you were there?"

"Oh, Tom, just shut up," snarled Homer.

"Yes, I did. Flora Foley followed me. I invited her to come in." Tom looked around at the circle of expressionless faces. "Was it Flora? Flora Foley? Is she dead?"

The little regiment of police officers took him away. Fern watched from the top of the stairs. Among the heads and shoulders descending below her she could see only a tuft of Tom's carrot-colored hair. Bringing up the rear, Homer Kelly glanced at her over his shoulder and raised his fist, meaning, *Don't give up, we'll fight back.*

Fern walked into the great chamber, shut the door softly, and looked up at the inner surface of the dome. Over her head the painted progress of the Lewis and Clark expedition had hit a snag in the rapids of the Columbia River.

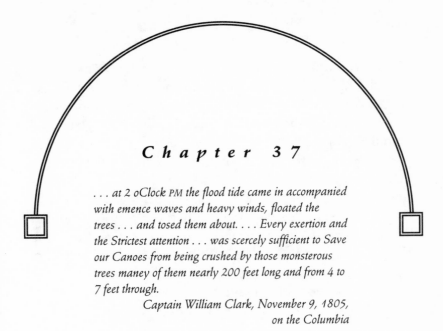

Chapter 37

. . . at 2 oClock PM *the flood tide came in accompanied
with emence waves and heavy winds, floated the
trees . . . and tosed them about. . . . Every exertion and
the Strictest attention . . . was scercely sufficient to Save
our Canoes from being crushed by those monsterous
trees maney of them nearly 200 feet long and from 4 to
7 feet through.*
Captain William Clark, November 9, 1805,
on the Columbia

George Dryer always watched the news on the TV in the
bedroom of his house. Today he turned it on too early,
and he had to sit through the commercial. While the cute
children ate their breakfast cereal and said cute things, and a
shining car sped at ninety miles an hour along a curving
mountain road, he noticed that the top of the set was dusty.
He took a wet cloth from the bathroom and cleaned off the
dust, giving the screen a good wipe at the same time. He
arranged the rabbit ears just so.

When the news anchors came on at last, smugly declaring
the end of the serial-killer ordeal in Charlottesville, George
was electrified. He stared at the film clip of a redheaded guy in
a Laurel and Hardy sweatshirt being shepherded in handcuffs
into the magistrate's office in the Charlottesville-Albemarle
Regional Jail.

Who the fuck was this-son-of-a-bitch, Thomas Arthur

Dean? Well, apparently he was the guy the tent belonged to, but who did he think he was, taking all the credit? Shit like him couldn't do what George could do, not in a million years. Oh, sure, this jerk had been to *college,* he wanted to go to med school and dissect *cadavers.* Motherfucking shit!

But the thing that most infuriated George was the claim that this son-of-a-bitch was an expert on Lewis and Clark. Jesus fucking Christ, Lewis and Clark belonged to George Dryer. Nobody understood those men the way George did. What did this jerk know about the lusty fornicators, the bloody butchers, the wrestlers with grizzly bears? They were George's own personal property. And, Jesus, what did the asshole know about the bravest man of all? George was sick and disgusted. He felt violated and brushed aside.

⌒

"Homer, what on earth is this?"

Homer was pulling a T-shirt over his head. He uttered a muffled "Just a sec." When the inside of his shirt gave way to a view of the dark bedroom, his wife Mary was looking at him accusingly. She stood beside the dead fern with a book in her hand.

He winced. It was *The Mind of the Monster,* the grisly report loaned to him by Chief Pratt. It had been squeezed into the bookcase beside the complete works of Sir Walter Scott. Unfortunately, Homer had tucked his notes into the pages.

Mary read one of them aloud. *"Serial killers, gratification from killing, desire to repeat, taking of mementoes, victims turned into zombies, sex toys."* She looked at Homer and shook the book at him. "Homer, this is sick. It's really sick."

"Of course it's sick. But it explains what's been happening. You know, the serial killer."

"Oh, of course, of course, I should have known. Oh,

Homer, *dear!*" Mary lifted the book to the ceiling as though appealing to God. "You just can't keep away from it, can you? This sordid murder case, you've just got to get mixed up in it, isn't that right?"

"Well, I suppose so." Homer was overcome by a feeling of wounded pride. His wife was scolding him for helping in the pursuit of a genuine monster. "But, Mary dear, they're accusing that friend of Fern's. I'm trying to help that young kid we met the other day. You know, Tom Dean. They've clapped him in jail."

Mary was scandalized. "But, Homer, how do you know he's not guilty? You don't know anything about him."

Homer could think of a couple of unsatisfactory answers— *I just feel it in my bones,* or *He has such an honest face.* Instead he growled stubbornly, "Well, I like him."

Mary stared at Homer, and then she dropped the book on the bed and burst out laughing. "Oh, Homer, I do too, I like him too. But, oh, *damnit,* Homer."

⌒

Of course Chief Oliver Pratt would not be open to any feelings in Homer's bones nor to his trust in honest faces, and he would certainly have no faith whatever in Homer's amiable fondness for young Tom Dean.

Therefore Homer abandoned any thought of pathos. In setting out to prove Tom's innocence, he pounded on the Chief's desk and asked an urgent and rational question. "Listen here, Oliver, what about Tom's DNA? You gotta test it. It won't match the real killer's DNA. So you'll have to release him. Hurry up. This is a wrongful arrest."

Pratt looked at him balefully. "We already got Dean's DNA. First thing they do at Intake."

"Well, fine. How does it compare with the weirdo's DNA?"

"Whaddayou mean, the weirdo's DNA? We ain't *got* no DNA."

"You ain't got—but, Christ, Oliver, he raped all those women."

"Correction. He made it *look* as if he'd raped all those women."

"You mean he didn't? He strangled them and tore off their clothes and then he didn't do it? He just carved them up and that was all?"

Pratt gazed at the ceiling and twiddled his thumbs. "Apparently so."

"But—!" Dumbfounded, Homer flapped his hands.

"So maybe the guy's incapable—you know, impotent."

"Then why does he molest these women at all?"

"Damned if I now. Those FBI profilers at Quantico, they're looking into it. These sleazeballs hate women for some reason. Usually it's the mother. They've got it in for the mother, so they take vengeance on the entire female sex."

Faintly Homer said, "Oh," and sank back in his chair.

Pratt smiled. "So your young friend is the best news we've had so far."

Homer was surprised to see that the Chief looked altogether different. His face was pink and healthy, his eyes were no longer hot coals smoldering deep inside his skull. "The kid admits inviting the woman into his tent, her body was found nearby, his motorbike chain was the murder weapon." Pratt stretched his neck and pretended to strangle himself, bulging out his eyes and sticking out his tongue.

Homer gasped and recoiled.

"And get this. A silver cigarette lighter engraved with the initials 'FF' was found in Dean's tent. It shows a clear imprint of the fingers of his right hand."

"'FF'? You mean 'FF' for 'Flora Foley'?"

"Right you are. 'FF' for 'Flora Foley.'" Pratt smiled blissfully. "'Flora'—such a pretty name." Then his forehead creased with puzzled wrinkles. "Was Flora a goddess or something? Wait a sec, I'll look it up."

Homer addressed the Chief's back as Oliver reached for the FAL–HIL volume of his *Oxford English Dictionary* and began riffling the pages. "So where is he?"

Pratt was in a trance, mumbling, "*Flambeau, flicker, flossy*—where is who, Homer?"

"Tom Dean! Where have you put Tom Dean?"

Pratt rammed his forefinger down on the book and cried, "Flora, goddess of flowers. Well, naturally, she was the goddess of flowers."

"Well, she didn't look like the goddess of flowers to me," said Homer testily. "With or without her wig. Tell me, did you find it anywhere, her wig?"

"Wig? No, what wig?"

"Aha, you see? When we saw her that day, up in the Dome Room, Flora was wearing a bushy black wig. So, if Tom Dean killed her, what did he do with it?"

Pratt stared blankly at Homer. He opened his mouth to say something, but closed it again to pick up the ringing phone. Homer sank back, his mind whizzing in circles and spirals, as the Chief muttered, "Pratt," and then fell silent, listening. Homer was amused at the gradual change in his expression. Pratt smiled, then grinned, then beamed, and at last, putting down the phone, he laughed out loud.

"DNA! You want evidence from DNA? Well, you've got it. That note, did you see the note? You know, like he always puts one on the bodies, sort of like adding bells and whistles? Well, as usual we don't know what the hell the crazy message means, but this one came from an envelope, a *licked* envelope. And we just got the lab report."

Homer groaned. "Don't tell me it's the same as—"

"Pre*cisely* the same. The DNA in the saliva on the envelopes exactly matches your young friend's." Pratt smiled triumphantly. Homer closed his eyes in pain.

Then Pratt's vainglory faded a little. "It's true, I have to admit, the voiceprint doesn't match the one we got from Dean."

"Voiceprint?"

"New electronic technique. There was this 911 call, some nut, we recorded it, the way we always do. We assumed it was the UNSUB—I mean, this nut said where to find the body, and he was right."

Homer was all at sea. "UNSUB? You mean the suspect?"

"Of course. The Unknown Subject. This guy talked really crazy. But his voiceprint doesn't match Dean's. So maybe it was just some crank on the phone."

"But you said he directed you to Flora's body?"

"Nutty hiker, maybe, came across it, rushed to a phone, called 911." The Chief frowned more deeply. "And there was the apple core. Spittle on that didn't fit either."

"Apple core? What apple core?"

"Somebody threw a half-eaten apple on the ground. Tom Dean had a bag of apples in his tent. Same kind of apples. You know, Macs. Only this time the saliva doesn't match."

Homer grinned, and burst into the last line of a comic song, which was all he could remember—*"I can prove that I'm the guy that ate the core."*

"What's that, Homer?" said Pratt.

"Adam and Eve in the Garden of Eden. The guy in the song was an eyewitness and he's got the apple core to prove it."

"Very funny."

Homer was feeling better. He rose to his feet. "Tell me, Chief, where's the jail? Is it okay if I pay him a call?"

"It's out Interstate 64. You can't miss it. But I don't know if they'll let you in. Visitors are strictly limited." Pratt thought it over. "But I suppose as a district attorney from Massachusetts you won't have any trouble. Here, I'll write you a pass."

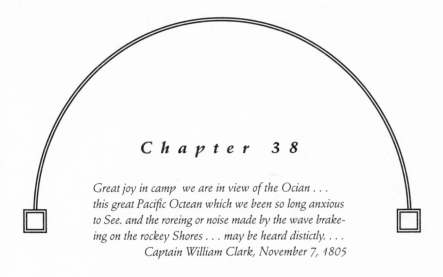

Chapter 38

Great joy in camp we are in view of the Ocian . . .
this great Pacific Octean which we been so long anxious
to See. and the roreing or noise made by the wave brake-
ing on the rockey Shores . . . may be heard distictly. . . .
Captain William Clark, November 7, 1805

Soon after he had met Fern Fisher for the first time, a gush of affection for the girl had filled the heart of Augustus Upchurch. His aging glands had swelled with youth. He was like a dying oak that drops a thousand acorns on the ground.

At first his affection had been a pure and innocent emotion, totally unlike his sexual fantasies. But now his feeling was more than affection. After the appearance in Fern's company of that terrible young invader, Tom Dean, the separating wall between Fern and the sexy sluts had collapsed. Astonishing new images of the sweet, virginal young girl began to mingle with the others. His dreams grew more and more lurid.

How he had envied Tom Dean! Simply by being young, the boy had everything that he himself did not, including the sympathy and companionship of dear, adorable Fern.

But now Augustus was happy and excited. His fears for Fern's safety had been justified. He had saved her from the beast who had been so dangerously close, the monster who was threatening her life. From now on she would be grateful, she would see him at last as her protector, she would wrap her arms around him, weeping, and whisper her thankful-ness.

But to his bitter disappointment Fern failed to oblige. The next time he wheezed up the stairs to the Dome Room, he found her standing at the top of the ladder. She gave Augus-tus a wild glance, tossed out an arm holding a paintbrush, nearly throwing herself off balance, and whispered, "It's not finished, you see. I've got to finish it." A piece of paper flut-tered down. "Oh dear," wailed Fern, "I need it. Oh, please, Mr. Upchurch, would you pick it up?"

Alarmed, Augustus glanced at the paper as he handed it to her. It was a map. He gripped the ladder. "My dear, be care-ful. Oh, please, my dear, come down."

Fern stared at the map, then dipped her paintbrush in a jar and stroked it on the ceiling. "No, no," she said softly, "not now. I'm fine up here, Mr. Upchurch, I'm really just fine. I've got to finish the river. I've got to finish it for Tom."

For Tom! Augustus couldn't believe it. He was stupefied. The child was still deluded, she was still under the spell of that dangerous young snake.

But then Fern stopped painting and cried, "Oh, Mr. Up-church!"

Hope returned. Augustus smiled up at her. His tie was red as blood, a pulsing scarlet. "Yes, my dear?"

"Those pins. They think Tom's paper of pins proves he's guilty."

Augustus was bewildered. "Pins? What pins?"

"Do you know why Tom had pins? It was because he pinned his time line to the wall of the tent." She glared at Au-gustus fiercely. "I mean, that's why he had that paper of pins."

"Oh," said Augustus, "I see," although he didn't see.

"If they look, they'll find the pinholes. Tell them to look for the pinholes, Mr. Upchurch." Fern scrambled down the ladder, took his arm, and dragged him to the long strip of paper encircling the wall. "And look, there are pins here too. Ouch!" She waggled her pricked finger at him to show the drop of blood. "You see?"

What was the child talking about? Augustus left the Dome Room in a state of confusion. Descending the stairs with extreme care, he remembered to his horror something poor dear Flora had told him about murderers and their victims. *Killers, lots of times they're highly attractive to helpless young females. Some women are gluttons for punishment.*

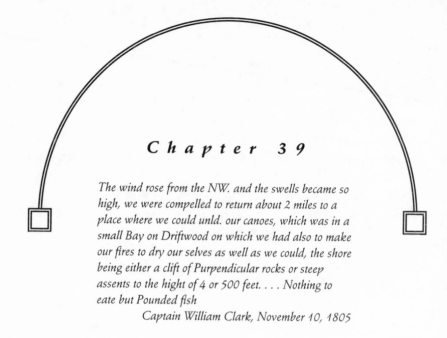

Chapter 39

The wind rose from the NW. and the swells became so high, we were compelled to return about 2 miles to a place where we could unld. our canoes, which was in a small Bay on Driftwood on which we had also to make our fires to dry our selves as well as we could, the shore being either a clift of Purpendicular rocks or steep assents to the hight of 4 or 500 feet. . . . Nothing to eate but Pounded fish

Captain William Clark, November 10, 1805

Of course it took Homer several tries to find the Charlottesville-Albemarle Regional Jail—two or three high-speed plunges in different directions along Interstate 64. He was damp with sweat when at last he presented Pratt's handwritten introduction and his own feeble credentials to the admitting officer at the desk.

He was not permitted to see Tom face to face. Four inches of tempered glass divided them. Tom sat on one side, Homer on the other. They were connected by telephone.

Monuments of catastrophe rose around them. Tom had been officially arrested on suspicion of murder, processed, and classified, and his DNA had been determined from a blood sample. He had been arraigned before a camera connected by fiber optics to a judge far away, and the judge had refused bail.

Tom's face was blank. At first he said nothing.

But Homer had something important to ask him. It was an embarrassing question, and the telephone was an impediment to intimacy. He decided it could wait. "Do they let you have books in this place?"

Tom brightened and picked up the phone. "I've got a book on Jefferson's presidency." His voice sounded buzzy and faint, as if he were somewhere on the other side of the world. *Which,* thought Homer unhappily, *in a way, he is.* "He sent off the expedition during his first term."

"The expedition?"

"Lewis and Clark. You know." Tom gripped the phone and rambled on about all the things President Jefferson had done to prepare Meriwether Lewis for the journey. "He had all these friends in the American Philosophical Society. You know, like Benjamin Rush. Dr. Rush gave Lewis a list of the medicines he should take along."

Homer listened. Tom might have been one of his own young teaching assistants rather than a poor soul imprisoned on a charge of multiple murder, facing a lifetime behind bars or even a sentence of death.

"I've been collecting them myself," said Tom. "Tartar emetic, epsom salts, gum camphor, laudanum—"

"Laudanum! Oh, of course, I saw them in your tent. All those little jars on the floor."

"On the floor?" Tom looked startled. His face fell. "Oh well, it doesn't matter now."

"Of course it does," said Homer, trying to sound comforting. He cleared his throat, wondering how to introduce the difficult subject. He came from a generation that found it hard to talk about sex. He and Mary didn't talk about it, they just did it. Therefore, his questions were so vague and roundabout that Tom was puzzled.

At last he guessed what Homer was trying to say. "Do you mean, can I fuck⸮"

Homer laughed, and his inhibitions melted away. "Exactly."

"Oh, God, Homer, of course I can." There was a pause, and then Tom blushed and cleared his throat. "Well, there's a couple of old girlfriends you could talk to. You know, politely." He scribbled on a piece of paper and held it up against the glass.

Homer copied the names and addresses and went away, satisfied.

If Tom Dean had been the killer he would have raped those women soundly. It was a point in his favor.

Chapter 40

*A hard rain all the last night, dureing the last tide the
logs on which we lay was all on float, Sent Jo Fields to
hunt, he Soon returned and informed us that the hills
was So high & Steep, & thick with undergroth and
fallen Timber that he could not get out any
distance. . . .*

Captain William Clark, November 11, 1805,
on the Columbia

It took Homer only two days to track down Tom's ex-
girlfriends, a couple of former students at the university.
Gently he succeeded in persuading both of them to sign affidavits attesting to the sexual adequacy of Thomas Arthur
Dean.

With the affidavits triumphantly in hand, he burst into
Oliver Pratt's office and found him closeted with a stranger.

"Oh, excuse me," said Homer, beginning to back out. "I
just wanted to pass on some information."

"No, no, Homer. Come right on in. Meet Lieutenant Detective Basil Partridge. Bazzie, this is my friend Homer Kelly
from the Attorney General's office in Massachusetts."

"No, no, Oliver," said Homer. "You were wrong before,
and now you're more wrong than ever."

"Well, whatever," said Pratt. "Okay, Homer, what do you
want to tell me?"

Homer relayed the news about Tom Dean's sexual prowess, putting it as delicately as he could.

Sergeant Partridge was not impressed. "Doesn't mean a thing."

Pratt wasn't impressed either. "How do we know how the kid would have responded at the—uh—critical moment?"

"You mean," said Homer, "he might have failed to—?"

"Ejaculate," said Bazzie crudely, getting right to the point.

"So you see, Homer," said Pratt, "in spite of his self-proclaimed masculine prowess, he might not have left any DNA on those women."

"But that's absurd. You can't possibly believe it."

It was an insult. Lieutenant Detective Partridge frowned at Homer and began itemizing the counts against Tom Dean. Homer had heard most of them before.

"One, the kid tells a piece of shit about this woman following him to his tent in the woods. *She* followed *him,* he says, you get that? Not the other way around. Two, he admits inviting her inside—God! —and they talk for a while, he says, and then they both leave. He goes one way, she goes another. Three, we found heroin in his tent."

"Oh, for God's sake," interrupted Homer. "It wasn't heroin. It was laudanum. Laudanum is tincture of opium. You have to do all kinds of things to opium to turn it into heroin. It's purely medicinal. Lewis and Clark—"

"Medicinal?" Bazzie snickered. "Oh, sure." He carried on. "Four, his possession of a silver lighter bearing the initials of the murdered woman, the lighter *with which*"—Bazzie's face shone with gloating triumph—"he lit the fire that was meant to destroy the evidence against him. Five, your young friend was seen *in person* at a crime scene, not once but twice."

Bazzie Partridge and Chief Pratt were both grinning at Homer. This item was a shocker.

Bazzie explained. "One of the county cops noticed this

redheaded guy at the library. You know, while the body of the victim was being removed."

"Serial killers," said Pratt comfortably, "it's what they like to do, come back to the—"

Homer said it for him—"scene of the crime." He sighed heavily. "You don't believe that first so-called eyewitness, do you? There were probably all kinds of people in the neighborhood at the time—blond, brunette, gray-haired men in derby hats."

Bazzie went on mercilessly. "And there he was beside the road at the place where the hitchhiker was dumped. Claimed he was fixing his motorbike. Our guy identified him positively. Oh, and, incidentally, the motorbike leads us to item six."

"Item six," repeated Homer, his voice sepulchral.

"Victims all throttled with a chain. The bike belonging to Tom Dean has a chain with a padlock." Like Chief Pratt, Bazzie took a melodramatic pleasure in acting out the garroting of the victims by wrapping his hands around his neck and pretending to strangle himself. "Just the right size," he said cheerfully, dropping his hands and grinning. "Item seven—"

"Oh, for God's sake, there isn't any more," said Homer. "You're making it up."

"Item seven, the vagueness of the suspect about his whereabouts. Ask him, go ahead and ask him where he was on particular days. Wait a sec." Bazzie groped for a piece of paper on Pratt's desk. "Here we are. Ask him where he was on May 14, May 23, June 1, June 11, and June 16—you know, the dates of the most recent killings. Claims he never budged from the woods around that goddamn tent."

"Well, maybe he didn't," whined Homer.

"Item eight. The bloodstained notes on the bodies were fastened with common pins. A paper of identical pins was found in Dean's tent."

"What?" Homer was scandalized. "Pins! But everybody uses pins."

They grinned at him, and he sank back defeated.

There followed a gruesome half-hour examining photographs of murdered women.

Homer did his best to seem unmoved. He didn't want to look like a fool in the presence of Chief Pratt and the loudly self-confident Lieutenant Detective Partridge. But in all of his experience as a sometime investigator of criminal behavior he had never before come across a serial killer. His culprits were usually of a refined and genteel nature—professors, college presidents, art historians, people of that ilk, men and women of exquisite taste. If they had to use a gun, they raised their little pinkie. But—Homer tried to control his revulsion—these pictures were truly abominable.

"Same heavy chain every time," said Pratt calmly. "See? They've all got the identical marks on the throat. Chain links an inch long, three-sixteenths-inch steel."

Homer forced himself to look through them all again. "You know," he said, struck by an idea, "they're all so neat."

"Neat?" Pratt was scandalized. "What do you mean neat" Holy Jerusalem."

"I mean they're all so nicely arranged. All lying flat with their arms and legs just so. And look at their hair, all neatly combed. Makes me think of morticians, the way they lay out a body in a coffin."

Pratt was interested. "Oh, right, I see what you mean."

"Even poor Flora. Without her wig there wasn't much hair to arrange, but she was propped up inside that tree stump like a queen on a throne."

"Wig?" said Bazzie Partridge. "She had a wig?"

"Oh, right," said Chief Pratt. "I forgot to tell you. Homer says she was wearing a black wig when he saw her alive that afternoon."

Partridge was disconcerted. "You mean it's missing?"

"A trophy, Oliver," said Homer. "It's in that gruesome book you gave me. These bastards, they take keepsakes to remember their victims by. It's like a lock of your girlfriend's hair, just looking at it gives you a thrill. I don't know what kind of thrill it gives your typical scumbag, maybe some kind of sexual gratification." Homer remembered the bewigged Flora Foley and shook his head in wonder.

"Of course," said Pratt. "Bazzie, remember the hitchhiker? The librarian's name tag was attached to her shirt. Classic example of trophy-taking. Then there was the earring. Same with the wig, I'll bet. It's another memento."

"The question is," said Bazzie—his voice was harsh, and it ricocheted from wall to wall—"where will the wig turn up next?"

They brooded for a moment in silence, and then Pratt shook himself and shuffled his papers. "Got another job for you, Homer." He handed him a typed sheet. "It's the list of those weird notes, the ones we've found on the bodies. You'll notice there's a couple of new ones at the bottom. See if you can figure them out. I keep forgetting you're a professor. Piece of research, right up your alley."

Homer looked at the list and said doubtfully, "I'll see what I can do."

"I've already looked into the first one." Pratt was suddenly enthusiastic. "See, Homer, where it says 'old bawd'? Fascinating word, *bawd*. Woman who keeps a brothel. It goes way back. Old French *baude,* Old High German *bald*—"

"After all," said Homer dryly, "it's the world's oldest profession."

"What the hell are you talking about?" said Lieutenant Detective Partridge.

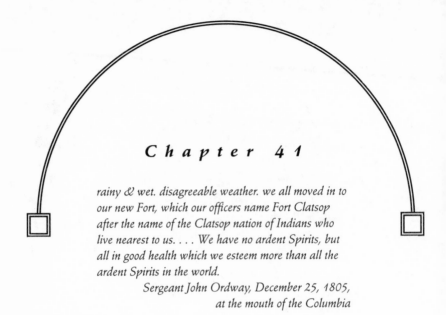

Chapter 41

*rainy & wet. disagreeable weather. we all moved in to
our new Fort, which our officers name Fort Clatsop
after the name of the Clatsop nation of Indians who
live nearest to us. . . . We have no ardent Spirits, but
all in good health which we esteem more than all the
ardent Spirits in the world.*

*Sergeant John Ordway, December 25, 1805,
at the mouth of the Columbia*

After staring at them all evening and thinking about them
all night, Homer had made no progress in deciphering
the weird messages on Pratt's list, the eccentric notes found
on the bodies of the murdered women. Next day, in despera-
tion, he showed the list to Mary. Now that she had stopped
protesting against his interest in Tom's case, she had begun to
share his fervor.

They took their morning coffee outside and sat down carefully on the porch swing. Poising their cups in their hands
and steadying the swing with their feet, they studied the
list solemnly, trying to penetrate the perverted mind of the
madman.

The swing creaked. An unfamiliar Southern bird uttered a
bell-like note. Cars passed on the street. A couple of summer-
school students emerged from the house next door, laughing
and talking in a foreign tongue, Urdu perhaps, or Hindi.

The porch, the swing, the cars on the street, the students

and the singing bird were all part of the normal world. Pratt's list was an aberration:

> *Old bawd*
> *Article of traffic*
> *Presents neked*
> *Pocks & venereal*
> *All in scabs*
> *Venerious & pustelus*
> *Sport publickly*
> *Old tobacco box*
> *Honour of passing a night*
> *With the daughter of*

"Maybe he's talking about himself," suggested Mary. "Maybe he's got some kind of venereal disease, and he blames it on women. Maybe he's HIV-positive."

"What does that tobacco box have to do with anything else? It's just crazy."

Mary sipped her coffee and studied the list. "I suppose *Sport publickly* is about sex too, but somehow it sounds more frolicsome."

Clatsop hat

"As a matter of fact," said Homer, putting his coffee cup on the floor and pulling her to him tenderly, "I like a little frolicsome sport myself. Strictly privately, of course."

"Watch it, Homer dear," said Mary, holding her cup out of harm's way.

⌒

Ed Bailey was getting ready for a weekend fishing trip in the Blue Ridge. He had bought a lot of new equipment, the latest thing in flexible rods and artificial lures to mesmerize every kind of fish.

After packing all the stuff in his car, along with a camping icebox full of beer, he ran back in the house to shout a goodbye. "Don't forget, Mary honey, the Fourth of July's just around the corner. Me, I'm gonna use my new camera at the celebration. All digital, amazing. Where's Homer?"

"At the library." Mary looked up from her book. "He's looking for more stuff like this." Shuddering, she held up the grisly book that had been loaned to Homer by Chief Pratt. "It's about serial killers. It's loathsome."

The Jefferson-Madison Public Library was the one in which the poor young librarian had been so brutally killed. Today Homer's errand was an exercise in masochism, because he had already learned more than he wanted to know about the cannibal practices of Jeffrey Dahmer and the twenty-nine bodies buried in John Wayne Gacy's cellar.

But he sat down gamely at one of the library's computer monitors and looked for more books about serial killers. Soon a grim list appeared on the screen:

BESTIALITY: A HISTORY

MONSTROUS ACTS: A CATALOGUE

MULTIPLE MURDER IN THE USA

CASE STUDIES OF SERIAL KILLERS

There was even a jocular title:

GIVE YOUR MOTHER FORTY WHACKS:

THE LIZZIE BORDEN SYNDROME

Homer copied down the entire list and brought it to the librarian at the reference desk. "Can you tell me where to find some of these?"

Homer didn't know it, but the woman at the desk was Victoria Love, the director of the library. It had been Victoria who had gone to lunch one day, leaving her young assistant to be lured into the stacks and murdered. Now, looking at Homer's list, she turned pale and whispered, "One moment, please."

Turning on her heel, she walked quickly away, looking back at him furtively.

Homer trotted after her cheerfully, making complimentary remarks about libraries in general and her library in particular, and about the splendor of Benjamin Franklin's original magnificent concept, and the glories of the system of interlibrary loan, and the saintly devotion of dedicated librarians, their love of learning and eagerness to assist the bewildered scholar. But when Director Love snatched up a phone in trembling fingers and touched three buttons—three buttons only—he stopped short.

Oh, God, the woman was calling the police.

"No, no," shouted Homer, grasping her arm. "Look, wait a sec."

He was too late. The officer on duty in the Charlottesville Police Department heard her breathless whisper and then her squeal as she dropped the phone—obviously the cry of a woman in the clutches of a vicious killer.

Soon a herd of cops came thundering up the library steps and crowding in the door.

By this time Homer had managed to calm the fears of the

librarian. There were explanations, red faces and guffaws. The cops went away.

Homer put aside his list of gruesome books and asked Victoria, "Do you have a minute?"

"Of course." Victoria was ashamed of her panic. They sat down together behind the call desk, among carts loaded with books to be reshelved and rows of dictionaries.

Homer was distracted by the dictionaries. "The *OED*, I don't see it. Do you mean to say the library hasn't got the *OED*?"

Victoria was confused. "The *OED*? You mean the *Oxford English Dictionary*? Of course we do. It's in the reference room."

Homer came to his senses and started over. "Could you tell me who was using the library on the day your colleague was killed?"

"They've already asked us that. We gave them a list of everybody who took out books that day. But there were others. If someone comes in and doesn't borrow a book, then we have no record. Of course we've all tried to remember, but there are always so many people coming in and out, sometimes it's just a blur." She groped in a drawer. "Here's the list of the borrowers and the books they took out." She tapped a name. "This one's interesting, Flora Foley. She took out three books on firearms and one on poisons. She was writing a thriller, that's what she said."

"I guess you haven't been reading the paper," said Homer sorrowfully. "Flora Foley was the latest victim."

"Oh, heavens," gasped Victoria. "I didn't know that."

Homer ran his finger down her list. It stopped at the name of Augustus Upchurch. Wasn't Upchurch the guy who had discovered Flora's body and called 911 and warned the police about Tom? Homer remembered something from his monster book—*sometimes the UNSUB calls 911 himself, offering "helpful"* information. What if this guy Upchurch had killed poor old Flora?

Homer glanced up at Victoria. "Pornographic books? That's what he was interested in?"

She made a face. "I'm afraid so. Oh, he doesn't use his real name. He always pretends to be somebody else. But one of the retired librarians came in one day and recognized him and told us who he was, because she used to know him well. She said Mr. Upchurch was a successful retired businessman and a highly *respectable* old gentleman." Victoria held up a cautionary hand. "I hasten to say that we don't have many pornographic books in this library, because everything in our collection is supposed to have"—she put her hands together in a prayerful gesture—"literary quality. But some of the stuff is pretty raunchy."

"And you're sure he was here that day?"

Victoria turned to her computer and began swooping up and down the screen, rollicking in the vastness of cyberspace. "Yes, he was here, all right. Do you think—?"

Homer shook his head. "You say he's elderly? I'm afraid it doesn't fit the usual pattern for serial killers. They're usually men in their twenties or thirties."

"Oh, too bad," said the librarian, crestfallen.

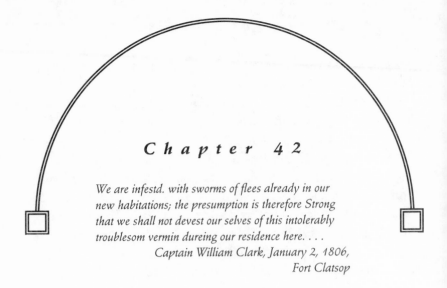

Chapter 42

We are infestd. with sworms of flees already in our new habitations; the presumption is therefore Strong that we shall not devest our selves of this intolerably troublesom vermin dureing our residence here. . . .
Captain William Clark, January 2, 1806,
Fort Clatsop

It was the last week of June. To Chief Pratt's relief, the sensational articles in the local paper about the failure of the police to capture the stalker/slasher/killer had been replaced by enthusiastic profiles of the highly educated young pervert now awaiting trial in the Charlottesville-Albemarle Regional Jail.

Standing in line at the post office, Mary heard one woman say to another, "Wouldn't you know it would be somebody totally unexpected? Didn't I tell you?"

"Those quiet types," agreed her friend, "they're the worst."

Tom's family was besieged. They had to lock their doors, pull their curtains, and unlist their telephone.

Behind the drawn curtains there were mortified conferences, whispers, and sobs.

Grandmother Dean and sister Myrna were for disowning Tom altogether. Tom's mother disagreed, although she was humiliated and ashamed. How would they ever again hold up their heads? They should never have allowed that boy to go off somewhere and live in a tent by himself. Look what it had led to! Not nature study, the way he said, but the acting out of hideous and unnatural sexual fantasies.

Tom's father paced the floor, growling and muttering.

$\frown$

Mary clipped Tom's picture out of the *Charlottesville Daily Progress* and showed it to Homer. There he was, poor old Tom, handcuffed between a couple of uniformed officers, walking into the jail. He looked gawky and solemn. His arms were so thin and childlike! Mary's long-suppressed maternal instinct welled up, and she said, "Oh, the poor kid."

"You know what will happen if his name isn't cleared," said Homer gloomily. "He'll have a section all to himself in one of those gruesome books, right between Jeffrey Dahmer and John Gacy."

He called the jail and made an appointment to see Tom that afternoon at three o'clock. And then he was late—not because he lost his way, but because he ran into a classic example of road rage.

The infuriated driver was all alone, driving very slowly in a big gray van. When Homer tried to pass him, the driver honked angrily and swerved viciously into the middle. Then, to Homer's dismay, he slowed down to a surly crawl. Homer had to jam on his brakes and proceed at fifteen miles an hour. For the next five miles he was stuck on the winding road behind the rancid driver of the van.

He wanted to blat his horn, but it was exactly what the creep wanted him to do. Who was this guy? From the rear he looked like a young white male with a small head and a black buzz cut. His van had a license plate, but the numbers were daubed with mud. Well, thank God, at last it was time to turn off.

As Homer made the left turn in the direction of the jail, the van's exhaust pipe emitted a loud fart. A cloud of oily black smoke smeared the air. *So long and up yours,* said the smoke.

◠

On the other side of the thick slab of glass, Tom's freckled face was blanched from a week in solitary confinement. He mumbled a greeting into the phone.

Homer wasted no time on sympathy. He said, "Tom, I've got something to show you." Then he put down the phone and held a sheet of paper against the glass. Pressing it flat with one hand, he picked up the phone and said, "These are the notes that were left on the bodies. The killer uses pins. Oh, God, the pins, that's another thing. Well, never mind the pins. Look at the notes. The originals, they're nicely lettered, he takes a lot of trouble. Some are bloodstained, but they're all still legible, so I suppose he uses waterproof ink. Do you have any idea, any idea in the world, what they mean?"

Tom sat forward and stared at the paper. Time went by.

At last he sat back and smiled at Homer. He picked up the phone and said, "I know what they are. At least I remember the tobacco box. It's from the journal of Sergeant Gass."

"Sergeant Gass? Who's he?"

"Sergeant Patrick Gass was a member of the Lewis and Clark expedition. He was one of the journal-writers. Oh, God, it's terrible, his journal. I mean, he was just a simple guy, like most of them, but he hired a schoolteacher to pretty up his language. It's a godawful shame. But his facts are right. I mean, they agree with the other journals. And I remember that tobacco box." Tom grinned at Homer. "It was the price of having sex with the chief's daughter. The last two, I'll bet they go with it."

"The last two?" Homer turned the list around and looked at it. "You mean this one, *honour of passing a night?* Oh, right,

I see how they go together—*honour of passing a night with the daughter of.*" He looked up at Tom. "The daughter of who?"

"I'm pretty sure it was the daughter of the head chief of the Mandans." Tom's face fell. "The guy who leaves these notes, all he cares about is their sexual exploits. What a travesty."

"Sexual exploits?" Homer was astonished. "You mean the men of the expedition had sex with Indian women along the way?"

"Sure, sure. It comes up in the journals every now and then. There doesn't seem to be any tut-tutting or disapproval. The only trouble was the physical results, the symptoms of venereal disease."

Homer laughed. "It isn't the usual image of Lewis and Clark. Tell me, did the captains themselves—?"

"Sleep with the women? Probably not. But maybe they were careful not to leave any record. Somebody suggested that Lewis's suicide later on was the result of an advanced state of syphilis, but I don't think anybody takes that seriously."

"Oh, God, I forgot." Homer shook his head sadly. "I forgot he killed himself."

"Homer," said Tom, looking at him solemnly, "the sentence isn't finished."

Homer nodded gravely. "It means he'll kill again, is that what you mean? He'll finish the sentence by killing again."

"I'm afraid so."

Homer cheered up. "But that would be good news, for you anyway. Well, of course it would be horrible, but it would mean the serial killer is still on the loose, while you've been innocently locked up and out of circulation. They'd have to let you go."

"No, Homer." Tom shook his head. "The fact that the notes come from the journals of the Lewis and Clark expedition is one more strike against me. Tell me, who's the big

Lewis and Clark enthusiast around here? Who's been vandalizing the walls of Thomas Jefferson's Dome Room with quotations from their journals? Who's been painting the course of the Missouri River on the ceiling, another act of illegal violence to Thomas Jefferson's sacred premises?"

"Oh, God, you have, I'm afraid," agreed Homer. "I see what you mean. But since the killer is not you, it means there's somebody else out there, some godawful bastard with a similar fixation on Lewis and Clark."

"No, no," protested Tom. "Not similar, not similar at all. This kook doesn't care about anything in the journals but a few passages about the men sleeping with squaws. He's sick."

"Well, of course he's sick." Homer stood up to go. "But it may give us something to go on."

"Wait." Tom scrambled to his feet, dropped the phone, picked it up, and then, with elaborate casualness, said, "I just wonder if you've seen Fern?"

"Fern? Oh, Fern Fisher. No, sorry, Tom, I haven't."

Tom's face fell. "I thought she might come," he said gloomily, "but she hasn't."

Unable to think of anything comforting, Homer said, "Clever girl. Have you ever heard her whistle through her teeth?"

Tom brightened. "No. Can she do that?"

"She sure can. Blasts your ears off."

Tom looked pleased and murmured goodbye.

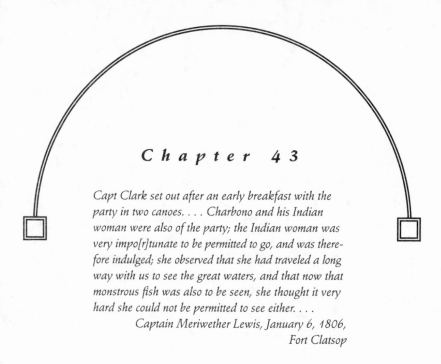

Chapter 43

*Capt Clark set out after an early breakfast with the
party in two canoes. . . . Charbono and his Indian
woman were also of the party; the Indian woman was
very impo[r]tunate to be permitted to go, and was therefore indulged; she observed that she had traveled a long
way with us to see the great waters, and that now that
monstrous fish was also to be seen, she thought it very
hard she could not be permitted to see either. . . .*
Captain Meriwether Lewis, January 6, 1806,
Fort Clatsop

July 1 was unbearably hot. In decades past, the citizens of
Charlottesville had sat on their front porches cooling their
faces with paper fans. Now they turned their air conditioners
to HI-COOL and stayed indoors.

Air-conditioned too were the classrooms and laboratories
at the University of Virginia. Sprinklers watered the lawn and
cooled the air in front of Jefferson's Rotunda. Tourists took
refuge from the sun in the shadowy arcades. On Fraternity
Row a small army of groundskeepers, mostly black, rode
lawnmowers up and down. But there were African-American
students as well as white among the kids who sweated
up the hill on Emmett Avenue to buy textbooks in the air-
conditioned bookstore.

On Hydraulic Road the pavement in front of the Bargain

Mart was unbearably hot, but inside the huge store the recirculated air went around and around, making shopping endurable.

Lazy ceiling fans did nothing to cool the air in the convenience store where Augustus Upchurch bought his magazines. It was a sweltering dark cave. Augustus dodged in and out and hurried home, his pink scalp and thinning hair protected by a Panama hat.

But at Monticello the air was fresh, the temperature cooler than in Charlottesville. The great trees around the house were islands of whispering leaves. Mary Kelly stood under the tall *Liriodendron tulipifera,* the last remaining healthy tree from Thomas Jefferson's time. From its high branches a canopy of shade dropped straight down over terrace walk and lawn, and she was reminded of Concord's vanished elms— Thoreau had called them *chandeliers of darkness.*

The house itself was not air-conditioned. The basement offices were the coolest part of the building. In the Dome Room, Fern's electric fan hummed softly.

There were no fans in the public rooms because the entire first floor was authentically unelectrified. Even so, the tourists in their shorts and duckbilled caps and sunhats were grateful to come in out of the sun to listen to the patient guides.

Cleverly, Gail Boltwood had thought of something cool to tell them about. "If you walk around the house you'll see the ice house under the North Terrace Walk. The deep pit was once filled with blocks of ice for the preservation of meat and the making of ice cream."

"Ice cream!" exclaimed one of the tourists. "Jefferson had ice cream?"

"Indeed he did. In fact, the first American recipe was written in his own hand. It was one of the dishes he enjoyed in France. But"—Gail raised her voice—"you must stay well

back behind the fence in front of the ice house. The iron railing has been removed for"—what should she call the removal of dead rats?—"necessary repairs."

The tourists came and went in their usual orderly succession. But there was nothing orderly about the tempestuous activity in the offices of the curator and his assistant on the second floor. Preparations for the Fourth of July were at a pinnacle of nervous excitement.

A horrid thought had occurred to Henry Spender. What if someone planted a bomb among the fireworks? What if the President of the United States and the President of France and the Prime Minister of Great Britain were blown to kingdom come? Three great nations would be thrown into chaos at the same time!

Gail's morning stint was over. She followed her last batch of tourists out of doors and met Mary Kelly, who had invited her to lunch.

Fern Fisher had been invited too. Fern drove to the Kellys' house in her own car, after running her finger over a map to find University Circle.

Homer had not been invited, but it didn't occur to him to stay away. Lunch, after all, was lunch. The fact that there were only three place settings at the table meant nothing in particular. "Wait a sec," he said cheerfully. "I'll get another bowl."

It was not a successful meal. Fern was a distracted and anxious guest, although she ate her spinach soup hungrily and held out her bowl for more.

Gail was distracted too. For once her calm face was not smiling. "I went to the funeral," she said unhappily.

Mary's spoon stopped in the air. "You mean—"

"Flora Foley's. She was an old friend. It was the most ridiculous service. If it hadn't been so sad, I would have laughed out loud."

"Why?" Mary had been present at a few absurd funerals herself.

"Oh, the minister was into pop psychology. *Griefwork.* You know the kind of thing. As if people didn't know how to cry."

"Ah," said Homer gloomily, "they call it the stages of grief." He put down his spoon and said something so wise, his wife forgave him for crashing the party. "It's too bad there aren't any stages for the dead. All they get is a sudden end and eternal darkness."

Mary squeezed his hand under the table, and Gail changed the subject.

"You people are coming to the Fourth of July celebration, aren't you? Oh, God, there's so much to do. And the security people, they're such a pest. They're all over the place already."

Mary passed the salad. "Is this in honor of our so-called serial killer? Don't they think he's already in custody?"

Fern half rose from her chair and said in a choked voice, "Well, if they do, they're wrong. The real killer is still out there somewhere." She plumped herself down again and muttered, "Sorry." Her spoon clattered on the edge of her plate.

"Well, of course it's not Tom," said Mary soothingly. "Homer knows that, don't you, Homer?"

Homer opened his mouth, but Gail hurried on. "No, no, I'm talking about the preparations for the arrival of the President. Two presidents in fact. The President of France will be here too, in honor of Jefferson's friendship with Lafayette, and the Prime Minister of England's coming, although I can't imagine why." Gail put her hand to her head. "It's terrible. They've grilled everybody on the staff. Politely, of course, but it feels like a police state up there."

"They talked to me too," said Fern." And they have a key to the west door of the Dome Room. They're going to have a sharpshooter out there, over the portico."

Gail's sense of doom had popped loose all her hairpins. Fussing them back into place, she continued to worry. "I don't know how the invited guests will ever get up the mountain. Henry says there'll be thirty local patrol cars as well as twenty-five Secret Service vehicles and a whole parade of limousines."

Homer snickered. "I've been reading about Jefferson's travels from Monticello to Washington when he was president. He had no guards at all. It never occurred to anybody to keep him safe with a whole company of militia."

"Well," said Gail uncomfortably, "it was a different age."

When lunch was over, Fern thanked Mary, hurried to her car, and drove dangerously fast down Interstate 64 in the direction of the Charlottesville-Albemarle Regional Jail.

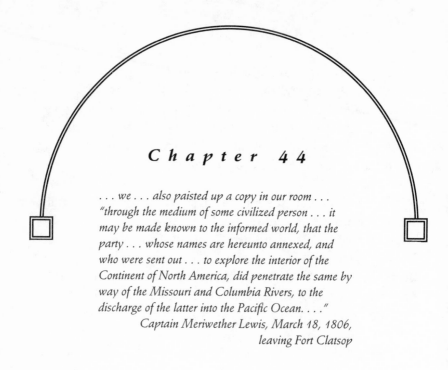

C h a p t e r 44

*. . . we . . . also paisted up a copy in our room . . .
"through the medium of some civilized person . . . it
may be made known to the informed world, that the
party . . . whose names are hereunto annexed, and
who were sent out . . . to explore the interior of the
Continent of North America, did penetrate the same by
way of the Missouri and Columbia Rivers, to the
discharge of the latter into the Pacific Ocean. . . ."*
Captain Meriwether Lewis, March 18, 1806,
leaving Fort Clatsop

Fern had to lie her way in.

"You're his girlfriend?" The officer in charge looked at her, wondering how any female could be so dumb as to get mixed up with a serial killer. "Well, I suppose it's okay."

Fern was disappointed to find a barrier between herself and Tom. She had meant to give him an impulsive hug, a purely friendly embrace. It was hard to be friendly through a telephone line and four inches of glass.

"Oh, Tom," said Fern, talking into the phone, "this is so ridiculous."

"Ridiculous, right," agreed Tom. "Har, har." He was looking at her hungrily.

"How can anybody think you could possibly have done all those things?"

"You mean, me with my college education and all? Too hoity-toity to carve up helpless females?"

"Well, yes, I guess so. Yes, that's exactly what I mean."

Tom's cheerfulness faded. "Well, they do, that's the trouble."

"What does Homer Kelly think? I saw him just now. His wife says he's trying to help."

"Oh, Homer's great. Makes me laugh. But I don't know if he can do anything. I mean, he's a complete stranger around here, doesn't know anything about Charlottesville or our own comfy Virginia kind of serial killer. Well, neither do I, of course. All I know is what any kid knows who grew up around here in the lap of middle-class suburban stupidity, plus of course I can draw you a picture of the human pelvis. You want to see? It's no mean achievement."

For some reason this sent Fern into a fit of crying, which soon turned into a fit of laughing. She mopped her wet cheeks. "I'm sorry. I'm really sorry."

Tom stood up. Holding the phone close to his mouth, he said, "Fern—"

"Twenty minutes," said the man in uniform, appearing in Fern's compartment. "Time's up." He picked up the phone and spoke to Tom. "You got a couple more visitors out there, won't take no for an answer." He waggled his head comically at Fern.

Tom's troubles had concentrated his mind. He held his arms wide, as though to enfold her, and his lips shaped words she couldn't understand.

She waved her hand very slightly and said, "Goodbye, Tom, goodbye."

The newly arrived visitors were Tom's mother and father. As they passed Fern in the corridor they stared at her blankly. She looked straight ahead and whistled softly through her teeth.

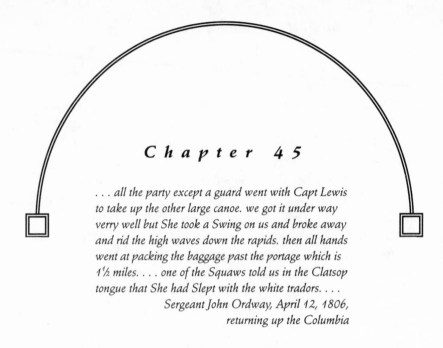

. . . all the party except a guard went with Capt Lewis
to take up the other large canoe. we got it under way
verry well but She took a Swing on us and broke away
and rid the high waves down the rapids. then all hands
went at packing the baggage past the portage which is
1½ miles. . . . one of the Squaws told us in the Clatsop
tongue that She had Slept with the white tradors. . . .
— Sergeant John Ordway, April 12, 1806,
returning up the Columbia

"Who was that woman?" These were the first words of the loving mother to her incarcerated son.

"What woman?"

"That woman in the hall. She whistled at us."

"Oh, that woman. Her name's Fern. Friend of mine. Professional whistler."

Tom's father took the phone. "Why the hell didn't you call us? We didn't know a thing about it until Myrna saw it on TV."

Tom shrugged his shoulders.

His father sighed, but he was prepared to be generous. "I've hired a prominent Richmond attorney to defend your case. Top of the line, a thousand dollars a day." Mr. Dean raised his hands in wonder at his own heroic sacrifice. "After all, who wants a forty-foot sloop anyway?"

"Oh, God," said Tom. "Please don't. I don't need an attorney. I've already got one."

An argument ensued, insistence on one side, stubborn refusal on the other.

At last Tom's father, deeply hurt, agreed to speak to Homer Kelly, the interfering stranger.

Then Mrs. Dean gave Tom a parting stare that meant, *Oh, Tom, we're so ashamed,* and at last they went away, leaving Tom gasping for air.

Arthur Dean did not bother to call Homer to make an appointment. The matter was too urgent. With Grandmother Dean and Tom's sister, Myrna, in the back seat, the sport-utility vehicle bombed right over to the house on University Circle. The entire family spilled out of the car and marched up the porch steps. Mr. Dean leaned angrily on the doorbell.

The weather was still sweltering. All the air conditioners in Albemarle County had been turned on at once, sucking energy from the power company. Refrigerators shuddered and worked overtime. A transformer failed. Blackouts were predicted.

When he heard the doorbell, Homer was in the shower trying to cool off. He swore, climbed out of the tub, wrapped himself in a towel, and came downstairs in his bare feet.

Even when he was dressed, Homer Kelly's great height and alarming growth of whisker made him something of a human spectacle. Now, standing damply in the doorway in his enormous towel, he looked like a wild man, an escapee from the circus—pink shoulders steaming, whiskers dripping, a frenzy of gray hair standing out from his head. His towel, in fact, said FRANKLIN PARK ZOO.

"Good afternoon," he said politely, gazing in surprise around the circle of staring faces.

Arthur Dean was a tall man, accustomed to cowing lesser mortals. Now he had to look up, way up, at Homer. "Mr. Kelly? My name is Arthur Dean."

"Well," said Homer affably, "why don't you all come in?" He stood back while they paraded past him, daughter Myrna shrinking away from the bulge of Homer's stomach. When they were settled on chairs and sofas, he galloped upstairs to snatch up his bathrobe and slippers. As he plunged downstairs again, Mary came in the back door. She had been walking the dog. Homer rolled his eyes, and she wisely retreated to the kitchen.

Arthur Dean came to the point at once, beginning on a friendly note. "I understand you have taken upon yourself the role of defense attorney for my son."

"I have?" Homer's brain processed this information instantaneously and analyzed it from top to bottom. He had taken an immediate dislike to the entire family. "Oh, yes, that's right, you're right, I have, I certainly have."

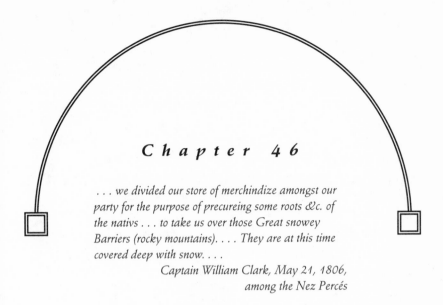

Chapter 46

. . . we divided our store of merchindize amongst our
party for the purpose of precureing some roots &c. of
the nativs . . . to take us over those Great snowey
Barriers (rocky mountains). . . . They are at this time
covered deep with snow. . . .
                    Captain William Clark, May 21, 1806,
                                    among the Nez Percés

On July 3, the day before the Monticello celebration, Henry Spender was the center of a storm of last-minute preparations. He had a fearful headache.

Heavy rain was forecast for the next day. Rain was unthinkable. It would be a disaster.

People kept popping into Henry's office with urgent questions. Through some appalling oversight, the Governor of West Virginia had received no invitation. Would Henry make a personal phone call? And would he call the agent of the famous film star, who was trying to back out?

Also—a highly ticklish predicament—the organization of the blood relatives of Thomas Jefferson had invited only a few of the descendants of Sally Hemings, the ones whose claim of kinship was backed by DNA evidence. The rest were boiling mad.

And that wasn't all. One of the caterers wanted to substitute finger sandwiches for the asparagus rolls, and was that all right? Because if it was, it meant the enraged withdrawal of the other.

And there were glitches with the film crew and the phone banks.

"Sorry to bother you, Henry," said Richard Barbaro, Henry's second in command, "but the loudspeaker system is failing. None of their stuff works. I need your authority to fire the whole damn outfit and call in the competition. Is that okay by you?"

There was a pause, then Henry said sarcastically, "You know, Richard, a million miles in outer space at the remotest edge of the solar system in a temperature of absolute zero, the shutters of space-exploration cameras open at the touch of a computer keyboard back on earth. Why is it, in the name of Almighty God, that public-address systems here on earth never, *never EVER WORK?*"

Henry had reared up from his chair, he was roaring. Then, collapsing back down and holding his throbbing head, he whispered, "I ask you that, Richard, simply for my own information, as a matter of philosophical inquiry."

Gail Boltwood was unaware of the fragile state of the curator's nerves. Putting her head around the door, she said, "Henry, there's a problem about the schoolchildren."

"The schoolchildren?" said Henry softly, looking at her with a dangerous gleam in his eye.

"You remember we had a lottery, way last May, to see which kids would be invited. Now the teacher of another class claims the lottery was rigged."

Howie Plover heard the explosion as he ascended the stairs. Wisely, he postponed his complaint about the ice house. And anyway, it certainly wasn't his fault. Howie had done his part all right, removing the dead rats, but the iron gate had not been replaced.

The truth was, they should have hired a more ordinary

blacksmith. This one was not your typical mighty man with arms like iron bands, nor was he like the simple lads who had hammered nails in Thomas Jefferson's own Nailery, right here at Monticello.

He was a craftsman, an artist, skillful in the design and manufacture of rood screens for Anglican churches, works of art splendid with spear points and interwoven spirals. His fame was widespread.

A mean little job like fashioning a new metal grille for an ice pit after the removal of dead rats was not the sort of job the blacksmith cared about. He kept putting it off.

The last time Howie had called him to ask about the gate for the ice house, the blacksmith had stared at the iron rod cooling on his forge and said vaguely, "Oh, certainly. I'll get to work on it right away."

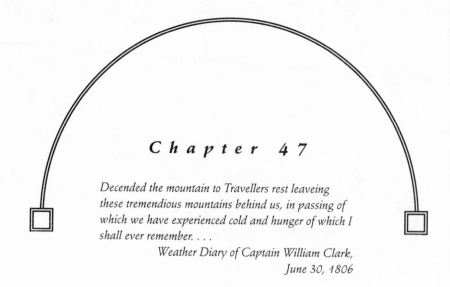

Chapter 47

*Decended the mountain to Travellers rest leaveing
these tremendious mountains behind us, in passing of
which we have experienced cold and hunger of which I
shall ever remember. . . .*

Weather Diary of Captain William Clark,
June 30, 1806

On the morning of July third, Homer woke early and
stared up at the ceiling, where there was a water stain in
the shape of a coffin.

Why did fits of depression come upon him without warning? On the other hand, why should he expect life to be one
thing all the time, and not a perpetual alternation from one
moment to the next of regret, shame, pride, guilt, confusion,
despair, pleasure, affection, loathing, gluttony, and lust? Why,
indeed?

"You know," he said aloud, "it's really sad."

"What, Homer?" Keeping her eyes closed, Mary turned
over and put her arm around him. "What's sad?"

"My ambition in life, that's what's sad. I used to look forward to glorious triumphs, magnificent achievements, castles in
the air. Now all I want is to keep from making a fool of myself.
It's my single supreme ambition. Don't you think that's sad?"

"Oh, Homer." Mary kissed him. "You know what? I like
you better this way."

They lay quietly on their backs, lost in thought. "Fern has a boyfriend," murmured Mary. "Did you know that?"

"A boyfriend?"

"Guy named Jim Reeves, old flame. Drove down from Baltimore yesterday."

The phone rang. Homer reared up, reached for it, and said a gruff hello.

"Mr. Kelly?" The voice was loud and peremptory. "Is that you? Arthur Dean here."

After a slight pause, Homer said, "Oh, Mr. Dean, good morning."

"I just want to know, Mr. Kelly, speaking as a father, how your investigation is progressing?"

It was an uncomfortable conversation, with Arthur Dean doing most of the talking, while Homer made noncommittal noises.

After a while it was Mrs. Dean's turn. She was anxious to know whether her son would be permitted to carry on his studies while he had so much time in prison with nothing whatever to do. She was eager to impress on Homer the fact that Tom had been the valedictorian of his high-school class and a member of Phi Beta Kappa at the University of Virginia.

Nor was Homer spared a whining complaint from Tom's sister, Myrna, who wanted him to know how *embarrassing* it was to have all her friends know about her *brother.*

When Homer visited the jail that afternoon, he was no longer separated from Tom by a window of glass. As Tom's officially designated attorney, he was permitted to sit with him in one of the compartments devoted to client-attorney interviews. A camera monitored their conversation, but Tom didn't want to talk about his case anyway.

Leaning his elbows on the table, he delivered a rambling lecture about Sacagawea, the Shoshone woman who had accompanied the Corps of Discovery all the way to the Pacific and back.

"She was just sort of an accident," said Tom. "They brought her along because she happened to be the wife of the French interpreter, and because she could speak Shoshone. There she was, this teenager, nine months pregnant, giving birth right there in the Mandan camp. Only she couldn't do it. I mean, the baby wouldn't come. So you know what Lewis did?"

Homer was amused. "No, what?"

"He ground up the rattle from a rattlesnake and made her a potion, and it worked."

"She delivered the baby?"

"Right. And then this baby"—Tom broke off—"actually it was Fern who pointed it out—the baby went all the way up the river and across the Rockies to the mouth of the Columbia and back again in the cradleboard on Sacagawea's back. Nobody talks much about the kid in the journals, but she must have nursed it and cared for it the whole way. The Indian woman, that's what they called her."

Homer laughed. "All those tough, gristly men, deerslayers, killers of grizzlies, can you see them disemboweling a carcass while this woman was sitting nearby, nursing her child? You mean they never mention the baby?"

"Hardly ever. Fern thinks it's really strange. When I told her that Sacagawea didn't get a red cent at the end, while all the men were paid in money and land, she was disgusted. And she's right, it was terrible that Sacagawea got nothing, after she saved their necks three or four times. Fern hates that statue."

"Statue? What statue?"

"In Lewis and Clark Square. The big bronze monument on the traffic island, those two big heroes gazing westward while this humble little Indian maiden crouches at their feet."

"Oh, right, I see what she means."

Tom's eyes were half closed. He was murmuring something, changing the subject. "Homer, you know the Beta Bridge?"

"No. You mean alpha, beta, and so on?"

"Bridge across the tracks on Rugby Road, made of cement. Kids at the university, they paint things on it."

Homer humored the boy. "They do? What sort of things?"

"*Josh loves Maureen,* that kind of thing."

"Oh, right. Matter of fact, I've seen it, the bridge. We're staying just around the corner."

"And sometimes they paint proposals of marriage. You know."

"Proposals of marriage, I see."

"Prison library, it's not that bad."

Homer was bewildered by the sudden leap from proposals of marriage. "They let you borrow books?"

"Right, so I've been reading about Thomas Jefferson. I mean, I don't have anything else to do. And I've sort of been coming to a conclusion. You know, about Lewis and Clark. He was right there with them the whole entire time."

"He?" Homer made a wild guess. "You mean Thomas Jefferson?"

"They don't say so, not in their journals, but he must have been like a wind at their backs the whole way, through every goddamn thing that happened, cold, hunger, the long portages, the rapids, the attacks by grizzlies." Tom shrugged. "You know. Whatever."

"Another case of obsession," said Homer, whose entire life was driven by obsession.

Tom changed the subject. "Have you seen her?"

Homer smiled. "My boy, you need a lesson in how to talk good. When you say 'her,' do you mean Fern?"

"Yesterday was visitation day, but she didn't show up."

"Oh, I suppose she's busy with her old boyfriend."

"Old boyfriend?" Tom stared at Homer, his dreamy expression changing to sharp attention. "What old boyfriend?"

Homer regretted that he had brought it up. "Oh, some guy's come to town, name's Jim Reeves."

After an unhappy pause, Tom said, "Oh."

Their time was up. A guard touched Homer's shoulder. He stood up, smiled at Tom, and left the prison. Tom was conducted back to his solitary cell.

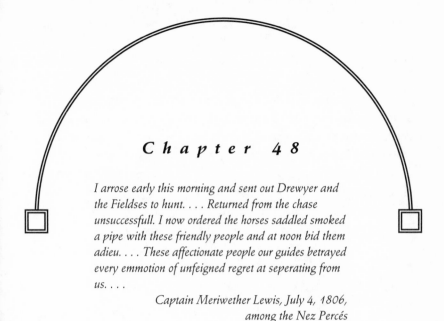

Chapter 48

I arrose early this morning and sent out Drewyer and the Fieldses to hunt. . . . Returned from the chase unsuccessfull. I now ordered the horses saddled smoked a pipe with these friendly people and at noon bid them adieu. . . . These affectionate people our guides betrayed every emmotion of unfeigned regret at seperating from us. . . .

Captain Meriwether Lewis, July 4, 1806,
among the Nez Percés

Augustus Upchurch knew perfectly well that his presence was distressing to young Fern Fisher. And yet he couldn't live without seeing her, talking to her, pleading with her.

At least he could call her. Surely she wouldn't mind a simple phone call?

"Oh, hello, Mr. Upchurch." Once again Fern sounded distracted and far away.

"My dear, I wonder how you're coming with the—with the river?"

It was the right thing to say. At once Fern sounded more lively. "Oh, it's moving right along. I've got as far as Butte, Montana, only of course it wasn't Butte, Montana, in the year 1805."

"No, of course not." Augustus cleared his throat. "I wonder if—I just wondered if you'd like to have dinner with me. Oh, wait, just something simple! What about one of those student places near the university?"

Fern was no fool. She was well aware that Augustus Upchurch was far too interested in her. It was terribly embarrassing. And she was furious because she had read in yesterday's paper that Mr. Upchurch was Tom's first accuser. His information had been directly responsible for the terrible thundering on the stairs, the bursting in, the capture.

But now, pulling herself together, she tried to be kind. "Oh, Mr. Upchurch, if you could only see what it's like around here. Henry Spender's nearly out of his mind. So many things still have to be done. And there's some kind of big emotional problem with one of the caterers, and Security is all upset because of the hot-air balloon."

"Balloon?"

"There's this hot-air balloon club, they want to come over Monticello during the President's speech. Security's going ballistic. What if they have sharpshooters up there aiming down at the President?"

"But surely, my dear, the Jefferson Studies scholar doesn't have to be involved in all these preparations?"

"Oh, yes, I do. I'm making name tags for all the folding chairs. Four hundred of them, hand-lettered."

Augustus was in anguish. "Oh, Fern. Oh, my dear."

"So I'm sorry, Mr. Upchurch, but I'm afraid I can't come to supper." Fern tried to soften the blow. "Are you coming to the celebration tomorrow?"

"I have an invitation," said Augustus with dignity.

"Well, then," said Fern cheerily, "I'll see you tomorrow." Gently she put down the phone.

In the dark den of the gloomy house on Park Street, Augustus hear the soft click and the buzz of disconnection. Bowing his head, he nearly wept.

He couldn't bear it. He couldn't stay away. Almost without willing it, he found himself behind the wheel of his car, zooming it backward out of the garage and then plunging down Route 20 in the direction of Monticello. Surely they would let him in. As a personal friend of Henry Spender's and a substantial contributor, he would certainly be welcomed just as usual.

By the time he turned off on Route 53, Augustus was sweating heavily. His eyes bulged as he imagined Fern's arms twining around his neck. Monticello, which had once been for him such a sacred shine, was now a place of feverish desire.

What had happened to Augustus? He was in torment.

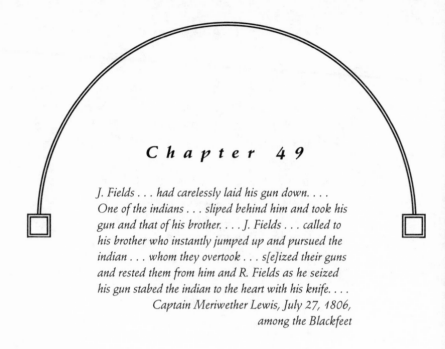

Chapter 49

J. Fields . . . had carelessly laid his gun down. . . .
One of the indians . . . sliped behind him and took his
gun and that of his brother. . . . J. Fields . . . called to
his brother who instantly jumped up and pursued the
indian . . . whom they overtook . . . s[e]ized their guns
and rested them from him and R. Fields as he seized
his gun stabed the indian to the heart with his knife. . . .
Captain Meriwether Lewis, July 27, 1806,
among the Blackfeet

George was sick of hearing about the exploits of *Thomas Arthur Dean*. The TV stations couldn't get enough of him. They kept gabbling about the amazing fact that this super-duper honor student had been accused of nine fatal assaults on the women of Albemarle County.

It was about time the son-of-a-bitch was exposed as an imposter.

George mopped the plastic top of the kitchen table and polished it dry. Then he washed his hands, pulled on his gloves, and sat down with his marking pen and a slip of paper.

Frowning, he gazed for a moment at the view out the window over the sink, the back yard with its freshly raked dirt and patches of new grass, the valley of dead shirts.

Then he bowed his head over the slip of paper. It would be the last note about the Mandan camp—

THE HEAD-CHIEF OF THE MANDAN NATION.

There, that did it. It was the end of the sentence. It rounded out the last four Jeanies. He'd take it up to Monticello and find the new Jeanie and ram the wig down on her head, the one he'd taken from that ugly old witch in the woods. What a joke.

Actually, the old witch had been a shock, not part of his plan at all. George had been working his way up the hill at Monticello, meaning only to take a look at the place and maybe see the Jeanie he'd spotted a couple of times in the Bargain Mart, and then this old hag had found him in the tent and croaked something about a perp, a twerp, a burp. Crazy old fool. She wasn't Jeanie, but he couldn't leave her alive.

The TV was muttering. George went into the bedroom to turn it off, but his attention was caught by the current scene at Monticello, the Secret Service roadblock at the entrance, the helicopter view of tents going up on the lawn and people running back and forth, getting ready for the Fourth of July.

Excited, George smacked his fist on the top of his dresser and laughed. In spite of his reclusive habits, he loved crowds. He loved the sense of himself as a secret hero, rubbing shoulders with strangers who had no idea who he was. Three heads of state would be there tomorrow. George loved celebrities. He'd be a celebrity himself someday.

And Jeanie would be there for sure.

But he'd never get past Security tomorrow. They'd be swarming all over the place. It would have to be tonight. He'd park a couple of miles away and walk in.

George took a bath, keeping his eyes closed as usual. Then

he ran a razor around his chin, patted his cheeks with after-shave, put on his new underwear, took the pins out of his new shirt, shook it out, and put it on. His jeans were new too, and so were his socks. His shoes were spotless.

He had an itemized list for his backpack, and he checked things off as he put them in:

> Water bottle
> Candy
> Couple bananas
> Knife and chain
> Plastic apron
> Clean shirt
> Towel
> Zip bag wet washcloths
> Plastic bag laundry

What else? The wig. George stuffed it in another plastic sack.

The note. He folded it carefully and tucked it in his shirt pocket. He studied his hands, which were pink and wrinkled from the bath. He looked at himself in the mirror and smiled. He looked nice. He was cleanshaven, his bristle cut was freshly dyed, his clothes were neat and new.

The mirror did not show the red and gristly globe surrounding George, the ugly boil crisscrossed with clotted veins. But it was there. He lived inside it, but he was so used to it, he didn't see it.

Oh, one more thing. George picked up two of the pins he had taken from his new shirt and stuck them beside the second button. There, he was ready.

But when he stepped outside, he had to put his backpack down, because the grass had grown an inch. He couldn't leave without mowing the lawn.

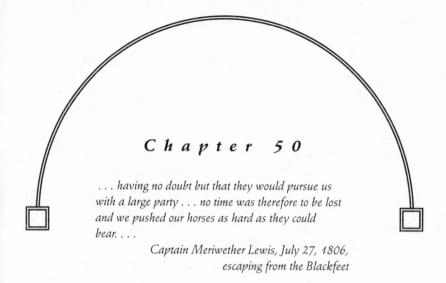

Chapter 50

*. . . having no doubt but that they would pursue us
with a large party . . . no time was therefore to be lost
and we pushed our horses as hard as they could
bear. . . .*

Captain Meriwether Lewis, July 27, 1806,
escaping from the Blackfeet

Homer came away from the Charlottesvile-Albemarle Regional Jail deeply concerned about Tom.

The poor kid seemed uninterested in his own fate. He had
been loquacious about Sacagawea's infant son, he had talked
about that crazy bridge on Rugby Road with its sentimental
messages, and then Homer had opened his big goofy mouth
and told him about Fern's old boyfriend. What a jerk.

Poor old Tom, passing his time reading books about Jefferson. It occurred to Homer that the kid wasn't the only Tom in
trouble. True, this one had been arraigned on nine counts of
murder, not to mention arson, trespass, and the possession of
an illegal substance, but there was a case against the other
Tom as well. Thomas Jefferson had been charged by the his-
torical revisionists with every sort of public failure and personal disgrace.

Grimly Homer told himself that he was powerless to res-
urrect the reputation of the presidential Tom. He was responsible only for saving the life of young Tom Dean. And
somehow he'd have to do it all alone, because Chief Pratt had

given up the search. It wasn't his problem anymore, the Chief said. It was entirely up to the courts. He had other things to think about, he said. "You know, trying to work with the guys from the Secret Service tomorrow at Monticello. And, Homer, that's not all. You'll never believe it, it's such an honor. I've been invited to give a paper before the Philological Society of Philadelphia—'Philological Musings on the Declaration of Independence.' What do you think of that?"

The invitation was obviously the darling of Oliver's heart. Well, so much for any help from the Charlottesville Police Department. And Homer suspected that the FBI profilers at Quantico Naval Base were equally uninterested in the case of Thomas Arthur Dean.

He was all alone, and he resented it. He didn't know where to begin.

For the moment, the only problem was how to find his way home. By now Homer had patches of the map of Charlottesville in his head. Surely if he dodged to the right on Avon it would take him to High Street, and on High Street he'd turn left, and the rest would be a piece of cake.

But no, High Street didn't look right. Homer had a sinking feeling he'd made this mistake before.

Well, what about the next right, Park Street? Following a sudden inspiration, Homer swung the wheel and turned onto Park, because it was the street where Augustus Upchurch lived, the old guy who had borrowed pornographic library books on the day the librarian was killed, the one who had called 911 and accused Tom of murdering Flora Foley.

At the first house he stopped to inquire. "I'm sorry to trouble you, but could you tell me where Mr. Upchurch lives?"

The woman merely jerked her head sideways, and slammed the door.

"Well, thanks a bunch," growled Homer. Stepping back on the grass, he looked up at the house next door.

It was a substantial homely dwelling from the same era as the house on University Circle. Homer pushed the doorbell, and then, hearing no ring, he rapped on the glass panel and peered into the gloom of the front hall. Inside he could see a lily-shaped bronze lamp, an umbrella stand, a Panama hat on a coatrack, and a shield-shaped plaque on the wall. Squinting, Homer could just make out the words *Charlottesville Rotary Club*.

No one answered his knock. No sex-crazed old gentleman emerged from one of the shadowy rooms. Augustus Upchurch was not at home.

From Park Street, Homer found his way back to University Circle by a series of random dodges and strokes of luck.

On the front porch he found Ed Bailey and Mary at a table covered with cameras. Mary's was automatic, simple, and cheap. Ed's were complex and expensive.

Ed was scornful. "My dear girl, you won't get good pictures tomorrow with that thing. Idiot camera, right? Point and shoot?"

Mary was incensed. She appealed to Homer as he climbed the steps. "Homer, tell Ed about my Venice pictures. They were pretty good, weren't they? I shot twenty-four rolls, and some of them were just fine."

"Well," said Homer tactfully, "one of your pictures made a big difference." He explained it to Ed. "There was this picture Mary took, it changed everything."

Ed wasn't listening. He was full of his own expertise. Homer went inside and closed the screen door gently behind him, while Ed explained the superior features of his Minoltas and Nikons and Hasselblads.

Oh, God, where should he start? In the untidy room they used as a study, Homer sat down in a fraying wicker chair and leafed through his notes. A lot of his scribbles were passages copied from the gruesome book loaned him by Chief Pratt.

After a while the notes slipped from his fingers. His head drooped on his chest.

Five minutes later Homer woke up and sprang to his feet. "Public places," he boomed to the glass-fronted bookcases, the faded curtains, the framed Old Testament prophets. "Public places full of crowds. Sometimes these freaks are just crazy about crowds, that's what the books say."

At once he hurried back out on the porch, where Mary was loading film into her idiot camera and Ed was packing his fancy equipment into form-fitting cases.

"So long, you people," said Homer, beaming at them. "I'm off to the celebration."

They stared at him blankly. "But, Homer dear," said Mary, "it isn't until tomorrow, the Fourth of July. This is only the third."

"Oh, I know, but I need to get there early," said Homer importantly. "I mean really early."

"*This* early?" said Ed.

"Oh, sure. I want to look around. Case the joint. You know."

"But, Homer, they'll never let you in. Wait a minute." Mary wrestled with the contents of her handbag. "Here's your ticket. But it's for tomorrow, not today."

"It's okay," said Homer, waving away the ticket. "I'm buddy-buddy with Chief Pratt. He'll let me in."

"The man's out of his mind," said Ed, watching him go.

Full of purpose, his fingers tightly gripping the wheel, Homer lost his way only once. To his surprise, he found himself breezing down a residential street with small houses left and right. He was reminded of something Chief Pratt had said, *He's here, God's whiskers, he's right here in Charlottesville, I swear he is. Maybe we can't find him because he's in plain sight, like the purloined letter.*

Driving slowly, Homer wondered if one of these small dwellings was the purloined letter. What would the creature's house or room or rat hole look like? Maybe a filthy pigsty. On the other hand—Homer remembered his foolish observation that the women's bodies had been mutilated quite *neatly*—maybe the place occupied by the killer was trim and tidy, just like the houses on this street.

Look at that guy mowing his lawn, for instance. It doesn't even need mowing. Super-meticulous kind of guy.

Homer glanced at the mailbox as he drove by. The name painted on it in big block capitals was GEORGE DRYER.

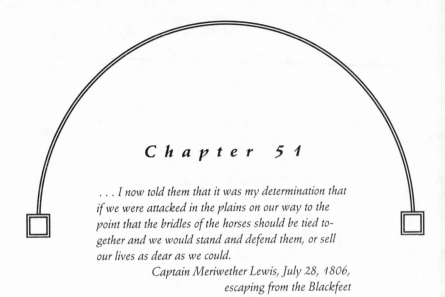

Chapter 51

It took Fern far into the evening to finish labeling the chairs.
On the west lawn she moved slowly along the first ten
rows, attaching her ribboned name tags one by one. Awe-
struck in spite of herself at the sublimity of some of the
names, she had been far too painstaking with the calligraphy.
It had taken her all day.

The light was fading. On the West Portico, behind the ros-
trum with its red, white, and blue bunting, a couple of men in
uniform stood with folded arms, talking quietly. Several of
Chief Pratt's men, removed from traffic duty, roamed among
the flowerbeds, inspecting the rows of chairs. Beyond the dying larch tree—one of the last survivors from Jefferson's
time—another platoon moved down into the Grove.

A sense of anticipation electrified the air. The flowers had
been fussed into an orgy of blossoming. The great trees
swelled in even greater splendor. The sunset blazed from the
west windows. The house waited in calm perfection.

Down the hill to the northeast, the fireworks were ready

for the match—the titanium salutes, the whistling serpents, the two-color chrysanthemum showers, the four-inch shell reports, and all the rest, including the grand finale—a ground display of the American flag and a fiery portrait of Thomas Jefferson.

At eight o'clock, Henry Spender went home in a state of exhausted euphoria. After the wild scramble and the disastrous portents of the past week, everything had fallen into place.

The furious captains of the catering teams had settled their differences and fallen into each other's arms. The public-address system was working at last. The offended Governor had accepted an apology. The phone banks were a miracle of electronic ingenuity. The film star had decided to come after all, and even the sparring Jeffersonian descendants had been reconciled.

To cap all these triumphs, a starry-eyed Gail Boltwood had bounced into Henry's office with the news that an unexpected weather front was passing through. Tomorrow there would be no thunderstorms, no rain, no summer hail. The day would be clear and cool.

"Look!" said Gail, pointing out the window at the crescent moon, a delicate bauble in the treetops.

In a rapture of thanksgiving, Henry pulled on his jacket. An avowed atheist, he almost regretted his cynicism as he drove out of the parking lot. Perhaps there was a God in heaven after all.

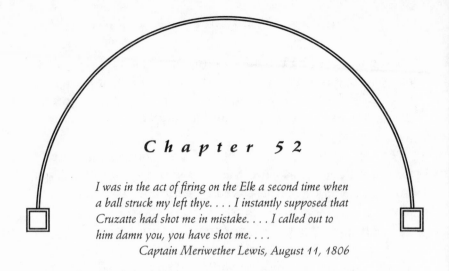

Chapter 52

*I was in the act of firing on the Elk a second time when
a ball struck my left thye. . . . I instantly supposed that
Cruzatte had shot me in mistake. . . . I called out to
him damn you, you have shot me. . . .*
  Captain Meriwether Lewis, August 11, 1806

So they were all there at once, in the dusk of evening.
George Dryer moved silently up through the trees,
dodging the uniformed officers patrolling the woods. He was
just in time to catch sight of Fern as she tied the last of her labels to the chairs on the west lawn.

Once again George had the sensation of being in two
places at once—both here and not here. Another George
Dryer was looking down at Jeanie from a great height. His
eyes were all-seeing. They followed her as she moved back
into the house, carrying a cardboard box.

For Augustus Upchurch, permission to enter the grounds was
not easy, in spite of his friendship with the curator and his
standing as a major donor.

A security officer stopped his car as it turned into the driveway. "I'm sorry, sir. No one is permitted to enter."

"But I have an appointment with Miss Fisher."

The officer consulted a list. "Miss Fern Fisher? We haven't checked off her departure. She must still be on the premises." He took a phone out of his pocket, consulted the list again, and pushed buttons. Augustus, waiting, was aware of the pounding of his heart.

"Sorry, sir, she's not in her office. She doesn't answer her phone." The security officer looked up doubtfully. It was an impasse.

Augustus tried another tack. "Mr. Spender! Call Henry Spender. He'll be astonished that there should be any question about admitting me."

"I'm afraid Mr. Spender has left for the day."

Augustus was desperate. In spite of the coolness of the evening, his seersucker jacket was damp with sweat. "Well, why don't you call him at home?"

The security officer sighed, then leaned over backward. Probably the old guy was important enough to get him in trouble. Once more he consulted his list.

When the phone rang in the Spender household, Henry was reclining happily in his bath. A telephone and a glass of whiskey sat side by side on the floor beside the tub. He was in a jovial mood. He picked up the phone and said, "Henry Spender here. What's that? Mr. Upchurch? Why, certainly. Anything Mr. Upchurch wants is okay with me. Good old Mr. Upchurch. Glad to oblige."

So Augustus was permitted to drive up the curving road while the officer at the gate called the other checkpoints along the way. A couple of women in uniform waved him on, and at last Augustus pulled into the privileged parking lot below the gift shop.

He was trembling so badly, he stumbled as he walked up the brick steps to the east lawn. Then, hurrying around the house beside the South Terrace Walk, he was stopped by another security officer. "Sir, may I ask your name?"

Augustus was badly out of breath. He could only gasp, "Upchurch, Augustus Upchurch."

The officer smiled at him. "Carry on, Mr. Upchurch."

Trying to look purposeful, Augustus walked quickly to the end of the terrace walk and peered around the corner. At once he saw Fern mounting the steps of the West Portico, carrying a box.

He wanted to cry out. If he shouted at her she would surely turn her head and look at him. But he was overcome with shyness. What could he possibly say? Fern would be startled, she might even be frightened. Somehow she would guess at the kind of daydreams that were teeming in his head. She would know why he was there.

◠

Homer Kelly had only a little trouble getting past the guard at the gate. Reaching his long arm out the car window, he took the guard's list, stared at it, and put his finger on the name *Oliver Pratt, Chief, Charlottesville Police.* Cowed, the guard called the number.

Fortunately, Pratt was still in his office. The MOUL–OVUM volume of the *Oxford English Dictionary* was open on his desk. He was deep in a blissful examination of the word *nature* in the preamble to the Declaration of Independence, as in the phrase *the laws of Nature and of Nature's God.*

In answer to the question about an after-hours visitor at the gate of Monticello, some guy called Homer Kelly, he mumbled, "Why certainly, yes, of course," and went back to the *OED:*

nature . . . *The essential qualities or properties of a thing . . .*

No, no, that wasn't it. Pratt ran his magnifying glass down the page of small print. Here, this was more like it:

The general inherent character or disposition of mankind . . .

Well, that was pretty good, but it was still not quite—here, what about this?

The creative and regulative physical power
which is conceived of as operating in the material world
and as the immediate cause of all its phenomena.

The examples were amusing:

Jonathan Swift, 1738: Oh! the wonderful Works of Nature;
That a black Hen should have a white Egg!

But wait, here was something else:

light of nature: *(see* LIGHT*)*

Aha! Pratt snatched volume 8 off the shelf, smacked it down on top of volume 10, and flipped the pages. At once he found what he was looking for:

light of nature, *the capacity given to man of discerning certain divine truths without the help of revelation.*

God's whiskers! That was it! Thomas Jefferson in a nutshell!

Absent from Pratt's mind was any premonition of catastrophe, any forewarning of approaching doom.

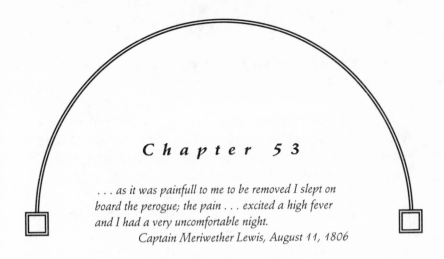

Chapter 53

... as it was painfull to me to be removed I slept on board the perogue; the pain ... excited a high fever and I had a very uncomfortable night.
Captain Meriwether Lewis, August 11, 1806

Fern climbed the stairs to the Dome Room and set her empty box down on the table beside the newest piece of the time line. Leaning over it, she read the last entries.

Tom had carried the journey of Lewis and Clark only as far as the Yellowstone:

The morning being fair and pleasant and wind favourable we set sale at an early hour, and proceeded on very well the greater part of the day; the country still continues level fertile and beautifull, the bottoms wide and well timbered. ...
Captain Lewis, May 6, 1805

It was a wonderful passage, revealing the fulfilled purpose of the expedition, the rich promise of the country opening before them.

Her own entry was from March of the same year. It was Jefferson's Second Inaugural:

I shall need, too, the favor of that Being in whose hands we are, who led our forefathers ... from their native land, and planted them in a country flowing with all the necessaries and comforts of life.

Fern was pleased with the symmetry of the two choices. In Jefferson's address there was an echo of the words of Meriwether Lewis, the trusted friend he had chosen to lead his cherished expedition, now working its way up the Missouri River a thousand miles away.

Ah, well. Fern lifted her arms to stretch her back. She was in a queer mood. She was physically exhausted and she was terribly afraid for Tom, and yet foremost in her consciousness was the room itself, and beyond the room its architect.

The sense of his presence was different from her playful summonings of an imaginary Thomas Jefferson mounted on his horse or working in the vegetable garden. Nor was it some sort of ghostly manifestation. Fern did not believe that dead people hung wistfully around the places where they had lived and died. Monticello was not haunted by Jefferson's astral soul.

From below she could hear feet descending the stairs, doors closing. Was she alone in the house? No, someone else had come in. There was a soft noise, a pause, another noise, the opening of a door.

No, Thomas Jefferson was dead and buried. He was not resurrecting himself to wander along the terrace walks and peer in the windows and whisper, *Dear me, the clock's run down.* And yet—Fern walked out of the Dome Room and started down the stairs—in some ways the house itself was an embodiment, an incarnation of the intricate turns of his mind.

She paused at the second floor and put her head in Henry Spender's office. The room was dark. She could see only the shuffle of white paper on his desk. Withdrawing, she looked down at the steep fall of the stairs below her, remembering the day Mr. Upchurch had fallen and sprawled on his back on the landing.

—*the intricate turns of a mind that had thrown out a web across history, a founding fabric that had clothed an entire people with the strength and will of kings.*

Slowly and carefully Fern began creeping down the last flight of stairs. *Not alone, of course, Jefferson hadn't done it alone. But the genius that was displayed in his house, in the shape of its rooms, in its books and furnishings and scientific instruments, was the same prophetic intellect that had envisioned the nature of a free republic, that had seen the promise of the westering land and stretched out a hand to the Pacific.*

Fern smiled, because the hand that been stretched out was Tom's own Corps of Discovery, the expedition that had traveled up the Missouri River, across the Rockies, and down the Columbia to the western ocean, with thirty men, a black slave, an Indian woman, a dog, and a baby.

Halfway down the last flight, she stopped and listened. One of the security people was moving quietly in another room.

Did slavery matter? Of course it mattered. However kind and good a master Jefferson had been, there was no forgiving the fact of the hundreds of slaves he had kept on his plantations, there was no way of overlooking the extravagance that had entangled him in debts so heavy that only a few of the slaves had been set free by the conditions of his will.

But the debt wasn't altogether his fault. Generously he had signed a note for a distant relative who had left him holding the bag. But the consequences were cruel. Most of his household servants and all of his farm laborers had gone to the auction block after his death.

One of the stairs creaked, repeating the word *death* in a calm whisper. So did the matter-of-fact bottom step.

Fern walked into the entrance hall. In her strange mood, everything was transformed. The walls were whispering the same word, *death*. No, that was wrong. It wasn't *death* exactly. She closed her eyes to listen. The word was *dead*.

Opening them again, she looked at the slave-built Joinery, the folding ladder, the Great Clock, the map of the new country on the wall, and tried to work it out. *Perhaps the truth about Jefferson's failure to free his slaves was part of a general failure of compassion and imagination. It was a stain across the entire commonwealth of Virginia, at least until the Emancipation Proclamation, and then much later still.*

The finger of blame could not be pointed at a single master, at one exacting setter of tasks—the number of nails to be fashioned every day in the Nailery, the number of acres of plowing at Shadwell, the number of oxcarts to carry the Tufton wheat, the number of hands to stump and dig Monticello's Roundabout roads—no, it could never be an indictment of a single exploiter of human life—it was a universal and general blame.

Beyond the glass door to the portico, Fern could see two uniformed guards. They were part of the security forces that were swarming all over the mountaintop on the eve of the Fourth of July celebration. One of them leaned against a pillar and tossed away a cigarette. The other nodded at Fern through the glass. She nodded back.

And then there were other noises. Fern turned quickly around. She could hear hammering, the fluttering of paper, the tuning of a fiddle. The soft syllable *dead* still whispered discreetly in the background, but the house itself had come alive.

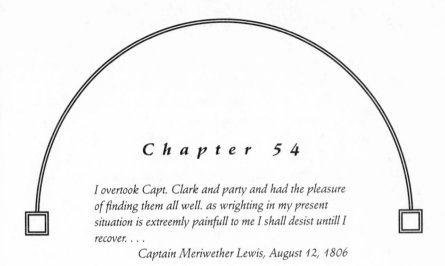

Chapter 54

I overtook Capt. Clark and party and had the pleasure of finding them all well. as wrighting in my present situation is extreemly painfull to me I shall desist untill I recover. . . .

Captain Meriwether Lewis, August 12, 1806

The things she saw were not really there, that was clear enough to Fern. And yet, in some strange way, they were true.

In the entrance hall, the ticking noise was the winding of the Great Clock. The ladder had been unfolded, it leaned against the wall, and the long wooden key was twisting around and around, first in one hole on the face of the clock, and then in the other. The pendulum began to swing, and in the corners of the room the cannonball weights were rising slowly, straining their ropes over the pulleys. Fern watched as the topmost ball on one side jerked to a stop at the painted word *Sunday.*

Yes, of course, the clock was always wound on Sunday. Now the gong on the roof was clanging eight o'clock.

When the gong stopped, the fiddle began. It struck up a dainty melody adorned with grace notes and trills. Fern listened, entranced, but after a few bars the music faded and the hammering began.

She ran to the greenhouse, but the hammering stopped

when she threw open the door. Yes, there was Jefferson's workbench, there were his tools, there was the hammer. She picked it up. It was still warm. If only she'd been quicker, she might have seen the carpenter himself.

Therefore, when a creaking began somewhere on the other side of the house, she turned on her heel, raced along the corridor, plunged under the balcony, and burst into the dining room.

It was empty. No tall host presided at the head of the table. No daughter Martha sat at the other end, the mistress of the house. There were no grandchildren, no guests—no Lafayette, no Daniel Webster or Margaret Bayard Smith, no George Ticknor or Abbé Correa de Serra. There was only the *crick-crick* of the rope of the dumbwaiter rising to the narrow closet beside the fireplace. Fern reached out her hand and opened the closet door. There on the shelf, still wobbling from its shaky journey up from the cellar, stood a dusty bottle of wine.

The midsummer daylight was gone. Fern blew off the dust and carried the bottle to the window to read the label. Was it one of the wines that had been ordered in such sumptuous quantities from Paris—crates of Château d'Yquem, hampers of champagne? The label said *Lafite, 1787*. What would it taste like now?

She set the bottle back on the shelf and closed the narrow door. At once there was another sound, bright and loud in the silent house, a sharp *scritch-scratch*.

Fern laughed. She knew what it was, but it was a miracle that it could be heard so clearly. It was the two pens of the polygraph in Jefferson's Cabinet.

Once again she ran. Would she find the great man sitting at his table, studiously at work?

In the Cabinet she found the polygraph writing busily, the two pens leaving identical trails of ink on the two sheets of

paper. No hand directed them, no long legs were stretched out on the bench below the table.

But the revolving chair was in motion, as though an invisible person were turning to look at her, and the bookstand was whirling, the books on its five surfaces sailing around and threatening to fall off. Beside it, on the table, the little ivory fan that was a pocket notebook spread itself wide and slapped shut. On the floor the round globe spun on its axis.

The two pens stopped scratching. Together they lifted from the paper and poised in air. What had they written? Fern bowed over the table and recognized at once the swift legible hand, the looping capital "T" and the lower-case "d"s with their curled-over tops. The word that had been whispered in the air, *dead, dead,* was part of Jefferson's last request to James Madison. Here it was in his own hand. Fern knew it by heart—*Take care of me when dead.*

Straightening, she was startled to see a movement in the small round mirror that hung on the wall. It was one of the

optical devices that had so interested the natural philosopher
in Jefferson. On its concave surface everything was reflected
upside down, including the master of the house himself.

There he was in the mirror, the grand old man of Monticello, standing on his head with one arm outstretched as if to
alert her, and his eyes were staring directly at her, urging her,
telling her in all but words, *Take care of me when dead.*

Fern could only nod and nod, and swear a solemn, silent
vow. *Yes, yes, she would try, she would really try.*

There was only one more vision in the transfigured house,
but it was the most remarkable of all. Walking slowly into
the parlor, Fern saw it at once, the object on the round marble table.

It was the traveling lapdesk that had been crafted so carefully to Jefferson's design, the desk on which he had written
the Declaration of Independence in July 1776 in an upstairs
room in Jacob Graff's boarding house in Philadelphia.

Fern knew perfectly well that the famous lapdesk could
not possibly be here in this house, because it was one of the
national treasures of the Smithsonian. And yet there it was in
the middle of the table, a neat box closed over on itself. She
reached out to open it, but at once there was a great clatter-
ing. The top fell back and the little drawer flew open with a
bang. On the hinged writing surface lay a heap of handwritten sheets.

Fern's eyes were magically keen. She knew exactly what they were—the four manuscript pages of the first draft of the Declaration. But they were rustling and lifting, and then, as the door behind her flew open and the glass cracked and splintered and a great wind rushed through the house, the precious pages sailed high over her head.

At once the entire room was aflutter with paper. It was a blinding snowstorm of letters and documents and architectural drawings and lists of garden vegetables and financial accounts and notes on the distribution of slaves.

Gasping, Fern reached up and snatched at the Virginia Statute for Religious Freedom, but it flew too high, and so did the bill against the Alien and Sedition Act, and the one against entail and primogeniture, and the Virginia law abolishing the importation of slaves, and—*look, look*—almost within her grasp was the famous letter to Captain Lewis, *The object of your mission is to explore the Missouri river.* For a moment Fern had it in her hand, but it whisked out of her fingers and flew away.

"Jeanie!"

What? Fern turned around and saw George Dryer standing within the shattered door. Between his fists was a heavy chain.

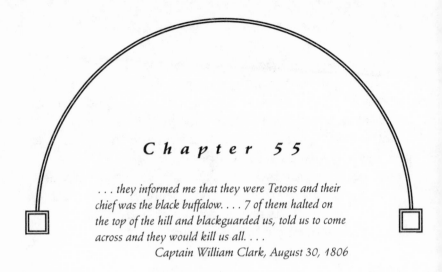

*. . . they informed me that they were Tetons and their
chief was the black buffalow. . . . 7 of them halted on
the top of the hill and blackguarded us, told us to come
across and they would kill us all. . . .*
Captain William Clark, August 30, 1806

The paper snowstorm had vanished. For an instant Fern
thought the man at the door was guarding the house.
Then she knew who he was. Slowly she began to back up.

George made a rush at her, lifting his chain. She cried out,
and he almost had her. But then something came between
them, a clumsy obstruction, a stumbling block.

It was an old man, weeping. He threw his arms around
George and sobbed, "No, no."

George cursed and tried to wrench himself free from the
fumbling clutch of the senile old fool. Fern slipped away and
dodged into the corridor. Grasping the banister, she hurled
herself around the turn of the narrow stairs and plummeted
into the basement below. With her heart in her mouth she
began clumping down the dark tunnel toward the square of
dim light at one end, her feet like slow stumps in a night-
mare. *Oh, poor Mr. Upchurch. What was happening to poor brave
Mr. Upchurch?*

But nothing was happening to Augustus Upchurch. Nothing
would ever happen to him again. To George Dryer, Augustus
was only a minor obstacle, a tiresome speck, a buzzing fly.

George swatted him dead with a single blow of his chain, then turned on his heel and bolted into the corridor after Jeanie.

In the narrow hallway there was a staircase going both up and down. Pausing, George heard the thump of Jeanie's feet going down, and he thundered after her, plunging four steps at a time.

Half a minute later a guard came running into the parlor. He had heard Fern's cry while making his rounds upstairs. Now he was shocked to find the body of an elderly gentleman spread-eagled on the floor. Where was the girl?

⌒

Homer felt more and more foolish. What the hell was he doing here? Driving up the mountain in the gathering dark, he had to stop and explain himself again and again. Even after he left his car in the privileged parking lot, he was accosted three more times as he walked toward the house.

The last two inquisitors were standing on the steps of the East Portico. They turned their flashlights on him as he loomed up out of the shadowy lawn, a gigantic stranger with wild hair and ferocious whiskers, a threat to the sanctity of the house and the safety of four hundred distinguished guests tomorrow morning, including the Prime Minister of Great Britain and the presidents of France and the United States of America.

"Stop," thundered one of the flashlights. "Stand where you are."

Blinded, Homer grinned in the friendliest possible way, but before he could explain himself there was a squawking babble of amplified static. The flashlights whirled away, the glass door was thrown open and the two men rushed inside. Homer could see their bright beams streaking back through the house.

Something violent must have happened on the West Portico, over there where the speakers would be standing tomorrow, all those important people from all over the world. What the hell was going on?

Homer turned away and began galloping across the lawn. Behind him there were hoarse shouts and rasping commands. At the corner where the North Terrace Walk made a sharp right angle, he glanced over his shoulder and saw armed men converging from all directions. No one was looking for a fool named Homer Kelly. He grinned as the last of them bounded up the steps.

No, not quite the last. Someone was pelting along the east front of the house, racing past the portico steps. Even in the darkness Homer recognized Fern Fisher. She was running toward him, stumbling clumsily, gasping, struggling for breath.

Then Homer could see why. Someone was darting after her, catching up, reaching out, snatching at her. He was faster on his feet than Fern, and he had a chain in his hand.

As a man of action Homer sometimes blundered, and sometimes his wits failed him in a crisis. It was certainly true that his great size was as much a liability as a blessing. (Homer had an unhappy history of crushing antique chairs.) But there were other times when his eccentric intellect grasped the nature of a problem and pounced on a solution. This was one of the times.

When Fern came panting around the corner, he thrust her roughly aside, and then, with a single powerful shove, he sent George Dryer spinning into the ice pit.

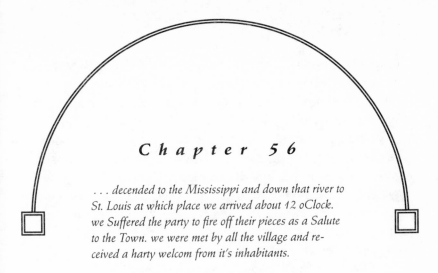

Chapter 56

. . . decended to the Mississippi and down that river to
St. Louis at which place we arrived about 12 oClock.
we Suffered the party to fire off their pieces as a Salute
to the Town. we were met by all the village and re-
ceived a harty welcom from it's inhabitants.

. . . had all of our skins &c. suned and stored
away. . . . In the evening a dinner & Ball
  Captain William Clark, September 23 and 25, 1806

Next day the festivities began on schedule. Henry Spender sailed through the day in a catatonic state.

He had arrived early, happy and ready to go, freshly showered and wearing a new suit, only to find the place teeming with police officers, Secret Service personnel, a medical examiner, and a team of forensic technicians.

Chief Pratt conducted him into the parlor and across the parquet floor to something shocking. "Mr. Spender," said Pratt, "can you identify this person?"

"Oh, dear me," said Henry, bowing over the body, "I'm afraid I can. It's poor old Augustus Upchurch." He wanted to reach down and close Mr. Upchurch's blue eyes, which were staring up at the portrait of Benjamin Franklin on the wall, or perhaps they were gazing at the Roman frieze, which— Henry told himself in a fit of scholarly irrelevance—had been copied by Thomas Jefferson from a book. Turning to Pratt, he whispered, "My God, what happened?"

"We don't know yet." Pratt crooked his finger at Henry. "There's something else."

"Wait," said Henry, looking back at the body, the blood on the floor, the floodlights, the men and women dodging around Jefferson's chairs and tables. In the mottled glass of one of the tall French mirrors he could see his own white face. "The celebration, Mr. Pratt. The President, the Prime Minister, they're all coming."

"Don't worry," said Chief Pratt. "We'll be through here in a jiffy." He put his arm reassuringly around Henry Spender's shoulders and led him back through the entrance hall and down the steps of the East Portico.

A couple of stretcher-bearers were crossing the lawn. "Good Lord," said Henry, "it's not another one?"

"No, not exactly," said Pratt, smiling. "This one's not dead, at least not yet. They've just fished him out of the ice pit."

"You mean he fell in?" A terrible thought gripped Henry Spender. "My God, what if he sues us for criminal negligence!"

Pratt laughed. "Don't worry," he said soothingly. "It won't ever happen."

"It won't? How can you be so sure?"

"Trust me," said Pratt.

Over their heads on the roof of the East Portico, the weathervane glittered like gold and swiveled on its axis in the gentle breeze blowing over the mountain. By ten o'clock, the sky was a faultless blue, the dew was dry on the grass, the President's helicopter had touched down safely, and all the invited guests had been shuttled up the hill to the west lawn.

During the mild confusion as they were guided to their seats, the Richmond String Quartet entertained them with delicate Mozart airs. In eighteenth-century outfits and spun-

nylon wigs, the four players were squeezed into an angle of the portico.

"He played the fiddle himself, you see," explained the Lieutenant Governor of Virginia, leaning across the Governor's wife to impart this information to his chief.

"I know he played the fiddle himself," said the Governor testily.

But the day was too fine, the air too fragrant, the bunting too bright for any of the four hundred assembled guests to be anything but cheerful. As the quartet played a last merry chord, there was a general gasp as a hot-air balloon rose above the trees, looming soundlessly out of the valley.

"He was interested in ballooning, you see," whispered the Lieutenant Governor, again leaning over the Governor's wife.

This fact was new to the Governor, but he said, "Don't you think I know that?"

"Shhh, shhh," said his wife, because the President of France was mounting the steps to speak. They listened as he began his talk with a salute to Jefferson's great friend the Marquis de Lafayette, who had been such a crucial supporter of the American colonies in their struggle to free themselves from Great Britain.

At this point the Lieutenant Governor was eager to explain that Lafayette had once been Jefferson's guest, right here at Monticello, but this time the Governor's wife, feeling his weight shift in her direction, said, "Please!"

Then it was the turn of the Prime Minister of Great Britain. Under the circumstances, he had no choice but to tell a few modest jokes at the expense of his own nation. He did so gracefully and subsided in favor of the President of the United States.

A staff researcher had written the President's speech. He had come up with a jolly fragment of history, a remark made by founding father John Adams, declaring that the Fourth of

July *ought to be solemnized with Pomp and parade, with Shews, Games, Sports, Guns, Bells, Bonfires and Illuminations from one End of this Continent to the other from this Time forward forever more.*

It was a perfect choice. The President delivered it well, and there was a tumult of applause.

So the events of the day rolled on. The catered luncheon was delicious—there were finger sandwiches *as well as* asparagus rolls—and then everyone sat down again to hear a dramatic reading of the entire Declaration of Independence by the famous Hollywood leading man.

He had rehearsed it well, he knew it by heart. Now his voice rose in outraged indignation at the perfidious behavior of King George the Third. *"He has PLUNDERED our seas, RAVAGED our coasts, BURNT our towns, and DESTROYED the lives of our PEOPLE! He is transporting large armies of foreign MERCENARIES to complete the work of DEATH, DESOLATION and TYRANNY scarcely paralleled in the most BARBAROUS ages, and totally unworthy THE HEAD OF A CIVILIZED NATION."*

While the rest of the audience went wild, the Prime Minister of Great Britain clapped politely, muttering to himself, "Poor silly old George the Third. It was hardly his fault."

The afternoon ended with the singing of "The Star-Spangled Banner," led by a famous African-American gospel singer. Most of the audience couldn't reach the high notes, and they didn't remember the words, but it didn't matter. The singer's mighty voice carried them along.

Throughout the day, Mary Kelly and Ed Bailey had been saving a seat for Homer.

"Where on earth do you suppose he is?" said Mary for the fiftieth time, looking anxiously around.

"Oh, don't worry about good old Homer," said Ed. "He'll turn up sooner or later. Hey, wow, will you look at that! Here comes the champagne."

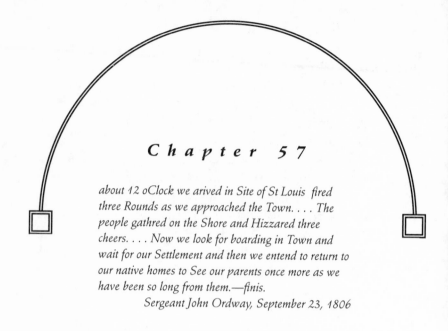

C h a p t e r 5 7

about 12 oClock we arived in Site of St Louis fired
three Rounds as we approached the Town. . . . The
people gathred on the Shore and Hizzared three
cheers. . . . Now we look for boarding in Town and
wait for our Settlement and then we entend to return to
our native homes to See our parents once more as we
have been so long from them.—finis.
           Sergeant John Ordway, September 23, 1806

While the four hundred invited guests assembled on the west lawn of Monticello, and Henry Spender tried to collect his wits, and an ambulance from the University of Virginia Medical Center raced along Highway 20 with the broken body of George Dryer, Homer Kelly shepherded Fern Fisher home to the safety of her own soft bed and then flopped down on her sofa to catch a few winks. At dawn he jerked himself awake just long enough to make a belated 911 emergency call (setting in motion a frantic chain of events), before sinking back again with a blissful smile.

When Fern at last poked Homer awake at noon, Oliver Pratt was back in City Hall. His office door was shut against interruptions because the Chief was trying to nerve himself to call the family of Augustus Upchurch.

Oliver hated informing an expired person's relatives that their nearest and dearest was dead. Courageously he dialed the number, hoping no one would answer.

But Roger Upchurch picked up the phone at once. Oliver cleared his throat and said mournfully, "Mr. Upchurch?"

"Speaking."

"I'm sorry, Mr. Upchurch, I'm afraid I have some very bad news about your father."

Roger Upchurch seemed startled, but he listened gravely as Oliver explained what had happened, then said "Thank you" politely, and hung up.

Of course the news shocked them all, especially the little girls, who burst into tears.

"But, Roger, what happened?" said his wife, gathering her daughters in her arms. "What on earth was your father doing at Monticello at that time of night?"

She never found an answer to this question, but she learned other things about her father-in-law's death after the funeral in Christ Episcopal Church on West Jefferson Street. As the family filed out of the sanctuary, red-eyed, deeply moved by the rector's praise of Augustus, someone touched Roger's arm.

She was a stranger, weeping. "Oh, Mr. Upchurch, my name's Fern Fisher. Your father saved my life."

Then Fern explained what had happened. She described the frightening apparition of George Dryer in the parlor of Monticello and the gallant intervention of Mr. Upchurch. "He was a hero. He sacrificed his life to give me time to run away."

"Good heavens, I didn't know that," said Roger. He shook her hand warmly. And then they all crowded around her, grateful to know that Augustus had died so heroically.

Of course Roger's wife again asked her bewildered question, "Do you know what he was doing there the night before the celebration?"

"I have no idea," said Fern. If she guessed at a possible reason, she kept it to herself.

◠

When one of the guards opened the door of Tom's cell in the Charlottesville-Albemarle Regional Jail and gave him papers to sign and conducted him outside, two people were waiting for him.

One was his father. Arthur Dean was eager to bundle his son into his car. He put a commanding arm around Tom's shoulders.

But Homer Kelly was there too, grinning at him. "Mary's expecting you for dinner. She's made a blueberry pie, worked her fingers to the bone."

Tom paused. He wasn't choosing between his father and Homer Kelly. He was looking around for someone else, but she wasn't there.

"Oh, well, then," said Tom, "we can't let Mary down." He shrugged his shoulders at his father and climbed awkwardly into Homer's car.

Arthur Dean was left open-mouthed on the sidewalk. A guard said, "Hey, guy, you his dad?" and handed him a bag of dirty laundry.

◠

Fern had not heard a word from Tom. Her feelings were hurt. Now that he was free, why didn't he call her?

Tom, in the meanwhile, after borrowing his mother's car to clear out his camp in Jefferson's sacred grove, began living uneasily at home, where he was the object of intense interest on the part of sister, mother, father, and grandmother.

Topmost in their concern was the importance of his return in good standing to medical school. Topmost in Tom's mind were three entirely different things.

One was his anxiety about the unfinished time line in the

Dome Room at Monticello. Had it been ripped off the wall and thrown away?

The second was his fear for the painted river on the ceiling. Had it been painted over?

His third concern was for Fern, who had so nearly become another victim of the brutal killer George Dryer. Was she all right? Why hadn't she called him? Well, it was obvious why she hadn't called him. She was all mixed up with somebody else now, her old boyfriend from Baltimore.

A week after his release from prison, Tom was again invited to dinner at the house on University Circle.

Mary was waiting for him on the porch. She hugged him hard. Homer slapped him on the back. Then a dim person rose from a folding chair at the far end of the porch and stood stiffly upright. In classic fashion her chair collapsed with a bang.

They all laughed. "I'll fix it," said Homer, and he wrestled with it manfully, but the chair understood its melodramatic role in this crisis, and once again fell flat. At this they all laughed harder than ever.

But there was some sort of impasse. At the table Homer and Mary had to carry the burden of the conversation all by themselves. Slightly illuminated by two glasses of wine, Homer babbled gaily about nothing in particular. Mary was embarrassed. "Homer, please, you're talking our ears off."

"Oh, that's no problem," said Homer. "Don't worry. You just stick 'em back on with library paste."

Mary turned apologetically to Fern. "You'll have to forgive Homer. He can't help it. He was born babbling."

"Oh, that's right," cried Homer, flourishing his serving spoon. "As soon as I popped out, do you know what I said? I said, 'Hi, Ma!' The doctor was amazed."

Fern and Tom smiled politely. They still had nothing to say to each other. As Homer passed around the plates of lasagna, he told himself that a couple of wild animals wouldn't make such a big thing of it. They'd go right at it, whereas highly educated humans merely pussyfooted around and shuffled their feet and then trotted off in two entirely different directions.

The butterscotch cake was a safe subject of conversation. Tom was lavish in his praise. He had three helpings, Fern two.

It was a hopeful beginning. Then Mary had a good idea. "How would you people like to take the dog for a walk while Homer and I clear up?"

"Well, okay," said Tom.

"Certainly," said Fern.

Trembling with joy, Doodles yipped noisily as Tom attached her leash. Then they set out, the little dog trotting ahead, Tom and Fern ambling after her down the driveway. At the sidewalk Tom turned to the left, and they walked in the direction of Rugby Road. "How's your friend Jim?" he said, elaborately casual.

"Jim?" Fern was bewildered. "What Jim?"

Tom looked at her in surprise. "Isn't there some guy named Jim?"

"Oh, you mean Jim Reeves." She laughed. "He's gone back to Baltimore."

"Wasn't he—?"

"Wasn't he what?"

Tom grinned and dropped the subject. At the corner he urged Doodles to the right. "This way," he said. "I want to show you something. It's just a little way down the street."

It was the Beta Bridge, a short piece of asphalt between lumpy cement walls.

Tom said nothing. He merely glanced at Fern to see if she noticed. When she walked nearly all the way across the bridge without looking at the wall, his heart sank. He had spent half the night painting it in the light of a camping lantern while passing students snickered and made remarks.

Then she saw them, the silly orange words, TOM + FERN, on a background of Day-Glo green.

"Oh," said Fern. "It says—" Then she stopped, because it was probably some other Tom, some other Fern.

"Fern—"

"Does it really mean—?"

Swiftly Tom cleared the matter up, Doodles found a perfect patch of weedy dandelions, and everyone was glad.

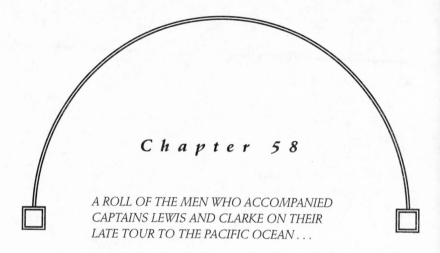

Chapter 58

A ROLL OF THE MEN WHO ACCOMPANIED
CAPTAINS LEWIS AND CLARKE ON THEIR
LATE TOUR TO THE PACIFIC OCEAN . . .

George Drulyard [Drouillard, "Drewyer"] Interpreter.
A man of much merit; he has been peculiarly useful
from his knowledge of the common language of gestic-
ulation, and his uncommon skill as a hunter and woods-
man; those several duties he performed in good faith,
and with an ardor which deserves the highest commen-
dation. It was his fate also to have encountered, on
various occasions, with either Captain Clarke or myself,
all the most dangerous and trying scenes of the voyage,
in which he uniformly acquitted himself with honor. . . .
                         Meriwether Lewis,
                  Captain 1ˢᵗ U.S. Reg't Inf.,
           City of Washington, January 15, 1807

The identification of the dying killer in the intensive-care unit of University Hospital turned out to be child's play. George had been careless, or perhaps he had simply been cocky.

Homer's monster book devoted a whole chapter to the subject. *Your typical serial killer feels himself invulnerable, godlike, under divine protection.*

The gray van was found in the woods, the mud was

washed off the license plate, and the glove compartment ran-
sacked. The plate number soon led to the name of the owner,
one George Dryer.

There were no papers in the glove compartment, no regis-
tration, no flashlight, no dark glasses, no handy tools, nothing
but a petrified doughnut and a plastic library card. The name
on the card was George Dryer.

Chief Pratt passed the information on to Homer, who
found it hard to believe.

"A *library* card? Not a Handy-Dandy Manual for Serial
Killers? *In*-credible."

"So, anyway, Homer, how about visiting him in the hospital? See if you can get him to say something. You know, just
ask him a few questions before he goes to a better world—or,
in his case, a worser."

"You mean, interrogate a dying man, grill him on his
deathbed?"

"Well, yes. That's it exactly."

The intensive-care unit in University Hospital was a ring of
small rooms. All were open to the center, where a team of
nurses kept track of all the patients at once.

George's shattered leg was in traction and he was suffering
from uncontrollable internal bleeding, but he was wide
awake and talkative, even garrulous. He didn't seem to recognize Homer as the attacker who had hurled him into the
ice pit. Instead he whispered eagerly, "Aren't you the Harvard man?"

"What?" It wasn't at all what Homer had expected.

Then George told him all. It was one long brag.

"My name's not Dryer, it's Drewyer. George Drewyer.
That name mean anything to you?"

"I'm afraid not," said Homer.

George grinned, lording it over the Harvard man. "I'll

give you a hint. Lewis and Clark. Ever heard of Lewis and Clark?"

"Yes, but—"

"George Drewyer. The best hunter. Brought home the bacon. You know, deer, bear, buffalo. All those guys, they couldn't have survived without George Drewyer."

Homer put two and two together. "You mean you're descended from *that* George Drewyer, a member of the Corps of Discovery?"

"Indian women. You know. The men fucked the squaws." Again George asserted his superiority over this know-it-all. "See, I'm from Bismarck, North Dakota."

Homer shook his head. "I don't follow you."

"Bismarck? You don't know Bismarck, North Dakota? Right there on the Missouri River? Jesus! You don't know shit."

"Well, of course you're right about that," agreed Homer, nodding his head, a glimmer of light beginning to dawn.

"Mandan villages, that's where they were. You know, this Indian tribe, the Mandans? Lewis and Clark, they spent the winter at Fort Mandan, George and all the rest. And the Mandan braves, you know what they said? They said, Hey, boys, help yourself. So the squaws—well, you know."

"I see," said Homer. "You mean—?"

"My name, right, Dryer? Just like Drewyer? So my great-great-great-grandmother, she must have been a Mandan squaw, slept with George Drewyer, got pregnant."

"Of course, of course." Homer slapped his knee, asking himself whether any upstanding Mandan squaw would have given a child the name of some passing white man when she didn't speak English, never saw the name written down, and probably couldn't read anyway. He pretended to be impressed. "So I'm talking to a direct descendant of a member of the Corps of Discovery? How fascinating."

George grinned with pride, but then his expression changed. His mouth gaped open but no sound came out, his face was suffused with blood, he reared up and fell back. One of the nurses ran to his side.

Homer got in his question quickly. "But why, George? Tell me, why did you do that to all those women?"

It was too late. The nurse pushed him out of the way and shouted at the others. They came running. A doctor appeared from nowhere.

Homer waited in the corridor, watching through the window, hoping to get another chance. But the crowd of experts around George's bed hovered over him for an interminable half-hour.

They thrust a tube down his throat, they worked over him with CPR, they leaned convulsively on his chest. At last they looked at each other and stepped back. The doctor shrugged her shoulders and departed. A sheet was pulled up. The head nurse made a face at Homer. They all dispersed.

Homer gave a last regretful look at the body of the murdering, mutilating serial killer, George Dryer or possibly Drewyer. In the silent compartment George lay still while a nurse swiftly disconnected his life-support systems and detached from his fractured leg the complicated arrangement of pulleys and cables.

A hospital aide appeared within minutes, rolling up a gurney. The body was transferred and whisked off to the hospital morgue, while another aide snatched the sheets off the bed, scrubbed the mattress with disinfectant, and ballooned over it a clean sheet, slapping it down and tucking it in.

George was dead. The red boil of anger that had enclosed him for so long had burst at last.

Leaving the hospital, Homer pondered the dying man's insistence that he was descended from a Mandan squaw. The crudity of his claim was like the squalid insinuations about Jefferson's "blackamoor wife."

Of course any comparison between the exalted refinement of Thomas Jefferson on the one hand and the filthy coarseness of George Dryer on the other was unthinkable. Homer tried heroically not to think it.

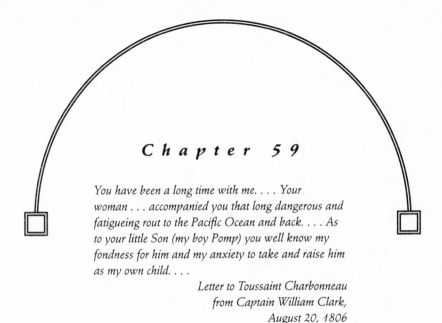

Chapter 59

You have been a long time with me. . . . Your
woman . . . accompanied you that long dangerous and
fatigueing rout to the Pacific Ocean and back. . . . As
to your little Son (my boy Pomp) you well know my
fondness for him and my anxiety to take and raise him
as my own child. . . .

Letter to Toussaint Charbonneau
from Captain William Clark,
August 20, 1806

It was lunchtime at City Hall. The officer at the police reception desk was out sick, and the sergeant who normally handled emergency calls at this time of day had been summoned to the divorce court across the street, hoping to salvage a few scraps from the vengeance of his ex-wife.

Therefore, Chief Pratt, left alone, was not free to accept Homer's offer of lunch under the trees in the Downtown Mall.

So Homer brought a bag of hamburgers and set it down on Pratt's desk.

The Chief was not to be outdone. "Hey, looky here. I just happen to have a pint of booze." He reached behind the last volume of the *OED* and brought out a bottle. It was full of dark liquid. It had no label. "Liberated, so to speak, from a couple of moonshiners."

"Moonshiners? Don't tell me you've still got old geezers in the hills making sourmash whiskey?"

"We sure do. And it's still a federal offense." Pratt produced a couple of glasses from a desk drawer, dabbed at them with a paper napkin, removed the cork from the bottle, and poured an inch into each glass. "Watch it," he said, "it's pure rotgut."

Homer took a fiery sip and grinned. "Strong stuff." He wiped his mouth and said, "Well, let's see, now, where are we?"

"Hospital," said Pratt. He took a large bite of his hamburger and chewed it slowly. "The head nurse, did she tell you what she told me?"

"The head nurse? No, she didn't tell me anything. I was just in her way."

"Well, she told me why none of those poor murdered women was raped. He didn't have anything to rape them with."

"What?" Homer was dumbfounded. "You mean he'd been castrated? For Christ's sake, we should have thought of that."

"Okay, then." Pratt wiped ketchup off his chin. "You said Dryer maybe came from North Dakota, someplace around Bismarck. So Quantico, they talked to the hospital out there, found the record. Guy by the name of George Dryer came into the emergency room three years ago, bleeding like a stuck pig, yelling and hollering. They fixed him up and discharged him, but one of the medicos wrote something in the margin of his medical record. You know, all they have to do is fill in the blanks, cardiac arrest or something. But this guy wrote a comment in the margin. It was the name Dryer kept yelling, the name of the woman who did it to him. *Jeanie*, the note said. Woman by the name of Jeanie."

"Jeanie!" Homer slapped his forehead. "Oh, my god, Oliver, I forgot to tell you. That's what Fern said. It slipped my mind. She said he called her Jeanie."

"God's teeth, no kidding?" Chief Pratt took another swig of moonshine. "Well, they found her."

"Already? They found Jeanie?"

"Jean Lighthorse, that's her name. She had a friend in Bismarck who kept in touch with her after she ran away."

"Jeanie ran away? You mean, after she did that to George?"

"This friend's a local prostitute, Beatrice Winn, sensible woman who sometimes works with local law enforcement. She saw it in the paper, all about this former resident of Bismarck who turned out to be a killer, only now he was dead. Well, it was great good news, because now Jeanie wouldn't have to be afraid any more. So Beatrice got in touch with her again and persuaded her to come back and tell exactly what happened." Pratt looked at his empty glass, leaned his chair back, and said, "Hooee." He picked up the bottle of moonshine and waggled it at Homer.

"Oh, no thanks." Homer wiped his red face and collected himself. "So what did she say?"

"What did who say? Oh, you mean Jeanie." Pratt opened his eyes wide and shook his head to clear his brain. "Grisly story. Dryer kept her locked up in an abandoned shed somewhere out of town, padlocks inside, outside, used her whenever he felt like it. Brought her food when he remembered to do it, as though she were some kind of farm animal. Jeanie bit and kicked and yelled and screamed, but nobody heard her. Then, one day, she found some kind of tool in the shed, maybe a sickle or, you know, some kind of pruning instrument." Pratt jerked his elbows in and out as though clipping an overgrown bush.

Homer winced. "She used it on Dryer?"

"Right. One night he made the mistake of falling asleep. It was what she'd been waiting for. His pants were right there on the floor, so she stole his keys. Then she—uh—did what she did. And naturally he woke up and howled, but Jeanie got away. Dryer had to crawl to the nearest road, yelling bloody murder, and somebody picked him up, took him to the hospital."

"Bloody murder," said Homer dryly. "That's exactly what he did from then on, avenging himself over and over again on Jean Lighthorse."

Pratt opened a folder and handed a piece of paper across the desk. "Here she is. Picture came through the computer, I don't know how the hell they do it, we've got a whiz kid in the office. So what do you think?"

"Handsome woman." Homer studied the picture. "Looks Native American."

"Right. She's Chippewa. Wears her hair in a pigtail."

"Ah, I see." Homer nodded wisely. "You mean like that poor librarian. And the girl at the fast-food place."

"And your young friend Fern." Pratt picked up the whiskey bottle, looked at it regretfully, put it down again, and sighed. "It sort of goes along with what Dryer told you."

"About his so-called ancestor, George Drewyer?" Homer brightened. "And all the Indian squaws the men slept with—the Chinook women at the mouth of the Columbia River and the Mandan women on the Missouri, right there where the city of Bismarck was going to be, the place where George was born." Homer reached for the greasy paper bag and looked inside. "Hey, there's another burger in here, Oliver. How about it?"

Oliver groaned and shook his head.

"Me neither." Homer put the bag on the floor. "My God, Oliver, those notes he left on the women's bodies, he was teasing us with Lewis and Clark. Poor Jeanie! He must have thought he was recapitulating the men's lusty freedom with the willing squaws along the way."

Pratt glowered. "You couldn't exactly call Jean Lighthorse a willing squaw."

"Of course not. But after what she did to him, he had to keep finding new Jeanies and punishing them in her honor."

"Punishing them? God's whiskers, he butchered those poor young women."

Homer made a sick joke. "Well, at least he didn't eat them. I mean, he wasn't a cannibal like Jeffrey Dahmer."

Pratt wasn't listening. He rocked back in his chair and stared dreamily at the ceiling. "Remember, Homer, I've been looking up the original meanings of words in the Declaration of Independence? Remember that?"

Completely befuddled, Homer tried to switch his attention from the depths of depravity to the heights of glory. "Sure, I remember. You wanted to find out what the words meant way back then, when Jefferson wrote them down."

"Exactly. Well, guess what?"

"My God, Oliver, I don't know, what?"

Pratt's face shone. "Well, I've been working on my talk. You know, for the Philological Society of Philadelphia. Wait till you hear this." In a fever of excitement he swiveled around in his chair and snatched out six volumes of the *Oxford English Dictionary* and piled them on his desk. For the next half-hour he lectured Homer on his philological discoveries.

Homer listened with tipsy attention. At last he thumped Oliver's desk and cried, "They were gods, Oliver, our founding fathers were gods walking the earth among mortal men."

Pratt stared at him, a little taken aback. "Well, jeez, I don't know if I'd go that far."

Homer drove back to University Circle in a daze of awe and wonder. Recognizing a whiskey stupor when she saw one, Mary wisely put him to bed.

Afterward, fully awake and sober, Homer remembered his ecstasy in Pratt's office. He hated to set it aside. "Well, they were demigods anyway," he said to Mary ruefully.

"Who were?"

"Washington and Jefferson, John Adams, Benjamin Franklin, James Madison, all those people. It's just dawned on me how lucky we were in our founding fathers. I mean, everybody always says that, but now it's not just a truism, it's a huge, enormous, overwhelming—"

"Vast and gigantic?" suggested Mary helpfully.

"Colossal, stupendous—"

"Immense and titanic?"

"Right. It's an immense and titanic fact. I now appreciate it for the first time. What are all those boxes for?"

"Homer, the landlord's coming back on Monday. Ed told us in the beginning we could only stay for a month, remember?"

"Oh, that's right. Too bad. I'll really miss this lovely town and the hills all around and the whole state of Virginia. But I won't miss you, you ratty little dog." Doodles was looking up at Homer, her violet nose quivering.

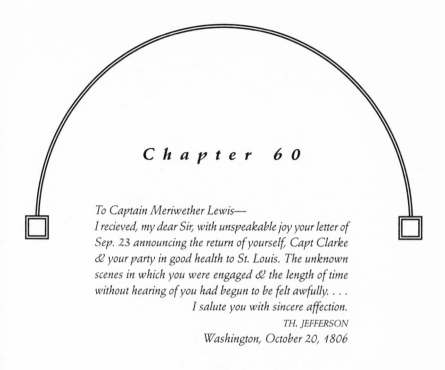

Chapter 60

To Captain Meriwether Lewis—
I recieved, my dear Sir, with unspeakable joy your letter of
Sep. 23 announcing the return of yourself, Capt Clarke
& your party in good health to St. Louis. The unknown
scenes in which you were engaged & the length of time
without hearing of you had begun to be felt awfully. . . .
I salute you with sincere affection.
TH. JEFFERSON
Washington, October 20, 1806

At Monticello things had long since returned to normal.
The captains and the kings had departed, the four hundred folding chairs had been whisked away, the men and women of the Secret Service had vanished, the caterers had swooped up their leftovers and garbage and mobile refrigeration equipment, their tent had come down, and a cleanup crew had walked slowly over the trampled lawn collecting plastic glasses, cigarette butts, toothpicks, dropped asparagus rolls, and paper napkins.

They missed some of the napkins, because a few had fluttered up into the trees, where they perched like doves for days. The remaining crumbs among the blades of grass were carried away by ants.

During the cleanup Howie Plover put a new set of sawhorse barriers in front of the ice house. But first he looked down into the pit and saw something strange and disgusting at the bottom. It wasn't a dead rat, it was a tangled mop, hairy and black.

He fished it out. Howie did not recognize it as the wig that had once belonged to Flora Foley. Instead of turning it over to the police, he tossed it into the trash.

Indoors, the blood of Augustus Upchurch had been washed away from the parlor floor. The wet mop was followed by a waxing machine, and now the parquet gleamed with its usual geometric perfection. The parlor was once again a room in a museum, a place where nothing happened.

When Fern came back to work she looked around downstairs, half expecting to see the key of the Great Clock turning, the pens of the polygraph moving, the concave mirror still holding in its shallow bowl an image of Thomas Jefferson, the lapdesk lying open on the marble table, and a storm of paper floating down from the ceiling. But of course everything was perfectly still and motionless, and all the things belonging elsewhere were back in elsewhere.

She climbed the stairs, looked in on Henry Spender, and wished him good morning.

Henry glanced up absently and smiled, then looked down again and frowned at his accounts. The bill for the fireworks was ten times more than he had expected. The itemized list was four pages long. The last page was the worst:

60 Spiral Screamers @ $60	$3600
45 Golden Starbursts @ $75	3375
4 Blue Blockbusters @ $550	2200
15 Vesuvius Rockets @ $300	4500
1 Forty-Second Final Bombardment @ $1000	1000

1 American Flag, Red, White, and Blue, @$1500	1500
1 Portrait Display, Thomas Jefferson @ $2000	2000
Total	$18,175
GRAND TOTAL	45,112

Opening the official checkbook for the Thomas Jefferson Memorial Foundation, Henry thought sourly that John Adams would never have called for Bonfires and Illuminations if he'd known what they would cost the future citizens of the nation.

He scribbled the check anyway, rammed it in an envelope, and slammed his fist down on the stamp.

In the Dome Room, Fern found Tom standing on the ladder with paintbrush in hand. "I didn't get it exactly right," he said apologetically, looking down at Fern. "I had to add another fifty miles of the Columbia River, here at the end, or it would never have reached the Pacific. This blue here, that's the Pacific."

"Well, I think it looks great," said Fern. "The time line's finished too. We should celebrate."

"Right you are," said Tom, descending the ladder with the can of blue paint. "After all, we deserve it. We've been all the way to the Pacific and back." He gazed up proudly at the completed map on the ceiling, the meanderings of the rivers, the Great Falls, the jagged mountains, the Continental Divide, the Lolo Pass. "I mean, we really have, you and me. Snags tearing up the canoes, grizzly bears, cold and starvation, hostile Indians, generous Indians, dead horses, falling off cliffs, serial killers, ghastly parents, murderous attacks, wrongful arrests, solitary confinement." Tom put down the paint can and gathered Fern in his arms. "Right? We got through it all. We made it all the way."

"Oh, yes," agreed Fern, laughing. "We made it all the way."

"And, hey, I've got just the thing." Tom picked up his knapsack, reached in, and pulled out a bottle.

"Where did you get that?" But Fern knew perfectly well where it came from.

"Dining room downstairs. The door of the dumbwaiter was standing open, so I looked inside, and there it was."

"Château Lafite," murmured Fern. "Seventeen eighty-seven."

Tom looked at the label. "That's right. How did you know?"

"I just did," said Fern. "But, Tom, we can't drink it."

"Well, I suppose not," said Tom wistfully. "It wouldn't taste like anything anyway, not after all these years."

Fern was puzzled. "But why didn't it disappear along with everything else?"

"Everything else?"

"Oh, sorry, I mean, I wonder how on earth it got there, an old bottle like that."

"Ghostly hands," said Tom.

That evening they celebrated in Fern's place with a bottle of two-year-old California Chardonnay, and the next day Tom filled out an application for admission to the university. This time he wasn't applying to the medical school, he was switching to the graduate school of education.

"My parents won't like it," he told Fern. "Teaching history in high school won't put me in the upper income bracket. I doubt I'll earn seven figures."

"Probably not," said Fern.

She too was going back to work. Although two members of the Grant Committee were dead, the rest gave her their blessing, and by Christmastime she was able to show them a finished draft of her book.

The task had been easier than she had expected. Even her chapter on the Sally Hemings affair was no embarrassment. It ended serenely—

However scandalous they might have seemed during Thomas Jefferson's lifetime, a widower's out-of-wedlock sexual relations would not be shameful now, two centuries later.

After all, his wife had died decades earlier. And Sally Hemings, however illegitimate, was his wife's own half-sister. The two women were daughters of the same father.

In the memoir of Isaac, the Monticello slave, Sally is described as handsome. Perhaps it was love on both sides. Why can we not be grateful that Thomas Jefferson enjoyed this very ordinary human pleasure?

After finishing her book, Fern moved out of the Dome Room and set up housekeeping with Tom, camping out in the house on University Circle. There they coped happily with the exploding coffeepot, the collapsing lawn chair and the reversed hot and cold water faucets. They also cared tenderly for Doodles, the toy poodle, because the little dog had, after all, brought them together.

The owner of the house was still away. "I think he's hunting butterflies in Costa Rica," said Ed Bailey. "So never mind, just move right in. If he turns up, you can always leave."

And at Monticello the tourist season was at its peak. Cars choked the parking lot, crowds of visitors were bused up the hill to the top, where they waited on the path between the hedges for their turn to climb the steps of the East Portico and enter the house.

Why did they come in such patient droves? It was not only to see the handsome house, nor to experience a surviving piece of American history. Nearly all of them felt a desire to come closer to Thomas Jefferson himself, to someone they were proud to think of—rightly or wrongly—as a very great man.